FAT FREE
AND
Fatal

Books by G.A. McKevett

Just Desserts

Bitter Sweets

Killer Calories

Cooked Goose

Sugar and Spite

Sour Grapes

Peaches and Screams

Death By Chocolate

Cereal Killer

Murder à la Mode

Corpse Suzette

Fat Free and Fatal

Published by Kensington Publishing Corporation

A SAVANNAH REID MYSTERY

G.A. McKevett

KENSINGTON BOOKS
www.kensingtonbooks.com

KENSINGTON BOOKS are published by

Kensington Publishing Corp.
850 Third Avenue
New York, NY 10022

All Kensington titles, imprints, and distributed lines are available at special quantity discounts for bulk purchases for sales promotion, premiums, fund-raising, educational or institutional use.

Special book excerpts or customized printings can also be created to fit specific needs. For details, write or phone the office of the Kensington Special Sales Manager: Kensington Publishing Corp., 850 Third Avenue, New York, NY, 10022. Attn. Special Sales Department. Phone: 1-800-221-2647.

Library of Congress Card Catalogue Number: 2006939878

ISBN-13: 978-0-7582-1550-5
ISBN-10: 0-7582-1550-9

First Printing: May 2007

10 9 8 7 6 5 4 3 2 1

Printed in the United States of America

For the baby named Eve,
Our angel with heaven's starlight in her eyes.

Acknowledgments

I would like to thank Jennifer Hald and Leslie Connell, Moonlight Magnolia detectives extraordinaire!

Also, I want to thank all the fans who write to me, sharing their thoughts and offering endless encouragement. I enjoy your letters more than you know. I can be reached at:

sonjamassie.com
or
gamckevett.net

Chapter 1

The tiny, southern California town of San Carmelita had its picturesque areas where Hollywood celebrities browsed for antiques, shopped quaint boutiques, and sunned themselves on pristine beaches. But Saul's pawnshop wasn't in any of those areas. Saulie's was on the other side of town, the part of town that the city council frequently discussed at meetings, trying to figure out new, cheap ways to spruce up the neighborhood. Or at least keep tourists out of it, so they wouldn't get themselves mugged or perforated by a stray bullet.

Nestled snugly between a tattoo parlor and a porn store, Saul's shabby little hockshop had been trading valuables of questionable ownership for instant cash for over fifty years. But Saul himself was neither shabby nor questionable. He was a character, and he also *had* character . . . which made him one of Savannah Reid's favorite people.

As she and her friend, Detective Sergeant Dirk Coulter, left Dirk's old Buick and walked up the sidewalk toward Saul's shop, she stepped off the walk to allow a teenage boy and his pit bull to pass, giving the dog and his master plenty of room.

Wearing full gang attire and a surly, wanna-piece-of-me? scowl on his face, the gangbanger looked threatening enough without his wide-jawed, excessively toothsome companion. And while the streetwise Savannah had kids like him for lunch on a bologna sandwich spread with plenty of mustard and a dab of mayo, she made it a point to avoid pit bulls whenever possible.

Dirk nudged her with his elbow. "Afraid of a little puppy dog?" he said.

"Puppy dog, my hind end," she replied, her Southern drawl thick, despite all her years on the West Coast. "Remember when we saw a 'pup' like that one take a chunk out of a patrolman's thigh a few blocks from here? All because the cop jumped over a fence and into the wrong yard, chasing a perp?"

Dirk shuddered. "Gross. Like I'm gonna forget that one. We saw some pretty nasty stuff when we worked graveyard back then."

Savannah felt her own little chill. During the years she and Dirk had served together on the San Carmelita police force, they had seen some pretty nasty stuff in the noonday sun, too. Heart-wrenching, soul-scarring images that kept you awake at night. Unless you read a lot of trashy novels right before bedtime and ate a lot of chocolate—Savannah's remedies for just about any of life's unpleasantries.

Dirk was still a cop—still collecting nightmare material.

Savannah had moved on to greener pastures and become a private detective. Well, sometimes the grass was greener . . . when she actually had a paying client or two. Then there were the other times, like this one, when she had absolutely nothing to do except tag along with Dirk.

As they passed one seedy establishment after another, she wondered if there wasn't a better way to spend a Saturday afternoon than hanging out on the bad side of the tracks with a guy who had been gruff in his twenties and grumpy in his thirties. And now that he and she were solidly in their forties, he had worked his way up to a five-star curmudgeon.

Dirk let go with a deep, chest-rattling cough, which he tried his best to suppress. She knew why. And it wasn't going to work.

"That's the third chest cold you've had this spring," she said. "Not to mention the four sinus infections and all the sore throats."

He growled under his breath. "So, *don't* mention it. Don't you start nagging me, woman. I won't stand for it."

"Since when? I've nagged you to quit smoking since the day we met. Pointing out all of your faults keeps me from having to focus on my own. So, why stop now?"

"Because I'm gonna fly into a blind rage if you don't. I've had enough of your—" More gagging and coughing took his breath away, along with the rest of his argument.

"Yeah, yeah, yeah. You and your blind rages," she said. "I live in fear."

When they reached Saul's front door, Dirk opened it and stood aside for her to enter. Savannah liked that. Right after a cigarette, he might smell like a Las Vegas casino, but Dirk was still an old-fashioned gentleman.

Dark and dank, the tiny pawnshop needed a good airing. The only bright spots in the glum establishment were the glass-front counters that held treasures ranging from estate jewelry and fake estate jewelry to dented French horns and antique typewriters.

A small gnome of a man appeared at the tinkling of the silver bells that hung above the door. He was wiping his hands on a dirty cloth as he came out of the back room, a hopeful look on his wizened face. But at the sight of Dirk, his bright, entrepreneurial grin disappeared. "Oh, it is only you," he said with a slight Slavic accent. "I must say this to you, I'm not a happy man. Not at all. Saul does not like to lie to his customers, to deceive them, to deliver them into the hands of the law. If word gets around that I do this . . ."

"The guys who are trying to unload their stolen crap will take it elsewhere," Dirk told him. "That's a *good* thing, right?"

Saul grimaced. "I suppose so." He turned to Savannah and his eyes lit up ever so slightly. "I am happy to see you, though, Savannah, my dear. It is not every day a pretty woman comes into Saul's store."

"Forget about the pretty girls for a minute, Saulie," Savannah said, giving him the benefit of a brief smile before turning all-business, "and tell us about the ugly mug you're expecting to come in here this afternoon."

"Ah, that one." Saul shook his head. "He's a bad fellow, I tell you. About a month ago, he comes in here and tries to sell me a gun that he has no papers for. And when I refuse to buy it, he gets so very angry, I swear I think he is going to shoot me with it."

"And you were probably right," Savannah told him. "Always trust your instincts, Saul. In your business you can't afford not to."

Dirk glanced down into one of the glass cases, then bent over, taking a better look at a bowie knife with a rosewood handle. "Tell me exactly what he said when he called you this morning."

Saul cast a quick look at Savannah. "I will not repeat exactly what he said in front of a lady, but he told me he had a woman's Raymond Weil watch and a gentleman's Tutima. Said he wanted to be rid of them this afternoon. Well, that Tutima rang a bell in my brain. Saul may be old, but he's not so stupid as some think. I grabbed the . . . what you police call . . . the hot sheet and looked at it really quick while I still had him on the phone. And there it was, third item on the page: a Tutima with 'Merry Christmas, Uncle Carl' engraved on the back of it. So, I asked him if it was clean, mint condition, and he said, 'All except for a short message on the back.' Claims he'd had it engraved for his beloved uncle, but dear Uncle Carl—may he rest in peace—passed away before he could give it to him on Christmas."

"Heartbreaking story," Savannah muttered.

"Ain't it though?" Dirk added. "Let's get this bastard."

"And return Uncle Carl's watch to him . . . whoever he may be," she said.

Saul's eyes brightened at the prospect. "I have suffered too many losses from these no-goods who come in here and sell me stolen items. And then you police come along behind them, take the merchandise and leave me with nothing but empty hands. It will be a good feeling to catch one of them in the act and let *him* take the loss for a change—let *him* be the one who is disappointed and upset."

"A good feeling?" Savannah laughed. "Oh, Saul, you have no idea how good you're going to feel if we nail this guy. Revenge is better than a hot fudge sundae . . . with two cherries on top!"

Half an hour later, they were ready for the vendor of fine, recently pilfered goods to walk through the door. Savannah stood behind the counter, trying to look like a proper pawnshop clerk—which meant trying not to stare at the pretty sparklies in the jewelry cases that were constantly snagging her attention.

And Dirk sat on a folding chair, just inside the door that led to the back room, within earshot, but out of view of anyone coming into the shop.

As Saul chattered nervously away in Savannah's ear, she wondered briefly if it might be a mistake, asking this frail, elderly man to cooperate with a sting like this. What if he had a heart attack right in the middle of the takedown? She was current on her CPR, but she couldn't imagine bouncing up and down on that skinny little rib cage. Savannah would never be accused of being a lightweight; she was a "real" woman, gifted with a sturdy, hearty frame and plenty of feminine embellishments to flesh it out.

She knew she had the capacity to mash old Saul flat as a flitter—as her Granny Reid would say. Savannah had never been sure exactly what a flitter was, but she was certain you could easily slip it under a tight door. And sure as shootin', nobody wanted to be one.

"So, tell me, pretty Savannah . . . when are you going to come in here and shop for an engagement ring?" Saul wanted to know as he rubbed some jewelers' rouge on a cloth and began to buff a candlestick.

"Uh . . . maybe when I find somebody I want to be engaged to."

Saul nodded his head toward the back door. "A nice girl like you with those beautiful blue eyes and all that shiny dark hair? You must have suitors lined up outside your doorway with flowers and candies. No?"

"Mmm, not so's you'd notice, Saulie." She gave him a flirty grin that deepened her dimples. "There's plenty of room on my porch if you want to show up with roses and a box of Godiva's chocolates."

"Ah, I'm too old to do anything but look. But how about that one in there?" He nodded toward the back room where Dirk sat. "Any chance of *him* wanting to put a ring on your finger someday?"

Savannah snorted. "More like, any chance of me holding still for it? Saulie, go wash your mouth out with soap, saying a thing like that. It'll never happen. That one in there wants to marry me about as much as I want to marry him."

"And how much is that?" Saul said, his eyes twinkling with a light that hinted at a younger, more virile fellow still lurking inside his timeworn body.

A cough rumbled on the other side of the door, followed by some throat clearing. "You two hens wanna stop cackling in there," Dirk said, "and stay sharp? In case you haven't looked at a clock lately, this afternoon is just about up. It's a quarter to five. This guy better show soon. I'm getting hungry."

"Oh, stop your griping," Savannah snapped. "I told you I've

got a chicken stewing on the back burner at home. You're getting a free chicken and dumplin' dinner tonight. Biscuits, too. That should enough to—oh—heads up. We got company coming." She turned to Saul. "Is that your buddy?"

Saul craned his neck to look out the window. He jumped to attention. "That's him! That's the one who calls himself R.L. Can you imagine a person wanting to be called by a couple of letters like that, instead of a proper name? That alone shows what a hoodlum he must be. I would wager he's already spent time in prison."

Instantly, Savannah thought of a dozen good ol' boys from her home state of Georgia who went by assorted initials in lieu of full names. She knew a J.D., a J.P., a J.R., and a J.B., just for starters. All fine, upstanding, proud sons of the South—they hadn't served more than thirty years of hard prison time between them. And most of that was for "thumpin'" on other, less upstanding, good ol' boys who'd been asking for it.

Nope. Saulie's theory just didn't hold water.

But R.L. looked like he might be an exception. He *did* look like a hoodlum, from the metal-studded leather vest that he wore with no shirt underneath, to the spiked dog collar around his neck, from the five-inch-high black Mohawk, to the swastika tattoo proudly displayed on his bare chest. Savannah took particular notice of the enormous skull-and-crossbones ring on his right forefinger that would be nasty in a fistfight, should one ensue in the process of taking him into custody.

No, R.L. didn't look like your average accountant or Sunday school teacher. He looked like exactly the kind of guy Savannah enjoyed busting—somebody who continually did nasty, ornery things to nice people, but was cocksure that they would forever get away with it.

She loved proving them wrong.

As he sauntered through the front door, she rearranged her

face from a self-satisfied smirk to the look of a moderately bored clerk who was looking forward to going home at five sharp. "May I help you?" she asked R.L. as her eyes casually scanned the rest of his person, looking for any telltale bulge that might signify a weapon—other than the oversized skull ring. But the ring was all she saw.

He walked past her and over to where Saul stood. "Nope. Saul here is my man," he said. "I called earlier."

"Ah . . . you're the good fellow with the Weil and the Tutima?" Saul laid his polishing cloth down on the counter. Savannah noticed that his hand was trembling. Again, she felt a pang of concern for her old friend. This sort of thing was nerve-wracking on anyone, let alone an octogenarian who had lost his wife only a year ago and had survived a triple bypass just last winter.

"That's me." R.L. glanced over at Savannah, then toward the front door and the back of the store. "Let's do some business. And don't take all day about it either, old man. I got places to go, things to do."

Saul bristled at the "old man" comment, pulled himself a couple of inches taller, and stuck out his chin. "Not so fast, *young* man. Saul takes his time and conducts his business in proper fashion. Let me see what you have to sell and, if you wish to do business with me, remember to address me in a respectful tone of voice."

R.L. gave a little snort, then dug into the front pocket of his jeans. He pulled out a couple of fine watches and dumped them onto the glass countertop as though they were nothing but a couple of carnival trinkets. "There," he said. "I told you they were expensive stuff. New. Never even worn. So don't go trying to cheat me. I want full price for these."

Saul pulled a pair of glasses from his shirt pocket, then took his time unfolding them and slipping them on. As he studied the pieces carefully, turning each one over and over in his expert hands, he said, "I'm sure you came by these fine pieces in a perfectly legal way. Eh, my impudent fellow?"

R.L. started to answer, then paused, mentally snagged on the word *impudent.* Then, unable to decide if he'd been insulted or not, he said, "Sure. Like I told you, legal all the way. Christmas presents I just never got around to returning."

Saul cleared his throat, looked up from the watches, and gave Savannah a big, toothsome smile. Suddenly, he looked years younger and decades stronger. "These watches," he announced in a loud, clear voice, "are exactly as we thought. We can conclude our business now if you like."

At his words, Savannah reached under her jacket and pulled her Beretta from its holster. She pointed the barrel at a spot a couple of inches below R.L.'s Mohawk. "Freeze," she told him. "Don't you even twitch, son, or you'll have a whole new hairdo with a permanent part."

Half a second later, Dirk came around the corner, his revolver drawn. When he saw the suspect, he smiled as brightly as Saul. "Well, hello again," he said. "I remember you, you worthless pile of dog crap. I busted you about two years ago for robbing a church's poor box. Remember me?"

As Dirk and R.L. reminisced about days of yore, Savannah was moving around the counter, intending to position herself between their suspect and the doorway. But she was watching him, his every movement . . . most importantly, his eyes. And she knew the instant he made the decision.

"No!" she shouted as he spun on his heel and headed for the doorway. "Don't you run, you little—"

She banged her hip hard on the corner of the glass cabinet as she rounded it, but she hardly felt the pain because of the jolt of adrenaline that had hit her bloodstream. She headed for the door, about six steps behind their now-on-the-run thief.

R.L. and his ugly leather vest shot out the door with Savannah on his heels and Dirk behind her. He took off down the sidewalk, running with the grace of a recently decapitated chicken, knocking his fellow pedestrians aside and a kid off his bicycle.

But what he lacked in beauty, he made up in determination.

The guy was pretty fast.

Too fast for Savannah's liking.

After only a couple of blocks, she could hear Dirk huffing and puffing behind her. An excellent runner with longer legs than hers, he normally overtook and passed her when they were in a footrace. But this time it was she who was in the lead when their quarry changed routes and headed down a side street toward the old mission.

A tourist attraction as well as a functioning church, the mission had a wide, shallow pool, decoratively situated in a courtyard at the entrance to the property. Inlaid with cobalt blue and yellow tiles, the pool provided some cool, refreshing wading for the town's children on hot summer days.

And, it seemed, for the occasional thief on the lam.

Rather than try to fight his way through a crowd of tourists who were taking pictures of the ancient adobe building and its picturesque surroundings, R.L. decided to take a shortcut through the fountain.

Splashing water like a Labrador retriever puppy gamboling at the beach, he galloped through it and was out the other side in less than five seconds.

Savannah didn't take the time or energy to even consider her new suede loafers. She plunged right in, making just as big a splash . . . much to the chagrin of the tourists within splash range.

She didn't take time to hate him either as she felt the cold water soak her new linen slacks up to the knee. She could always hate him at her leisure.

Once she had her hands on him.

He reached the other side of the plaza and its surrounding wall, where he hesitated a couple of seconds before deciding to turn right and head for the old graveyard near the back of the mission.

Those two seconds were all Savannah needed to close most of the distance between them.

And when he paused another half second before jumping up onto the wrought-iron fence that bordered the cemetery, that was all she needed.

She tackled him, grabbed one handful of leather vest and another handful of Mohawk, and yanked him down off the fence. A moment later, R.L. was face first on the grass and Savannah's right knee was firmly planted on the small of his back.

He let out a yelp as she tightened her grip on his hair.

"Make *me* run," she said, putting her full weight on him. "Make *me* have to hotfoot all over God's creation just to lay hands on you, will you? You're gonna pay for that!"

She glanced down at her soaked loafers. Now that her suspect had been apprehended she could afford to be fashion conscious again. "You're gonna pay for my shoes, too," she told him, "if I have to take it out of your mangy hide!"

At the sound of pounding footsteps behind her, she turned and saw Dirk racing up to them. At least, he was attempting to race. His face was red and his eyes slightly bugged as he huffed and puffed his way along.

When he finally reached them, he bent double, holding his stomach, fighting for breath.

"You okay there, buddy?" she asked him.

"Yeah, sure . . . no sweat."

But he was sweating. Profusely.

For a moment, Savannah forgot the struggling, groaning guy beneath her and did a mental checklist of heart attack symptoms.

"You feel any chest pain?" she asked him, fighting down a

surge of panic. Visions of doughnuts and too many beers while watching football games danced in her head, not to mention a chain of cigarettes reaching back for years and years and years. "Any sort of pressure? Pain in your arm or—"

"No," he said, still gasping, still bent double. "I'm not having a friggin' heart attack. I just can't catch my breath."

He reached into his bomber jacket pocket, pulled out a pair of handcuffs, and tossed them to her.

She quickly manacled R.L., then stood and pulled him to his feet. She gave him a shove in Dirk's direction. "There you go," she told him, "one bad guy—signed, sealed, delivered. He's yours."

"Thanks." Dirk grabbed R.L.'s arm and began to drag him back down the path they had just run. "I owe you one, Van."

"Another one," she corrected him, following close behind. "Another one in a long, long, long line of IOU's."

"Yeah, but that was the first time you've ever had to catch a bad guy for me," he admitted. The look on his face was one of utter devastation and deep humiliation.

It worried Savannah more than his previous breathlessness.

Dirk was seldom embarrassed—even on the frequent occasions when he truly should have been—let alone mortified.

"Dumb luck," she said, a little too cheerfully, even to her own ears. "Next time you'll nab 'em."

"That ain't it, and we both know it." He shook his head in disgust. "I can't run anymore. Hell, I can't even breathe anymore."

They reached the fountain, where the startled, thoroughly splashed tourists were still standing around, their mouths hanging open, watching for the next chapter of this unexpected drama that was playing out before them.

Dirk stopped at the edge of the pool and pushed R.L. toward Savannah. "Hold on to him for a minute. I got somethin' to do here."

Amazed, Savannah watched as he reached into the inside pocket of his jacket and pulled out a pack of cigarettes. She was even more surprised when she saw him toss them into the water.

"No way," she whispered. "I don't believe it."

"Believe it, Van. It's happening. It's happening right now." He squared his broad shoulders and lifted his chin a couple of notches. "The day that I can't chase down a perp—the day that you can catch one and I can't—that's the day I quit."

Savannah had seen Dirk quit before. Many, many times. He was an expert. He had "quitting" down pat.

He was as good at quitting smoking as she was at losing weight. They had both done it hundreds of times.

But after decades of "quitting" and "losing," he was still a smoker and she was still overly voluptuous, according to the surgeon general's weight charts.

This was no different than all the other times she had seen him give up the cigs.

Or was it?

Her breath caught in her throat when she saw what he did next. He reached into his pocket one more time, and pulled out his lighter. His silver Harley-Davidson lighter that he'd been carrying the day she had met him, back when polyester-clad dimwits were still dancing in discos and hitting on people with the line, "What's your sun sign?" Back when she had worn "big hair" and shoulder pads that made her look like a linebacker.

That lighter was as dear to Dirk as his bomber jacket. She had truly believed she would one day bury him with both.

But . . . but it looked like this time it was really going to happen.

Splash.

The lighter hit the water out in the middle of the pool and came to rest among the coins—mostly pennies—tossed by hopeful tourists who believed that the mission's patron saint would grant them a winning lottery ticket . . . in exchange for a lousy penny's worth of charity.

She looked at Dirk with amazement, total disbelief.

Dirk didn't own much: a decrepit house trailer, a battered Buick Skylark, his leather jacket, and some faded T-shirts. But he loved what he owned—with a fierce loyalty that bordered on psychosis. He never threw away *anything.*

He recycled paper towels!

With a smug look on his face and a swagger in his step, Detective Sergeant Dirk Coulter continued to escort his prisoner back toward the parked Buick, bringing a stunned Savannah in tow.

Lordy be! Granny Reid's right, she thought. *Wonders never cease!*

Chapter 2

Granny Reid was right about something else, Savannah decided when she took a bite of fried chicken: Soaking the pieces in buttermilk before cooking it *did* make it melt in your mouth. And the groans of appreciation from the others sitting around Savannah's dining table provided supporting testimony to the fact.

Even Tammy Hart, Savannah's friend and assistant in her detective agency, had set aside her usual healthy, vegetarian lifestyle and was violating her conscience with a juicy drumstick. She had arrived for the dinner party an hour ago, wearing a red silk kimono, her long blond hair pulled back and fastened with a pair of lacquered chopsticks. But now the sleeves of the elegant garment were rolled up to her elbows, and she was gnawing on the chicken leg like any other shameless carnivore. "Savannah, this is the best fried chicken I've eaten in ages," she said, laying the bare bone aside and reaching for a wing.

"Eh, it's the *only* chicken you've eaten in ages."

"That's true, but it's still the best I've had since . . . since . . . ?"

"Since the last time you ate Savannah's fried chicken," said

Ryan Stone, the reason for the dinner and the inspiration for Tammy's haute couture.

The tall, dark, and fibrillation-inducing Ryan was turning a year older, and Savannah had invited her closest circle of friends to celebrate—an intimate little sphere that just happened to encompass the members of her Moonlight Magnolia Detective Agency and no one else.

Savannah had never experienced even the slightest difficulty in drawing a line between her work and her personal life. It was quite simple: she had no personal life.

And other than one sainted grandmother and a batch of crazy siblings, whom she had left behind in Georgia, and the two black cats who were doing figure eights between her ankles, begging for table scraps, the people around her table constituted her family.

Them . . . and Dirk, who was conspicuously absent.

Dirk never passed up the opportunity to eat a free meal, and especially one of Savannah's.

"I can't believe Dirko isn't here," Tammy said. "And more than that, I can't believe I actually miss him." She washed down the final bite of chicken with a long drink of lemonade, made with real sugar—the plain old, refined, and much maligned white stuff.

Lots of it.

Savannah put only slightly less sugar in her lemonade than she did her iced tea.

Yes, Tammy was compromising her virtue right and left, in honor of Ryan Stone. Like all women between the ages of eight and eighty-eight, Tammy had fallen for Ryan within the first three seconds of setting eyes on him. And his courtly manners, countless kindnesses, and impeccable style did nothing to dispel the enchantment. She was totally, hopelessly hooked and too young to hide it.

Unlike Savannah, solidly into her forties, who was the epitome of "cool" around him. "Ryan, you darlin' birthday boy," she said, shoving an enormous bowl of mashed potatoes under his nose. "You eat up now! I won't have you fainting dead away from hunger out there in the street after having supper at *my* house." Savannah blushed slightly, hearing the adolescent titter in her own voice. He reached for the bowl, his fingers brushed hers, and she nearly dropped the spuds in his lap.

So much for "cool" in face of male perfection.

But Ryan was kind, as always, and pretended not to notice. It didn't become a demigod to react to mere female mortals slavering at his feet.

"Yes, I'm surprised to find that I miss the old boy, too," John Gibson agreed. He dabbed at his mustache with his napkin and took a sip of Beaujolais.

Although John was older than his life partner, Ryan, by quite a few years, he could still stop more than a few hearts himself. With his luxuriant silver hair, his pale blue eyes, and elegant British accent, he had the old-world charm of an English nobleman. But the occasional wicked sparkle in those eyes betrayed a far less than stodgy persona beneath those fine tweed jackets. "When the old boy isn't around," he continued, "I long for his insightful observations on the state of humanity, his stirring political exhortations, and provocative philosophical—"

"Yeah, yeah. More like, you miss sparring with him," Savannah said.

John chuckled. "Well, he *is* rather easily baited."

"And you," Ryan said, "have just enough British bulldog in you that you can't resist going after him."

"All in good fun," John replied. "All in good fun."

"Good fun. That's what the matador calls a bullfight." Savannah sighed and shook her head. More than once it had occurred to her that trying to merge her extremely diverse friends into one happy gaggle had resulted in the creation of an extended dysfunctional family.

The Moonlight Magnolia Detective Agency was basically a group of people who loved each other. Every one of them would readily defend the others from a rabid Siberian tiger attack. But even on a good day, not all of them actually liked each other. Especially Dirk and the couple sitting at her table.

"Dirk caught a case this afternoon. That's why he isn't with us," Savannah said as she stood and began to clear their plates from the table. "A homicide."

"The one over at Dona Papalardo's estate?" Ryan asked.

"Yes. How did you know about that already? It just happened around noon today. I don't think even the AP has picked it up yet."

Tammy perked up; Nancy Drew was on the case. "What? A murder at Dona Papalardo's place? No way! What happened?"

"Apparently her personal assistant was shot and killed right in Dona's front driveway," Savannah said. She gave Tammy a sideways smirk. "The gal probably caused Dona's computer to crash and lose all their billing data."

"That wasn't my fault!" Tammy's face crumpled into a pout, and she sank lower in her chair. "It's that stupid new computer you bought. I told you to let me do the consumer research online, pick out the best system, but no . . . you have to go shopping yourself at some stupid department store and pick out the first thing that—"

"It wasn't the first one I saw. It was the third one."

"And you bought it because . . . ?"

"It was blue. The other ones were gray or black. That one was prettier."

Tammy sighed. "I rest my case. Anyway, what's this business about Dona Papalardo's assistant?"

"Just that," Savannah said. "She was shot dead in the driveway of that fancy mansion Dona has up in Spirit Hills, while getting into Dona's limousine. Dirk seems to think the shooter may have thought she *was* Dona. She fits Dona's general description, and Dona had loaned her one of those fancy furs of hers—you know, the ones that PETA was giving her so much grief about?"

Tammy grimaced. "I don't blame them. Dona really overdoes that silver-screen actress bit."

"And especially for one so young," John agreed. "She can't be a day over thirty-five, and yet she dresses like Jean Harlow."

Ryan shrugged. "Hey, it's pure glamour, and it looks good on her."

Savannah sniffed. "Yeah, like *you'd* notice."

"I notice." He laughed. "Notice is all I do, but I notice."

"Did you notice my kimono?" Tammy asked, carefully adjusting one of the chopsticks in her hair in a gesture that was so sickeningly girlie that Savannah nearly gagged.

"Of course. The fabric is gorgeous." Ryan turned to John. "Don't you wish we had a few yards of that for throw pillows in the bedroom?"

Tammy groaned. "Oh, gawd, why do I even bother?"

"You look lovely, dear," John said. "And, as Ryan knows all too well, that shade of red is far too bold for our bedroom. He's just teasing you again."

She sighed and shook her head. Then, turning to Savannah, she said, "Just wait until the tabloids get a hold of this! Dona's been on the front cover of every rag in the grocery store checkout line for the past year, what with her weight loss and all."

"So true," John reached for a biscuit and began to butter it. "I've been shocked by how rapidly the pounds have melted off her. I guess these new surgeries really work."

"Of course they work," Savannah grumbled under her breath. "Cut out most of somebody's insides and there's bound to be some changes made."

"Actually," Tammy said, "I think she had gastric bypass—that doesn't actually remove—"

"Yeah, yeah." Savannah shook her head. "It's still messin' *big time* with what the good God gave you. It's a bunch of hooey, if you ask me. Dangerous hooey."

"That may be true," John interjected, "but you must admit, she's much thinner now. And healthier."

"Thinner? Yes. Healthier? Who knows? Chemo patients get thin. So do anorexics and bulimics. Doesn't mean they're healthy."

The table was silent for a tense moment, then Tammy said, a little too sprightly, "Well, so Dirk is out there now, processing the scene?"

"He is. And interviewing the staff there at her mansion and whoever was present when it happened." Savannah tried to keep the jealous tone out of her voice, but she wasn't at all successful. It was only at times like this, when Dirk was assigned to something particularly interesting, that she regretted her parting with the San Carmelita police department all those years ago.

She could take a day off, pretty much whenever she wanted. But Dirk had a pension, medical benefits, and juicy cases . . . like a murder at a movie star's mansion in the hills.

Sometimes she found herself wishing she had his job and he had a wart on his tail . . . as Granny Reid would say.

"When do you think he'll be finished over there?" Ryan wanted to know.

She glanced up at the clock on her kitchen wall, a cat whose tail swung back and forth and whose green, rhinestone eyes clicked right and left—a gift from Granny Reid, which made it a treasure. "Oh, he'll probably be wrapping up in an hour or so. Dirk doesn't exactly dally."

"Which means he'll be here in an hour and ten minutes," Tammy said. "He can smell your fried chicken and hear it calling to him from the other side of LA."

Savannah stood and began to clear the dishes. "Everybody ready for cake and ice cream?"

Ryan looked at John. "Oh, we can wait . . . for Dirk, that is."

"Most certainly," John said. "'Tisn't truly a party without him."

Savannah chuckled. Yes, they might be dysfunctional, but they were a family, this strange circle of hers. "We'll wait then," she said as she carried their dirty dishes to the sink. "But I'll go ahead and give you your gifts now that—"

The phone rang. Savannah wiped her hands on a towel and reached for it.

The voice on the other end was gruff and abrupt. Typical Dirk. He had never gotten the hang of "hello" and "good-bye." Pleasantries were a waste of time—unlike fishing and watching heavyweight bouts on Savannah's HBO.

"This sucks," was his greeting and pithy report.

"Oo-okay," she replied. "Details?"

"Come see for yourself."

"Really?" Savannah nearly jumped out of her skin.

"Yeah."

"When?"

"Now."

Savannah glanced over at the guests sitting around her table. Of course she couldn't just leave in the middle of Ryan's party, but—

"Uh, I can't right now."

"You sure? I got you a job here if you want it," Dirk said.

"A job? A paying job? Don't you toy with me, boy."

"It's yours if you want it. I told this spoiled rotten movie star bimbo that she needs a bodyguard. I told her either she hired somebody or I was going to assign my ugliest, meanest, nastiest cop to do the job. She fought me about it at first until I told her I knew a gal who could do it. You know, that you could watch out for her, even though you're a chick."

"Ah, how generous of you." Savannah reminded herself to

crack him in the head with a skillet sometime when he least expected it. "But really . . ." She lowered her voice. ". . . I can't right now. I could come over later after—"

"Go now," Ryan said.

Savannah turned around and saw that her friend had a wide smile on his handsome face. "But your birthday? The cake?"

"Hey," he said, "a homicide case and a paying gig for the Moonlight Magnolia Detective Agency? That tops a birthday party all day and all night."

Savannah weighed one against the other for two whole seconds.

A friend's party versus looking at a dead body?

Birthday cake or a homicide case?

It wasn't until she was in her '65 Mustang, speeding toward the Papalardo estate in Spirit Hills that she paused to consider what it might say about her character, or lack thereof—how quickly and shamelessly she had made that decision.

Murder takes the cake. Any ol' day.

Chapter 3

As Savannah drove her classic Mustang through the posh, gated community of Spirit Hills, she tried not to notice the dark smoke appearing in her rearview mirror, coming from the 'Stang's tailpipe. During the car's last garage appointment, it had been given a grim prognosis from Ray, her mechanic. "You're gonna need a ring job soon, Savannah, and maybe the valves ground, too. And that's gonna set you back some serious cash. You might consider trading her in while she's still running as good as she is."

The thought of getting rid of the 'Stang made Savannah's heart-strings twang with a sour resonance, and she usually managed not to think about it, not to notice the billowing black cloud behind her. One of her life mottos was: If you don't see it, it ain't there. But while that level of denial might work when it came to the size of one's buttocks, it was harder to maintain when you could look in your rearview mirror and see that you were a one-woman pollution machine in such a beautiful locale as Spirit Hills.

As she passed one palatial mansion after another with their vast property allotments, it was all too apparent to Savannah that she was a "have-not" in a "have-a-lot" community. She passed

Tudor and Greek revivals, Spanish haciendas, and the odd sprawling contemporary, but not a single driveway contained a smog factory like the one she was driving. Not even close.

"Eh, some people just got no taste for the classics," she muttered in a voice that sounded a lot like her Granny Reid's. "It takes a person of refinement to appreciate an objet d'art like you," she told the car, lovingly patting its dashboard.

As though on cue, the Mustang sputtered and spewed an especially foul emission from its rear.

"Knock it off!" she said, swatting the steering wheel. "You mess with me, you'll wind up with nobody to talk to but a junkyard Rottweiler."

But she knew she was no closer to getting rid of the Mustang than she was of dumping Dirk. Even though they were both guilty of the occasional objectionable "emission," she was loyal.

Often too loyal for her own good.

But her grandmother had taught her to walk that extra mile with a friend, and then another if they needed the company. And sometimes she felt like she had walked all the way around God's green Earth. Several times.

She wanted to believe that it was a mission of friendship that she was on now, coming to this crime scene to help her old friend. But she knew it had less to do with camaraderie and more to do with truth, justice, the American way . . . and the pure joy of catching a bad guy. It made her blood race faster than a three-pound box of gourmet assorted chocolates.

And, predictably, her pulse quickened when she saw, at the far end of the road, a Spanish-style mansion with half a dozen black-and-white police cruisers in front of it. She didn't need to scan the mailbox numbers to know that this was the Papalardo estate. Even without the parked units with their flashing red and blue lights, she recognized the mansion from pictures she had seen in magazines and on television. The seashell-pink walls, the ornate wrought-iron balcony railings, the red-tiled roof, the sheer size of the house, made it distinctive, even among the other mansions in this neighborhood.

It was a house fit for a diva. And no one fit that persona better than Dona Papalardo.

Only four years ago, Dona had been the queen of Hollywood, having won an Emmy and a Golden Globe for her roles as a steamy temptress in several television remakes of film noir classics. With her wavy blond hair, broad swimmer's shoulders, and svelte figure, Dona looked as though she had stepped right off the old silver screen into America's living rooms. And a new generation had been snared by the appeal of the classic femme fatale who used her sensual, womanly wiles to lure a perfectly good, unsuspecting, and overly horny guy down the path to perdition.

But for some reason, about which the public could only speculate, Dona had disappeared from the Hollywood scene, taking her leave almost immediately after receiving her major accolades. No one heard or saw anything of her . . . until the tabloid blitz began about a year later.

DONA PAPALARDO THE LARDO.

BEAUTY QUEEN PORKS OUT

DONA P—BIG AS A BUS!

The headlines at the grocery store checkout stands were ruthless, displaying candid and horrifically unflattering shots of the actress at her higher weight. The paparazzi ambushed her, even on her own property, photographing her from every possible angle to maximize her now-generous proportions.

Savannah had winced, seeing the pictures, reading the copy, and imagining how painful it must be for a woman once hailed as one of the most beautiful people on earth to be vilified in such a way.

She liked Dona. Having seen her interviewed many times, she

had always been struck by how down-to-earth and purely likable the woman seemed.

And no one deserved to suffer that sort of abuse.

Just because a person's job happened to be acting, that didn't make them hurt any less when they were maligned and ridiculed. Savannah felt sorry for Dona Papalardo and angry on her behalf that her fans were so fickle. They had held her in such high regard, proclaiming her one of the greatest actresses of her time. Had the woman suddenly lost her ability to act just because she had put on some pounds?

The tabloids, the gossip columnists, the late-night talk show hosts had all been merciless. There seemed to be nothing too insulting, too hurtful for them to say, as long as it got a laugh. And the world was enjoying a big laugh at a woman they had only a short time ago claimed to admire, even idolize.

And now this.

Once again, Dona Papalardo was the center of media attention. At least a dozen camera crews were milling about in front of the house. Their vans, bearing the call letters of their miscellaneous television stations, were parked helter-skelter along the roadside in front of the mansion.

Several policemen were lined up in front of the driveway, allowing none of the press to set foot on the property.

Among the SCPD cruisers in the driveway, Savannah saw the van with the county coroner's seal on the side. Dr. Jennifer Liu and her crime-scene technicians were already there, searching for evidence, collecting and processing whatever they found.

Savannah was grateful she could be here in the preliminary stages of the investigation. A fresh scene had so much more to tell than a stale one.

Dirk's old Buick was parked near the van, but she saw no sign of him among the white-smocked technicians or the uniformed police who were wandering around in the driveway in front of the mansion. But only a few of them were actually inside the yellow cordoned area directly in front of the house.

"Red marks the spot," Savannah whispered as she spotted the coroner's telltale drawings on the blood-splattered brick driveway. She had been hoping they hadn't removed the body before her arrival, but Dr. Liu and her team were both fast and thorough. No doubt, the victim was already securely bagged, inside the van, and ready for transport to the morgue.

Savannah found a spot about a hundred feet away, at the end of the media's impromptu parking lot, to leave the Mustang.

As she made her way through the throng of reporters, she had no problem elbowing them aside. As a cop, she had run the media gauntlet many times before. And while she realized that reporters had to be rude and relentless—it was their job—that didn't mean she had to be anything other than rude and relentless back to them.

"Nope, I'm nobody," she said in answer to their questions about her identity and her connection to the scene. "Nobody at all. So move out of my way and nobody'll slap you upside the head. That's it. Thank you very much. Step aside. You're too kind."

"But you aren't supposed to go onto the property," a particularly prissy anchor-type woman said to Savannah as she started up the driveway. "That policeman over there said nobody is supposed to go past the property line."

"And I'm just the nobody who can do it," Savannah returned, flashing her an icy smile. She looked the reporter up and down, taking in the designer suit, big hair, perfect makeup, and three-inch heels. "*You*, on the other hand, are obviously *somebody*, so you'd better stay where you are."

"What?"

"Eh, don't trouble your head about it. I know I'm not going to."

"What?"

Savannah chuckled and hurried on up the brick driveway to the white van and the tall, attractive Asian woman standing beside it. The lab coat did little to disguise Dr. Jennifer Liu's curvaceous body, and only an inch or two of a black miniskirt showed below the jacket's hem. Her long, black hair, although swept back and held with a bright aqua and green silk scarf, made her look more like a fashion model than a medical examiner.

To be sure, at first glance, one might think the good doctor was straight off the pages of Victoria's Secret, not on her way to an autopsy suite to cut up and evaluate dead bodies.

Until one looked into her eyes and saw a no-nonsense gleam of macabre fascination with the world of the dead that only someone who was truly called to do such work could have.

Though she did smile slightly when she saw Savannah coming her way.

The two women had bonded over chocolate so many times that they had formed a sisterhood of two. And a kinship born of and founded upon PMS cravings was as intimate and strong as any sorority could be.

"Hey, Dr. Liu," Savannah greeted her, foregoing their usual hug since the doctor was surrounded by subordinates . . . not to mention the press.

"Hi, yourself." The coroner pulled a pair of surgical gloves off her hands and dropped them into a paper bag that one of her assistants was holding. "Did Dirk give you a call?"

Savannah nodded. "He says Dona Papalardo may be in need of a bodyguard."

Dr. Liu glanced inside the open door of the van at the bagged body inside. "Yes," she said, keeping her voice low. "I'd say that some personal protection for Ms. Papalardo is a very good idea right now."

Savannah stepped closer and looked inside. The body bag's zipper had a lock on it.

And Savannah knew all too well . . . nobody ever wanted to end up in a body bag with a lock on it. Locked body bags were always bad news.

No one had a key to that lock, except Dr. Liu herself. When foul play was obvious, or even suspected, the chain of custody demanded that absolutely no one have access to the body until a thorough autopsy had been performed. If any trace of evidence was found and any charges brought, the prosecutor would want to be sure than no defense attorney could claim contamination of the evidence.

The last thing the state's attorneys would want would be someone suggesting that hairs, fibers, or any other sort of debris had been planted or even innocently transferred.

"So," Savannah said, "you think the other members of the household or staff could be in danger?"

Dr. Liu looked over at the reporters and stepped closer to Savannah. "Oh, I'm pretty sure of it," she whispered. "Dirk and I would both place a big bet that whoever shot the victim thought she was Ms. Papalardo."

"Really? Does she look that much like her?"

"From a distance, yes. Both of them are blondes, about the same size and height. And the vic was wearing that—" She nodded toward the front of the van.

Savannah had to step around the vehicle to see what Dr. Liu was referring to. And she gasped when she first saw it. It was a bloody, gory thing that at first looked like a slaughtered animal.

She had seen something like that once before, many years ago, in Georgia. Her brother had shot a rabid fox in the woods behind her grandmother's house with a shotgun. And he had brought the corpse home to show to everyone before burying it.

Savannah had seen that poor, mangled body in her dreams for months afterward. Such a beautiful animal, so graceful in life and so hideous in death.

The bloody pile on Dona Papalardo's driveway looked just like that dead fox.

"That's Ms. Papalardo's fur coat," Dr. Liu told her. "Red fox. She loaned it to her assistant, Kimberly Kay Dylan, for the evening. Kimberly had some sort of special date, and Dona let her wear the coat and one of her evening gowns. She also allowed her the use of her private limousine. The limo pulled up, here in front of the house, Kimberly walked out in the gown and coat, and was shot right over there." She pointed to the crime techs' markings on the driveway that showed where the body had fallen.

Savannah walked over to the spot. An impressive and depressing amount of blood covered the ground, and quite a number of individuals had tracked through it, spreading the gore for at least twenty feet in all directions.

It was hardly a virginal crime scene. Assorted medical garbage was strewn about; bloody gauze, discarded gloves, torn wrappers, bits of sparkling silver fabric, and even a stained brassiere lay among the forensic scribblings that marked distances and the locations where significant evidence had been found.

"Paramedics," Savannah said. She knew the signs of first-response critical care all too well.

Dr. Liu nodded. "They worked on her really hard," she said, "but it was pointless. If they'd had a surgical unit set up right here in the driveway they couldn't have saved her. It looks like it was a direct shot, through the back, right to the heart. She probably exsanguinated in less than a minute. Two minutes tops, I'm sure."

Savannah looked around, scanning the area for places where a shooter could hide, lying in wait and then fire. "Any idea where it came from?" she asked, noticing that someone could have gotten a clear shot from at least three of the neighboring mansions, not to mention numerous tall trees and a brushy hill to the side of the house. And, if they had a scope on a rifle, from a dozen more.

"Dirk thinks the shooter was up there," Dr. Liu said, nodding toward the sage- and marguerite-covered hill. "He had me send a couple of techs up there to look for a casing."

"Anything yet?"

"No. But they found some fresh footprints, and we'll be making casts of those. Looks like a man's size-thirteen hiking boot. Could be our shooter."

"Or it could have just been left by a guy who was hiking in boots," Savannah said.

Dr. Liu grinned. "That's what I like about you, Savannah, always looking on the bright side."

"Hey, Dirk's always accusing me of being a Pollyanna."

She sniffed. "Well, next to *him*, you are. *Anybody* is."

Savannah chuckled. "Speak of the devil, I've got to go find Mr. Morose. And Dona Papalardo, too. I can't believe I'm going to get to meet her. She's always seemed like such a nice person in TV interviews. I'm a big fan of hers."

Dr. Liu glanced at the front door of the mansion. "I'm sure she is under normal circumstances, but Dirk had his hands full with her earlier. She came unglued, was a real basket case for the first hour or so after it happened. Last I saw, Dirk had her there in the library and was trying to get her to calm down long enough to question her. I guess she and her assistant were very close, and she watched her friend bleed to death right here in her driveway . . . died in her arms, quite literally."

"That's rough."

"About as rough as it gets, next to losing a family member."

"I wonder if it's occurred to Dona that whoever took the shot probably thought they were aiming at *her*."

Dr. Liu nodded, a solemn look on her pretty face. "Oh, I think it's occurred to her, all right."

"How do you know?"

"Because the last time I walked through the house for something, I heard her crying and telling Dirk, 'They hate me. They always have. And they hate seeing me make a comeback. Some of them hate me enough to kill me.'"

"Hmmm." Savannah looked over at the mangled, bloody fox fur. The torn bits of finery left from the silver evening gown that the paramedics had cut off the victim's body. The medical supplies that had done nothing to halt the flood of precious blood from her ruined body. "Yep. It sure looks like somebody hated somebody," she said, "big time."

Chapter 4

Savannah left Dr. Liu to her crime scene and walked past a couple of uniformed policemen through the half-open front door of the mansion.

Even under the sad circumstances, Savannah couldn't help noticing and being impressed by the grandeur of the house. It reminded her of some of the mansions she had seen while touring the stars' homes in Hollywood. Although the mansions in Spirit Hills were less than three years old, this one had been built in a style reminiscent of the silver-screen era. The exterior was Spanish, like many of the homes in old, vintage Hollywood, the interior was markedly art deco.

The front door held a glass insert that was delicately etched. The stylized lily design was repeated in matching panels on either side of the door and in a transom above.

Savannah stepped into the cool, dim entry where a spiral staircase with a white wrought-iron banister curved gracefully from an expansive balcony to the pink marble floor at her feet.

In the center of the circular room stood a bronze, life-size statue of the goddess Diana, holding a hunting bow in her right hand and a crescent moon in her left. It was a particularly beautiful piece, and Diana was one of Savannah's favorite mythical characters, but she couldn't take the time to stand and enjoy it, as she would have under different circumstances.

To either side of her were two arched doorways, leading to opposite wings of the house. And through the one to her left she could see a dark, elegant library . . . and Dirk kneeling beside a wingback chair where a woman sat, sobbing, her hands over her face.

But Savannah didn't need to see the famous face to know it was Dona; her wavy, blond bob was her trademark, evoking memories of the classic silver-screen temptress. And even though her hair was mussed, her pale-green silk dressing gown smeared with blood, Dona Papalardo was the quintessential glamorous movie star.

Dirk glanced up and saw Savannah standing in the doorway. A look of relief flooded his face. "Savannah," he said, rising from his knee, "you're here." He turned to Dona. "Miss Papalardo, this is the gal I was telling you about. She can help you a lot more than I can, because she's . . . she's. . . ."

Not scared spitless of a crying female, like you are, Savannah thought.

Dirk didn't hold back even for a second when it came to charging through a door, knowing there might be an armed and dangerous criminal on the other side of it. But when a woman started weeping over anything from a deep family tragedy to a simple case of having her keys locked in her car, Dirk's carefully constructed facade of "cool" melted like a popsicle on a Georgia sidewalk in August.

Dona dropped her hands from her eyes and looked up at Savannah, her pretty face distorted by anger and bitterness. "You're going to help me?" she said. "You're going to tell me that you know how I feel, having someone I love die in my arms? You're going to sympathize with me and make it all better?"

"No," Savannah said, her voice as soft as the other woman's

was harsh. "I've had the sad experience of holding people while they died, but never one of my loved ones, thank God. So, I'd never tell you that I know how you feel. I wouldn't presume."

Dirk cleared his throat and crossed his arms over his chest. "Actually," he said, giving Dona a quick sideways glance, "my ex-wife was murdered. And she died in my arms. So, I know enough about it to tell you that there ain't nothing that's gonna make you feel okay for a long time. That's just the way it is. No getting around it."

Dona stopped crying and stared at him for several long, tense moments, then she gave him a small, sad smile. "Thank you for sharing that, Detective," she said. "I'm sure it isn't easy to think about it again."

Savannah herself was surprised at Dirk's candor. He didn't usually talk about Polly's murder. It had been one of the most difficult chapters of his life, and Dirk tended to keep that book tightly shut. It occurred to Savannah that he must have been particularly touched by Dona's sorrow to have been that open with her.

Savannah sat down on a chair next to Dona's and gave Dirk a subtle, dismissive nod. She could tell by the tight, pinched look on his face that, for right now, he'd had all he could take of this situation.

Cops—even good cops—had their limits when it came to dealing with the brutality of human sorrow at its worst.

And murder was always the worst.

Accidents happened and could be chalked up to destiny—a sad part of some great, higher, universal plan. Illness and aging were part of life also, nature in action.

But murder—there was just no way to reconcile it as "natural" or "meant to be." It was always so terribly wrong and so painful. And Savannah couldn't help hating the people who caused such unnatural sorrows in the world.

Just as she couldn't help the crushing sadness she felt when dealing with the families and friends left behind, the killer's other victims. She had learned long ago that no one who lost a loved one to murder ever got over it.

She knew that a part of Dona Papalardo had died in that driveway today, along with her friend. A part that she would never get back.

"I'm going to go talk to the ME," Dirk was saying to Dona, "the medical examiner. I'll leave you here with Savannah, if that's okay, Miss Papalardo."

Dona nodded, and he wasted no time making his exit through the arched doorway.

Savannah reached into her purse and produced a handful of fresh tissues. She handed them to Dona, leaning close to her as she did. The scent of the movie star's distinctive floral and spice perfume enveloped Savannah, reminding her of older, more gracious and elegant times.

Dona Papalardo was the epitome of Hollywood glamour, even in a moment of personal tragedy.

"Is there anything I can do for you?" Savannah asked, "Maybe get you a glass of water? Call someone for you?"

Dona shook her head. "No. Kim had no family to speak of, so there's no need to inform anybody. That pack of media jackals out there will make sure that her blood is splashed all over the evening news. This is what they live for. They feed off people's pain and suffering. They lap it up, the filthy, soulless scavengers."

Savannah was taken aback by the venom in Dona's words and the caustic tone of her voice. But only for a moment.

She couldn't really blame the woman for feeling that way toward the press. The media—especially the tabloids—had been ruthless and cruel to Dona Papalardo over the past few years, never giving her a moment's peace or treating her with even a modicum of common decency.

Savannah wasn't surprised that the star would hate anyone

with a camera or microphone—even the honest, hardworking reporters who were just trying to make a living by covering mainstream news items, like a deadly shooting in front of a celebrity's mansion.

"If you don't mind," Savannah said, "I'd like to ask you a few questions about the victim. She was your personal assistant, I understand."

Dona nodded. "And my friend, too. I don't know what I'm going to do without her." She reached up and patted her hair into place in a practiced, if vain, gesture that seemed inappropriate, considering the circumstances.

"Do you know why anyone would want to hurt her?" Savannah asked. "Did she have any enemies that you know of?"

"No. Kim didn't have an enemy in the world. She was a sweetheart." Dona wiped her eyes with the tissues Savannah had given her. Then she turned those famous green eyes on Savannah. Even though Dona's eyes were red and swollen, Savannah couldn't help but be struck by the woman's beauty. And even though she was past the first bloom of youthful beauty, Dona had the classic high cheekbones, the perfect skin and fine features that would assure that she remained beautiful for many years to come.

Her weight loss was equally obvious. The last time Savannah had seen her picture on the cover of a tabloid at the grocery store checkout, she had been at least fifty or sixty pounds heavier. And while Savannah thought Dona was lovely no matter what her weight, she could see that this drastic drop in size would be advantageous to her career in the ever weight-obsessed Hollywood.

"So," Savannah said, "if Kimberly had no enemies, why would someone kill her? Somebody must have had *something* against her if they would—"

"No." Dona shook her head and blew her nose loudly. "Whoever shot Kim wasn't trying to kill *her*," she said emphatically. "It was *me* they were after. That's obvious enough."

Savannah had already considered that possibility, taking into account the borrowed fur coat and gown, but she wanted to hear what Dona had to say. "Tell me why you think it's so obvious," she said.

"She was wearing my coat, my gown, and she was getting into my car. From a distance, she looks a lot like me. And *I'm* the one who has people mad enough to kill her."

"Who in particular is angry with you?"

"My former agent and my old boyfriend. I've had a parting of the ways with both of them recently. And neither one of them is very happy with me. They're both pretty infantile when they're upset about something."

"I'd call what happened in front of your house today a long way from infantile."

"I just mean that neither one of them handle conflict well."

Savannah took a pen and a small notebook from her purse, flipped the notebook open, and began to write. "What is your former boyfriend's name?"

Dona glanced down at the notebook and a guarded look came over her face. "Mark wouldn't shoot Kim. He and she were good friends."

"Yes, but you said yourself that the killer probably thought Kim was you. What's Mark's last name?"

"Kellerher. His full name is Mark Lee Kellerher. But there's no way that he would have done this."

"Did you break up with him, or vice versa?"

"I ended it, but. . . ."

Savannah began to write in her notebook. "Men hate getting dumped," she said, "Some guys more than others. It's one of the most common reasons in the world for a woman to get hurt or killed."

Dona shook her head. "No, really. You don't know Mark. He's a mouse. A total wimp. I was involved with him for seven years, and he never even raised his voice to me. Not even once." She gave a dry, bitter chuckle. "That's why I broke it off with him. Let's just put it nicely and say he was . . . passion-challenged."

Savannah thought of all the "quiet, soft-spoken, wouldn't-say-boo-to-a-goose" murderers she had encountered over the years. In spite of Dona's insistence to the contrary, she'd definitely tell Dirk to take a good, long look at Mousy Mark.

"And your agent?" she asked. "What's his name?"

"Miles Thurgood. Now there is somebody you should check out," Dona said. "He's furious with me. I fired him a month ago—an action long overdue—and he's suing me. He's a vindictive little bastard if there ever was one."

Savannah scribbled down his name, as well. "Okay. We'll check him, too. Have you had problems with him before?"

"Oh, please. Nothing but problems. And now that I've let him go, he's determined to ruin me. Somebody keyed my new Jag a week ago, and I'm just sure it was him. I was parked on Sunset Boulevard, having lunch with my new agent. I saw Miles sitting at the bar of the restaurant. A few minutes later, when I glanced his way again, he'd left, and when I went out to my car, I found a long, deep scratch all along the passenger side. It cost me six thousand dollars to fix it, and the body shop still doesn't have the paint job right."

Savannah looked up from her note-taking. "Is there anyone else that you're on the outs with right now?"

Dona shrugged. "Oh, this one and that one. Nothing all that serious. A person in my position has enemies, people who . . . let's just say . . . don't wish me well."

"Why?"

"This is a highly competitive business. Some people were

very happy to see me out of the spotlight for so long. And they aren't happy now that I'm 'back on the market,' so to speak."

"That's too bad," Savannah said, her voice soft with sympathy. "I'm sure you worked very hard and sacrificed a great deal to lose so much weight. And I'm sure it takes a lot of courage to step back out into that spotlight, knowing how closely you'll be scrutinized, and considering how unkind some people have been."

Dona stared at Savannah for a long, long time, saying nothing. Her green eyes searched Savannah's face with a guarded cynicism that had to come from years of emotional abuse. Then, just as quickly, she softened and even smiled. Apparently, she figured Savannah's words and intentions were honest and sincere.

"You have no idea," she said, "what this comeback has cost me. Is *still* costing me, for that matter. It's been nothing short of agony. The surgery, the complications that I'm still suffering, the pain and misery of it all. And for what? So that I can fit into a size five again and conform to an artificial standard of youth and beauty? This is supposed to make me a better actress?"

Dona shook her head, covered her eyes and, once again, began to softly weep. "And now this. The price wasn't high enough before. I sacrificed my health, the simple joys of living that everyone else takes for granted, like eating an ice cream cone. Now I have to pay with my friend's life? Where is it all going to stop?"

Savannah reached over and put her hand on Dona's shoulder. She was shocked to feel how thin—bony even—Dona felt beneath the silk robe.

Dona really *had* lost a lot of weight. She felt so frail, so fragile, as though if Savannah were to simply squeeze, she might break her shoulder.

She agreed with Dona. This was supposed to be better somehow? Becoming a bag of bones was preferable to enjoying the soft, feminine curves that nature gave most women once they entered their thirties and forties?

"I'm so sorry, Dona," she told her, stroking her shoulder. "But if it's any comfort at all to you, please know that I'll help Detective Coulter find the person who's responsible for your friend's death. And if you want me to, I can work for you, keep a close eye on you for a while, to make sure that nothing else like this happens."

Dona nodded, reached up and covered Savannah's hand with her own. "I want that," she said through her tears. "I want that very much."

"Then you've got it."

Savannah smiled—a small, grim smile that added no warmth to the cold blue of her eyes. Oh, she'd help Dona Papalardo, all right.

Catch a bad guy, a killer who would hide in the brush like a coward and shoot a helpless woman down in cold blood?

Protect another innocent woman and prevent him from doing the same to her?

Oh, yes. That was better than a bubble bath with a glass of champagne and a box of chocolate truffles.

Wa-a-ay better.

Chapter 5

When Savannah arrived back home later in the evening, she found Tammy sitting at the rolltop desk in her living room, working away at the computer. Although exactly what Tammy found to do at the computer that was "work" related, hour after hour, day after day, Savannah could only guess. Being ignorant of even the most rudimentary workings of all machines—except her Beretta and her Mustang's carburetor—Savannah didn't surf, chat, send or receive e-mail, IM, blog, or even Google.

And she was fine with that. Her ignorance was fully intentional. She had more than enough people to aggravate her in her everyday life. Why add a worldwide network of numbskulls to compound the problem? That was one of her favorite mottos, and she held it dear.

Savannah had a lot of mottos. She lived by them . . . when it was convenient. And when it wasn't, she revised or tossed them.

Life is complicated enough without bogging yourself down with a bunch of stupid rules—especially those that are self-imposed. And most are.

That was her main motto.

Tammy looked up with a bright smile on her face when Savannah came into the room. "Did you get the job?"

Savannah's cats—miniature panthers named Diamante and Cleopatra—bounded off their window perch and ran to her. She nearly tripped over them as they rubbed against her ankles and meowed loudly.

"Of course I got the job," she said, bending down to stroke their silky black coats. Ah, unconditional kitty love made it worth coming home every time.

Well, mostly unconditional.

A never-ending flow of Kitty Vittles and a clean litter box. Constant petting and never being able to sit down without a cat on your lap. Black cat hair on every garment you owned, and never being able to leave a half-eaten tuna sandwich on your coffee table . . . or kitchen table either, for that matter.

Okay. So kitty love wasn't all that unconditional. In Savannah's estimation, it was still good. There was something to be said for having someone to come home to—someone who didn't leave the toilet seat up and still miss the bowl.

Cleo let out a particularly plaintive yowl, and Tammy said, "Those beasts are lying to you. I fed them both half an hour ago."

"Celery stalks? Carrot sticks? Green tea?"

Tammy made a face. "No, that foul-smelling, fishy crap that they like. The canned stuff, not the dry. I nearly gagged."

Savannah thought of the blood and gore on Dona Papalardo's driveway and figured it was a good thing that Tammy hadn't been along. Anybody who gagged at canned cat food might do a lot worse viewing the aftermath of a homicide. And Dr. Liu took a dim view of people adding their own DNA to her crime scene.

"When does your gig start?" Tammy wanted to know.

"Tomorrow morning. I just came home to tie up some loose ends here and get some things together to take over there."

"You get to stay there? At Dona Papalardo's mansion?"

Savannah grinned and chuckled. "I do! I do! And you should see the place. It's gorgeous. Straight off the silver screen. Art deco glamour all the way."

Tammy's lower lip protruded like that of a three-year-old being told that it's still eleven and a half months to Christmas. "I wish I *could* see it. It's not much fun being your assistant if I don't get to assist you. Especially at cool places like Dona Papalardo's mansion."

"I'll see what I can do to get you inside as soon as possible."

The pout turned into a bright smile. "Really?"

"Do I lie to you?"

"Um . . ."

"Without good reason?"

"Uh . . ."

Savannah sighed. "I'll get you in. I'll deliberately leave something behind that I really need, and you can bring it to me tomorrow. How's that?"

"Will I get to stay and play?"

"We'll see."

Again the pout. "I have a mother. I know what *we'll see* means."

Savannah sat down in her favorite seat, an overstuffed, comfortable armchair that was covered with rose-print chintz. Propping her feet on an ottoman, she gathered the cats into her lap. They jostled each other, vying for the best spot. "But I'm not anybody's mother," Savannah said. "Unless you count these two varmints."

"No, but you're the oldest of nine kids. And big sisters can be as bad or worse than moms."

Savannah laughed. "That's true. And if you don't believe it, ask any of my eight younger siblings."

"Oh! That reminds me." She pulled a piece of paper from one

of the desk's cubbyholes. "A member of your Georgia brood called about an hour ago, asked to speak to you. I told her I wasn't sure when you'd be back, just in case you didn't want to talk to them tonight."

"Wouldn't want to talk to my own flesh and blood?" Savannah said.

"Well, I know that they can be . . . um . . . trying . . . sometimes."

"Trying? *My* family? Naw. I just *love* hearing about Vidalia's most recent fight with Butch, and how the morning sickness has hit her and her ankles are swelling already, and Marietta's latest fiancé—the guy she found on the Convict Penpal Web site—or Macon's current brush with the law, having burgled some junkyard for car parts or—"

"This time it's Jesup."

"Ah, the Princess of Darkness. And that's on a good day. How did she sound?"

"Gloomy."

"That's our Jessie. She can generate thunderheads on a cloudless day, just by crawling out of bed and looking out the window. What did she want?"

"Didn't say. Just asked to talk to you. She said she wasn't at home, but didn't want to leave a number."

Savannah felt a little guilty for the sense of relief she felt at not having to return the call. After all, Jesup was her sister, and who wouldn't want to talk to her *sister*?

A sister who harbored a morbid interest in murder, mayhem, and disease—the most exotic, gut-roiling ways that a human being could depart the earth.

A sister who wore nothing but black, who wrote twenty-stanza poems about Jack the Ripper, the Spanish Inquisition, the Donner Party, and Ted Bundy.

A sister who constantly asked Savannah if she had any new autopsy or crime-scene photos to share.

Who could resist the charm and appeal of a sibling like *that*?

Savannah decided that *she* could. And she could get rid of the guilt, too. She'd just toss it on the pile with all those pesky, outdated mottos.

"How long do you figure this bodyguard job with Dona will last?" Tammy wanted to know.

"Long enough for me to pay this month's mortgage and last month's utility bills," Savannah replied. "And I—"

The doorbell rang, followed by a loud pounding on the front door.

Savannah glanced at her watch. It was after nine.

Most of her friends were well-trained enough not to drop by without calling first, and certainly not after nine, which was usually her romance-novel reading/chocolate nibbling time.

And while Dirk wasn't particularly well-trained, she knew it wasn't him. She had said good-bye to him at the Papalardo mansion and sent him home with strict instructions to get a good night's sleep and let some uniformed cops stand guard at Dona's.

When it came to sleeping, Dirk usually followed directions.

"Who can *that* be?" Tammy said.

"A dead person walkin,'" Savannah replied, dumping the cats onto the floor and heading to the front hall. She mentally checked the fact that her Beretta was in its holster, lying on the table next to the door. If it was a burglar or a door-to-door salesman, they were living their final moments on earth.

When she opened the door and saw the faces of the people standing on her porch, Savannah instinctively slammed the door closed, threw the bolt and reached for the gun. She had it out of the holster and had chambered a round before she could form any conclusion about what she had just seen.

"Who is it?" Tammy asked.

Who? Savannah wasn't even sure *what* it was.

Her mind was churning with the possibilities. A person in a Halloween mask? It wasn't even close to Halloween. A burglar?

Violent, disturbing visions of all the home-invasion robbery scenes she'd ever processed raced through her mind, along with plans of action.

"Call nine-one-one!" she told Tammy. "And run to the back door. Don't open it. Make sure it's locked and turn on the porch light."

Then she pointed the gun at the center of her closed front door—her finger off the trigger, but ready.

"Who the hell are you?" she shouted. "And what do you want?"

"Your sister, you idiot," yelled back a voice with a thick Georgia accent. "Open up."

Sister? Sister?

Savannah's brain whirred, trying to process the vision of the white-faced, black-lipped, monster-clown faces on her doorstep with the concept of "sister."

And it just didn't compute.

"Open up, Van! What's the matter with you, girl? Slam the door in *my* face, will ya?"

Okay, the voice was right. The Southern twang, the bossy indignation—all rang Savannah's memory bells.

She ventured a look through the peephole, a definite no-no when expecting that the person on the other side might be an armed and dangerous criminal. More than one person had done so, only to find themselves looking down the barrel of a gun.

She saw the snow-white face again, with its black-rimmed eyes and black lips, surrounded by spiky black hair. The face was grinning and sticking its tongue out at her.

"Savaaa-nn-ah," it said. "Open the door this very minute! I want you to meet my new husband!"

Savannah looked past the first face to the one behind it, equally adorned with the macabre makeup. She could tell from the square set of the jaw and the strange goatee that it was male.

Husband? For half a second she considered that her sister, Vidalia and her redneck, mechanic husband, Butch, had gone stark raving crazy. Vidalia was the only one of her siblings who was married at the moment, Marietta being between hubbies.

"It's me, Jesup. Girl, have you plumb lost your mind? Let us in!"

Suddenly, the loose pieces snapped into place.

Jesup.

Over her shoulder, she shouted, "Skip the nine-one-one call, Tammy."

"I've already got them on the line," was the answer.

"Tell them it's a false alarm."

Tammy came into the hallway, the phone to her ear. "Then I should tell them that we aren't in life-threatening danger?"

Savannah sighed as she replaced her gun in its holster, laid it on the table, and opened the door. "Well, I wouldn't go *that* far. But, hopefully, you and I can handle it."

"Does Granny Reid know that you ran off and got yourself hitched?" Savannah asked, once she had her sister and her new-found brother-in-law sitting on the sofa, tall glasses of lemonade in their hands and a plate of pecan brownies on a plate in front of them.

"Nope," Jesup replied, munching on a brownie. "It's gonna be as big a surprise for her as it was for you."

"Dear Lord, I hope not! She's too old for a shock like I just had. Her ticker would seize up and stop for sure. Where does she think you are?"

"Oh, she knows that I went to Las Vegas. She just thinks I'm still there, gambling and dabbling in the devil's stagnant scum pond of wickedness and pure *D* iniquity—as she calls the place. And she thinks I'm alone. She doesn't know nothin' about Bleak. Nobody back home does. We met on Monday. It was love at first sight."

Savannah cast a critical eye over the object of her younger sister's affection, the latest member of her family, and she tried not to gag. He reminded her of a certain jewelry thief she had recently wrestled to the ground. The leather vest, the tattoos that crawled from his wrists up his arms and onto his neck, images of snakes, snarling demon faces, bats and spiders, vampire fangs dripping with blood—all without a "Mom," a heart, or a flower among them. Not to mention the spiky hair that, with the help of a jar of gel, defied gravity as well as society.

She also had to resist the urge to walk across the floor and slap her sister stupid. One whack would probably suffice.

She glanced over at Tammy, who was known for being far more tolerant and less judgmental than Savannah ever could be, even on her most benevolent, Sunday-go-to-meetin' behavior.

And she could tell that even Sister Tammy the Munificent was put off by his appearance.

Both Bleak and Jesup wore white, chalky foundation makeup, as well as lipstick that was the color of coagulated blood and black, dramatic eyeliner. But Bleak had used the liquid eyeliner brush to draw a spiderweb on his right cheek, complete with a spider, whose eyes were tiny rhinestones, apparently glued to his face.

All Savannah could think was that he looked like a demon-possessed drag queen. And an ugly one at that.

Yes, Gran would roll over in her grave—if she weren't still alive.

"You met on Monday," Savannah repeated in an ominously monotone voice that she usually reserved for questioning perps she suspected of child molesting or puppy drowning. "Monday, you say. And it's only . . . Friday. Now, if that don't just beat all. And you got married when?"

"Yesterday," Jesup announced proudly. "We wanted to on Tuesday, after spending the night together Monday night, but we decided to wait and think about it some more, you know."

"Oh, yes, wait, think about it, mull it over, weigh the pros and cons. Lord knows you wouldn't want to just jump into something as all-fired serious as marriage with both feet on a moment's notice like that. That would just be plain ol' loco."

"Exactly. It's a real commitment, marriage is, and—"

"No, Jessie," Savannah said, "bringing home a kitten from the city dump, that's a commitment. Marriage is a life sentence. At least, it's supposed to be."

Jesup looked at Savannah as though she had lost her mind, then rolled her eyes. "Well, duh, Van. Of course it's for life. Once you meet your soul mate who completes you, you'll never want to be without them. Not even for a moment."

"Soul mate?" Savannah shook her head. "What constitutes a soul mate? Somebody who shares the same tube of lipstick with you? The same bottle of black nail polish? Does that constitute a 'mate' who was ordained to be with you since the creation of the universe or some such hooey?"

Jesup reached over and grasped Bleak's hand in hers. Yes, their red-black nail polish *was* the same shade, although hers were extremely long dragon claws, and his were bitten to the quick. "Yes, we are soul mates and the very fact that you have to ask what a soul mate is means that you haven't met yours yet. So there!"

Jesup turned goo-goo eyes on Bleak and blinked at him with what must have been pure soul-mate adoration.

Savannah wasn't sure because, as Jesup had so tactlessly reminded her, she hadn't met hers yet. Or if she had, he hadn't announced himself as such, and she hadn't recognized him.

Although, watching her sister ogle her new hubby, Savannah was reminded of a few milk cows she'd known on neighboring farms in Georgia. The same shining eyes, the same gentle spirit, the same quiet acceptance, generosity, and quiet resignation—all the result of having a single-digit IQ.

Jesup had always been a bit ditzy, a little melancholy of disposition, a tad shy of the good sense possessed by most tennis balls. But this was a new low, even for her.

"Did the two of you meet in Vegas?" Tammy asked, sprightly, feigning fascination.

"Yes! At the Blood Fest," Jesup replied. "It was wonderful! Four full, beautiful days." She looked up at Bleak and batted her spiky eyelashes that were caked with clumpy, red mascara. "And four wonderful nights, as well," she added.

"So, Bleak . . ." Savannah said, helping herself to another brownie. It was going to take a lot of carbs to get her serotonin level up after this shock. She walked over to her comfy chair and lowered herself into it with a weary sigh. ". . . tell us about yourself."

Bleak fingered the stud sticking out of the right side of his nose and said, "Sure. Whatcha wanna know?"

"How old are you?"

"Thirty-three."

"When is your birthday?"

"January thirteenth. Why? Are you going to send me a birthday card?"

Oh yeah, Savannah thought. *Right after I run a check on you and see what sort of a record you've got, you jackass.* Then she reminded herself that, other than his bizarre personal grooming, she hadn't really seen anything too objectionable in ol' Bleak. *Keep an open mind, Savannah*, she told herself. *At least until you get that report back with his arm-long rap sheet and find out that he's a serial killer.*

"Do you have a last name, Bleak? Or is it just Bleak, like Cher and Madonna and—"

"Yeah. Manifest."

"Manifest." Savannah stared at him for a long time. In her peripheral vision she could see Tammy squirm and shoot her a warning look to "be nice." She could also hear Granny Reid's voice deep in her heart telling her to assume the best about people until they showed you the worst. Although, she was pretty sure that the minute Gran saw this guy, she'd call the elders of her church over to lay hands on him and cast out the devils out of him.

"So . . ." she said, ". . . about thirty-three years ago, Mr. and Mrs. Manifest had a beautiful, bouncing baby boy, and they looked down at him in his bassinet and said, 'Now, ain't he just the cutest thing you ever did see? Let's name this precious little bundle of joy "Bleak."' Is that what you're telling us?"

Bleak returned her level stare. "Nope. Bleak Manifest is a name of my own choosing. It better describes my view of this prison sentence we call life."

"It describes it better than . . . ?"

He hesitated. And Jesup filled in the blank. "Better than Milton Pillsbury."

Savannah checked him out again, the makeup, tattoos, piercings, the rattlesnake boots. Yes, Bleak Manifest did suit him a lot better than Milton Pillsbury. She had to agree with him there.

She wondered what he looked like under all that makeup. *Oh, well,* she thought, *I'll find out when I see his mug shot.*

"And are you from Las Vegas originally?"

He laughed. "Nobody's from Vegas originally. My family is in Barstow. They own the biggest mortuary there."

"I'll bet they do. And is that the line of work you're in?"

"No. I'm in school."

"To be . . . ?"

"I want to run a body farm."

"A body farm." She glanced over at Tammy, who nearly choked on her mineral water. "Do you mean a body farm, as in, forensic research?"

His eyes blazed with interest. And to her dismay, so did Jesup's. Suddenly, they both came alive with passion.

Bleak scooted forward to the edge of the sofa. "Yeah! Me and Jess are going to have our own body farm, there in the desert outside Vegas. I've already got the property picked out. It'll be perfect. Lots of wildlife to scavenge the corpses and hot enough that the decomposition rate will be—"

Savannah held up her traffic-cop palm. "Okay, Okay. Gotcha. I've been to body farms before . . . far more frequently than I've wanted to."

"Really? Wow!" Bleak was practically dancing in his black leather pants. "Oh man! That's so cool. When Jess told me about you, that you're a homicide investigator, I told her, 'Hey, I gotta meet this sister of yours.' And that's when we decided we'd spend our honeymoon here with you. Do you have any cool pictures of murder scenes? Stuff like that? Could we, like, go with you on some of your investigations, you know, before they actually clean up the scenes and—?"

"Whoa! Hold on a minute. In the first place, I'm not a 'homicide investigator.' I'm a private investigator."

"Who usually investigates homicides," Tammy said.

Savannah gave her a dirty look. "You aren't helping here, Tamitha."

Tammy giggled. "Sorry."

"And . . ." Savannah continued, ". . . it's usually all I can do to get myself onto a scene before it's 'cleaned up,' as you say. There's no way I could get you onto an unprocessed crime scene. That's illegal and, to be frank, it wouldn't be half as much fun as you think it would be."

Bleak and Jesup looked at each other, totally confused. "But why not?" Jesup asked Savannah.

"Why not *what?*"

"Why wouldn't it be fun?"

"Yeah!" Bleak added. "I think it would be great! I mean to see it firsthand, the blood and guts and brain matter and—"

"Oh, for pete's sake." Savannah shook her head. "What's the matter with you two chuckleheads? There's nothing fun or great or *cool* about somebody being murdered. It's the most horrific thing that can ever happen! Ever!" She jumped up from her chair, walked over and snatched the plate of brownies out from under their noses. "You guys are disgusting, and I've had just about enough of this conversation."

"Hey," Jesup said, grabbing her lemonade and holding it close to her chest before Savannah could nab it, too. "Death is what life is all about. We're all going to die someday. That's where we're all headed."

"Yeah." Bleak nodded so hard that his gelled hair nearly budged. "We're all going to be moldering in a grave someday, just like those bodies on the body farm. Might as well get used to the idea."

"Get used to the idea, yes," Savannah agreed. "But we don't have to wallow in it like a bunch of hogs in a mud ditch. Death is *not* what life is about. *Life* is what life's about."

Tammy cleared her throat. "And besides," she said, "not all of us are going to molder in a grave somewhere, monopolizing valuable land resources. Personally, I'm being cremated. It's far more environmentally conscious. Do you know, I read that cemeteries take up—"

"Oh, shut up, Tammy." Plate of brownies in hand, Savannah stomped off into the kitchen.

Once she was gone, Tammy snickered. "Sorry," she said. "Savannah's had a rough day. Someone was murdered at Dona

Papalardo's estate nearby here, and she's helping with the investigation."

Jesup shrugged. "Eh . . . you don't have to apologize to *me* for my big sister. She always was cranky and bossy."

Bleak nudged his new wife. "Did you hear that? We lucked out! She's investigating a homicide." He turned to Tammy. "Do you think she's got some cool pictures of the crime scene? You know, like clotted blood and . . ."

Chapter 6

The next morning, when Savannah came downstairs, wearing her bathrobe and fuzzy slippers, Diamante tucked under one arm and Cleopatra scampering at her feet, she could already smell the aroma of coffee wafting from the kitchen. She expected to see Tammy sitting at the computer, but she hadn't arrived yet. So Savannah was momentarily puzzled as to who might have made coffee. And if she wasn't mistaken, she was pretty sure she could smell toast, too.

When she entered the kitchen, she saw her sister standing at the counter, slathering butter and peach preserves on bread, a big sappy grin on her face.

Savannah wasn't a morning "grinner" and didn't tolerate cheerfulness very gracefully until at least ten o'clock.

Noon, if she'd been up late the night before.

As she had been last night.

After her initial huff off to the kitchen with the brownies, she had managed to adjust her attitude and had allowed them to spend the night. They'd made no lodging reservations and the seaside, vacation town of San Carmelita wasn't the sort of place where you could get a motel room on short notice. Not realizing this, a lot of naive tourists wound up sleeping in their cars, parked on the beaches on weekend nights. And Savannah had investigated too many robberies over the years, which had occurred under exactly those circumstances, to turn her kin over to the bad guys.

Even if they did look more like the bad guys than the law-abiding ones.

There was the added bonus that they wouldn't be roaming the beach, scaring away the local tourist trade and frightening small children.

Yes, Savannah considered it her civic duty to keep her weird relatives contained.

"What are you up to?" she asked with subdued interest as she rummaged in the cupboard for her favorite Minnie Mouse mug. Then she realized it was already on the counter, next to the Mickey mug. Both were already brimming with coffee and thick cream, and something told her that Jesup hadn't poured either of them for her.

"I'm making breakfast for the first time for my new husband," Jesup said. "I'm going to impress him by taking it to him and serving him in bed."

"Well, ain't that nice?" Savannah settled for the Snow White mug, which had a picture of the witch handing Snow a poisoned apple.

Briefly she considered putting chocolate-flavored laxative in a fudge cake and feeding it to her houseguests that night. If she couldn't get them to take their honeymoon elsewhere, it might be a plan.

But after she had swallowed several slugs of the thick, rich brew, her spirits began to lift slightly. And as she watched her sister smearing on the preserves with what could only be described as schmaltzy attention to detail, her heart softened.

Without her ghastly makeup, Jesup was, once again, her little sister.

Jess had always been the "runt of the litter," shorter and slighter of build than the rest of the Reid clan, who tended more toward the robust. "Horizontally gifted" was how Savannah liked to think of it. But Jess was barely over five feet tall, more than a head shorter than Savannah. And she couldn't have weighed more than a hundred pounds, even considering the metal studs that sprouted from her ears, lips, tongue . . . and probably a lot of other places that Savannah didn't want to know about.

But without the gel spikes in her hair, it fell in soft ringlets, framing her delicate, heart-shaped face. Her eyes were the same startlingly blue shade as Savannah's, and her complexion was the traditional Reid combination of peaches-and-cream perfection.

Savannah had lain awake for hours the night before wondering if drug addiction was part of this new culture of hers, not to mention the horrors of "cutting" and self-mutilation that some of that culture espoused.

But Jesup's skin and eyes were clear and bright, and there were no marks of any kind on her arms, which were totally exposed by the men's sleeveless undershirt she was wearing.

She was also wearing men's boxers, which were black with white skulls and crossbones.

Probably knucklehead's knickers, Savannah figured. She had already decided—in the future, anything new that she didn't like about her sister, she was going to blame directly on the dude still asleep upstairs in her guest room.

Which reminded her; she had to get Dirk on him right away, running his name and birth date to see if he had any outstanding warrants. If he was, indeed, a bad guy, this whole ridiculous marriage fiasco could be remedied before Granny Reid had to even hear about it, let alone fret over it.

The last thing Savannah wanted was for Gran to fret. Both because she didn't like to see her beloved grandmother upset about anything, and because Gran tended to fret very loudly . . . on the phone . . . to her . . . for hours.

"If you want to really impress your man," Savannah said, "how about some eggs and bacon to go with that toast? Maybe some cheese grits or cream gravy?"

Jesup brightened even more. "Really? Are you going to cook a full breakfast for us? You're so sweet, Van!"

"Not me, wide eyes. *You.* I have to down this coffee and get going."

"Going?" Her face fell. "Where are you going? Aren't you going to stay here and visit with us? I want Bleak to get to know you, and he's all excited about talking to you about the cases you've solved. He heard about the one where you found that woman's body out in a cabin in the woods and she'd been there for days and was all gross and—"

"Stop it. Right now." Savannah held the hot mug to her forehead for a moment. Yes, last night's headache was returning with a vengeance. "I'm sorry I can't stay here with you guys and entertain you for the rest of your . . . honeymoon . . . but I didn't know you were coming. And I accepted an assignment to—"

"A homicide? At that actress's house? Cool!"

"No, not cool. The body's already gone and by now the blood's been scrubbed off the driveway, so you two ghouls wouldn't be interested at all. I've been hired to be Dona Papalardo's bodyguard, starting today. So, you're on your own."

"That bites."

"Sorry. You should have let me know you were going to get married and spend your honeymoon with me."

"How could I? I didn't know myself until yesterday!"

"My point exactly. Doing things on the spur of the moment doesn't always work out best for everybody."

Jesup's chin began to quiver, and tears brimmed in her blue

eyes. "I hope this isn't the kind of support that my whole family is going to give me. I was hoping you'd be happy for me."

"I am," Savannah lied. "I'm plumb tickled pink about you finding your soul mate. And to prove it, I'm going to let you stay here in my house for the whole week, or until I'm done with this assignment. You guys can go to the beach or drive down to Malibu or go see Hollywood or hang out at Disneyland, whatever you want. But you're going to be pretty much on your own, because I have to work for a living."

"Bleak's going to be so-o-o-o disappointed."

Savannah sighed. "Well, it's your honeymoon, Jessie. Surely you can think of *something* to do to lift the guy's . . . ah . . . spirits. Just don't do it anywhere except in the guest bedroom. I don't want to have to disinfect the entire house when you've left."

An hour later, when Savannah arrived at the Papalardo mansion, her suitcase in her hand, optimism in her heart, and a finally-I-have-a-chance-to-make-a-lousy-buck grin on her face, she was met at the door by a woman she had never seen before.

The lady's straight, shoulder-length hair was bright red—a shade so bright that she couldn't possibly have been born with it. And the angora sweater and wool slacks she wore were the same red, bordering on fuchsia.

In contrast, her face had no color at all. Savannah had seen rosier cheeks on corpses in the morgue.

And while Savannah had seen many fair-skinned people in her day, and was relatively light complexioned herself, she couldn't help but think that the lady who had answered the door could benefit from a day on the beach, soaking in one or two of the famous California rays. Or at least a "dab from a pot of rouge" as Granny Reid called it.

But when she looked into the woman's eyes, she saw the palest shade of blue she had ever seen in her life. And she decided this lady must have a few Viking ancestors perched on the branches of her family tree. Maybe the red hair was natural, after all.

"Hello," Savannah said, holding out her hand. "I'm Savannah Reid. I believe Ms. Papalardo is expecting me."

The woman shook her hand, and Savannah couldn't help noticing that her fingers were cold and sweat-damp. And although she was nearly as tall as Savannah, she had a frail, delicate look about her. Even though the sweater and slacks were loosely fitted, Savannah could see enough to know that her body was thin to the point of being bony.

As Gran would say, Savannah thought, *here's a gal in desperate need of a week's worth of good homestyle cookin' . . . three meals a day of it . . . breakfast, dinner*, and *supper*.

The woman gave her a lackluster smile. "Yes," she said, opening the door wider and motioning her inside. "Dona is out, but your friend Sergeant Coulter told me you'd be coming. He asked me to let you in and show you to your room."

"Where *is* Dirk?" Savannah asked, stepping into the cool marble foyer.

"He's out in the backyard, I believe, questioning the gardener."

Savannah considered the fact that she should have stopped by the Patty Cake Bakery and gotten him a couple of cinnamon rolls and an extra large coffee. He had told her that he intended to arrive here very early to talk to Dona Papalardo again, to question anybody he could get his hands on, and snoop in general. He would be grumpy without his caffeine/sugar jolt to get him going.

She paused by the statue of Diana and turned to the woman, "By the way," she said, "I don't believe I caught your name . . ."

"Mary Jo Livermore," she said. "I'm Dona's friend. Her best friend, in fact. Have been since elementary school."

Briefly, Savannah flashed back on her conversation with Dona the day before. When she had offered to call someone for Dona, someone to perhaps offer her some comfort and strength in her time of need, Dona had flatly refused. Savannah wondered if Mary Jo and Dona were as close as Mary Jo seemed to think they were.

"That's nice," Savannah said. "I must admit I haven't stayed in contact with most of my childhood friends. But then, they're all in Georgia. It's really nice that Dona has a good friend to help her through this difficult time."

Mary Jo's pale blue eyes stared blankly into hers for a long time before she seemed to snap to attention. "Oh. Right. You mean about Kim getting killed. Yeah, that's a bad one, to be sure. I suppose Dona was pretty upset about that."

"Oh, you haven't seen Dona since it happened?"

"Not yet. She was gone by the time I got here this morning. I had an early morning session at the recording studio, so I couldn't come over right away. And Dona had a breakfast meeting with her new agent in Hollywood. Our schedules don't allow us to see each other as often as we'd like. It's a shame how busy everybody is these days."

She ushered Savannah toward the staircase, and together they climbed the steps to the second floor. "Your room is up here with the other guest rooms," she said. "Dona's bedroom is on the third floor."

"That's good," Savannah said. To herself she added, *Somebody would have to get past my door to get to her.*

She was doing a mental checklist of security factors in her head as she passed through the house. There was a state-of-the-art burglar system in place. She had seen the primary panel mounted on the wall next to the front door, and several motion and glass break detectors. She noted the mini-sensors on the windows and doors.

But the alarm would have to be activated and remain on at all times to be truly effective. And when she had passed through the foyer, it had been turned off. She was surprised that Dirk hadn't been on top of that himself. He might not be the most detail-conscious guy on the planet, but he usually took care of business when it came to security.

At the top of the stairs, she saw two long hallways, branching off in either direction. Mary Jo led her down the one to the right.

"Your room is here," she said, "second one on the left. Mine is across the hall."

"Oh, you're staying here, too?"

Mary Jo tensed and gave her a quick, defensive, and angry look. "Yeah. So?"

Savannah made a mental note to consider later what that might mean. "No problem," she said. "It's nice to know I have a roommate right across the hall. You know, if I need to get up in the middle of the night for a bowl of ice cream, you can join me."

Mary Jo gave her a long, confused look, as though the concept of late-night snacking was completely foreign to her.

A gal in need of a banana split with extra fudge topping and whipped cream, Savannah added to her former assessment of Mary Jo Livermore.

Mary Jo opened the door to the room, and Savannah stifled a gasp. It might not be "cool" to be overly impressed with one's accommodations, but it was hard not to be.

The room was larger than Savannah's living room and dining room combined and was a delicious shade of the palest, smoky pink. From the watered silk that covered the walls to the matching moiré draperies, and the bed curtains hanging from the canopy bed, it was a feminine delight—the sort of room Savannah adored, and the kind that would keep a "manly man" like Dirk awake all night.

And underlying the glamour of the room was that lovely, distinctive scent of Dona Papalardo's perfume, adding the final touch of elegance to the setting.

"Do you like it?" Mary Jo asked.

"It's *gorgeous*." Savannah walked over to the old-fashioned dressing table and ran her fingers over a matching silver comb, brush, and mirror. Beside the antique set was a perfume bottle—a pale-pink art deco design with a series of triangles and arches, creating a pleasing geometric pattern. Savannah lifted the glass stopper and sniffed. Instantly, the rich, complex scent enveloped her, sending her mental pictures of sunlit gardens and grand ladies in white dresses with parasols.

"Very nice," she said.

"It's Dona's own custom scent. She has it mixed for her every time she goes to Paris," Mary Jo said.

Savannah chuckled and said, "Well, don't we all?" as she reluctantly placed the stopper into the bottle and turned her attention to the other items on the tabletop.

Arranged on a lace doily was a series of small gilded picture frames, containing sepia-tone photos of women dressed in flapper attire. Savannah thought of a picture she had seen of her own great-grandmother, wearing a similar, if more modest, outfit. She wondered if those days had been half as much fun as they looked. Probably not.

Lighting the table was an exquisite lamp, a delicate porcelain creation that was obviously very old. It featured a man and woman dressed in eighteenth-century attire with powdered wigs, hair ribbons, and ruffles galore. The lady sat at a harpsichord, apparently trying to play, as the gentleman distracted her with a lover's embrace. Above them, the shade dripped with layer upon layer of beautiful handmade lace.

"That lamp is quite special," Mary Jo said when she saw

Savannah studying it. "Dona loves it. She found it at an estate sale. It once belonged to Norma Shearer."

"Norma Shearer?"

"Norma was an actress who was married to one of the uppity-ups at MGM during the golden age of the silver screen. She and William Randolph Hearst's honey, Marion Davies, competed for roles back then."

"Dona is into the Roaring Twenties, I see," Savannah observed.

"Dona is into old Hollywood, period." Mary Jo walked over to a dressmaker's form that stood next to an ornately painted dressing screen in the corner of the room. The form was draped with a long, beaded, fringed, velvet duster and had a feather boa draped around its neck. "Dona is, and always has been, more comfortable in almost any era other than this one. She's only truly happy when she's surrounded by things from . . . yesteryear. It's an escape, I suppose."

"An escape from what?"

"Being Dona Papalardo."

Savannah watched the play of emotions that crossed Mary Jo's face: sadness, pity, and maybe a hint of resentment?

"What's so bad about being a beloved actress?" She glanced around the opulent room. "And a rich one to boot?"

"You'd think it would be enough, wouldn't you?"

Yes, Savannah was sure she detected some jealousy, maybe even some bitterness there.

"But not everybody loves Dona," Mary Jo continued.

Savannah's detective antenna rose. "Oh? Anyone in particular who doesn't?"

Mary Jo was on instant alert. "Not anybody who would want to *kill* her, if that's what you mean," she said.

"So, what do you think that shooting was about yesterday?"

Mary Jo shrugged, a blank mask firmly in place. "Who knows? Some kook probably. Or maybe somebody who had it in for Kim. Just because she looked a bit like Dona, who's to say it was Dona they were trying to kill?"

"Do you know anyone who would want Kim dead?"

"I didn't really know Kim that well."

"Even though she worked for your best friend'?"

Mary Jo's chin raised a notch and her eyes narrowed. "That's right. I don't get close to the help. I hardly knew Kim at all, and I have no idea why that happened yesterday. I'm as much in the dark as anybody about it."

Savannah didn't believe her. After years of trying to squeeze information out of people, she was an excellent judge of which fruits had juice in them and which ones didn't. She was sure that Mary Jo had a lot more to give than she was offering.

And that's just not smart, lady, Savannah thought. *Hold out on me, and I'll look at you that much closer to find out why.*

Savannah gave Mary Jo a long, searching look designed to make her squirm—if, indeed, she had anything to squirm about. But the woman returned the look with a dead-level stare that Savannah could only describe as bordering on defiant.

Yes, she would definitely have to watch this one. It wouldn't be the first time that a so-called "best friend" had stabbed somebody in the back. Or shot them, as the case might be.

"It's very kind and supportive of you," Savannah said evenly, "to be here for your friend in her time of need."

"I *live* here," Mary Jo snapped, again with a defiant, defensive manner that made Savannah's right eyebrow rise a notch.

"Oh? You said you're staying here. I didn't realize you actually live here."

"There's probably quite a bit you don't know about us. The tabloids don't tell the whole story, you know."

The tabloids? Savannah wondered what the tabloids had to do with the price of pecans in Georgia. But she made a quick mental note to have Tammy get her hands on as many as she could that mentioned Dona Papalardo, and especially her good buddy, Mary Jo.

"I'm sure they don't," Savannah said. "In fact, I'm sure they tell a lot of half-truths, and that's on a good day when they aren't just plain ol' outright lying through their snaggled teeth."

For just a moment, Mary Jo's expression softened, as though she appreciated the fact that Savannah and she were on the same side when it came to the politics of supermarket rags. But their "strange bedfellow" bond was short-lived.

"I've been living here for a few months now, since I sold my house in Malibu," Mary Jo said, her chin a couple of notches higher than normal. "And Dona is very nice to have me here. But it isn't like the tabloids said. I wasn't homeless, for heaven's sake. She didn't snatch me off the streets, bring me home and clean me up. It wasn't like that at all."

"I'm sure they exaggerated it something awful."

"They did! They made it sound like she's this successful, totally together diva who, out of the goodness of her heart, reached down to pull her poor, loser friend up out of the muck."

"They didn't!"

"They did! And it's such a lie. Dona has plenty of problems of her own, I'll tell you. Lots of problems. And I've helped her more than she's helped me! I mean, not financially maybe, but there are other ways one friend helps another."

"Of course, there are umpteen dozen ways."

"I've helped her in ways that you wouldn't believe since she had that gastric bypass surgery. She's been sick as a dog. Throwing up . . . and other things I won't even mention because it's so gross and—"

"Thank you. I appreciate that."

"And only a friend, a *real* friend would stand by you at a time like *that*!"

Savannah nodded solemnly. "How true. Bathroom duty elevates a casual acquaintance to soul-sister status every time."

Mary Jo waved an arm, indicating the room they were standing in. "With all of this, everyone assumes that Dona has it all, that she's happy and fulfilled and doesn't have a care in the world. Except maybe her weight. But I've known her since we were kids and neither one of us had anything. We were going to be a world-famous singing duo. When we were in high school we won every contest we entered. We were going to go all the way to the top together. But then Dona was 'discovered' and had her face on the cover of *Teen Idol*, and as they say, the rest is history. She turned her back on her true love, singing, and started acting just because of the money. And she hasn't been happy since that day."

Savannah recalled the night when Dona Papalardo had won her Emmy, her tears of joy, her grateful and gracious acceptance speech. If she hadn't been happy that night, she was a better actress than even Hollywood was giving her credit for.

Savannah had a feeling that Mary Jo was rewriting history, coming up with a new version that she, herself, could live with. And this account played a bit better than: My best friend promised we'd make it to the top together, but she left me behind in her scramble to the summit. And here I sit in a mud puddle looking up at her, feeling bitter and sorry for myself.

Yes, Savannah decided, *the tabloids aren't the only ones who can spin a yarn when it suits them to do so.*

She had to ask Mary Jo *the* question.

She had to.

The question was a necessary evil in each and every investigation. And no matter how many times you asked how many people, nobody ever took kindly to being asked.

"Mary Jo," she said, using her soft, lulling voice . . . the one she usually used for coaxing her cats out of trees. "If you don't mind me asking, where were you yesterday when Kim was shot?"

Mary Jo's eyes opened wide. "Well, I *do* mind. I mind because the only reason you'd ask such a thing is because you suspect me of having something to do with it."

Savannah shrugged and gave her a half-smile. "Don't take it personally. I suspect everybody of everything. That way I'm never disappointed . . . or surprised. In my line of work, you can't afford to be surprised. It could be deadly."

Mary Jo seemed to consider Savannah's words and decide, perhaps, they had some merit. She relaxed a little, her body less rigid and her expression less hostile. "Okay," she said. "I guess that's a fair question. I was out jogging."

"Where?"

"In the hills behind the property. There's a beautiful valley back there, and except for a few rattlesnakes, it's a great place to run. I run every day."

"Did you see anything unusual while you were out there?"

"Some stupid kids throwing rocks at a rattler they had cornered between some rocks. I told them they were idiots and made them quit. Other than that, no."

"And when you got back here? What was happening at that point?"

Mary Jo looked down at the rug at her feet and a look of great sadness washed over her face. "Kim was dying," she said simply. "There on the driveway. Dona was holding her in her arms. And she was dying. I'd never seen anyone die before. Not even of natural causes, let alone . . . like that . . . "

She swallowed hard, then looked up at Savannah, her eyes filling with tears. "I didn't particularly like or even know Kim, but that was really awful. I guess you've seen a lot of that sort of thing in your line of work. You're probably used to it."

In her mind's eye, Savannah saw a line of bodies, the dead and the dying, stretching back over the years—during both of her careers as a private investigator and as a police officer. By now, literally hundreds. And she could remember every single one of them vividly. Far too vividly, sometimes, in the middle of the night.

"No," she said. "I'm not used to it. And God forbid I ever will be."

Chapter 7

Savannah found Dirk standing in the backyard next to an exquisite swimming pool shaped like an octagon. It was rimmed with pastel pink and aqua tiles with an Egyptian motif, and in the center, a fountain sprayed an iridescent jet of water into the air. The tiles were accented with flecks of gold and something told Savannah that in this case, if it looked like gold, it probably was.

Elegant palms grew along the back side of the pool, partially shading it and providing bathers with a sense of jungle verdure.

The yard was expansive with numerous areas that had been designed for gracious entertaining. A natural stone barbecue pit was surrounded by chaises with thick, inviting cushions. A garden filled with native wildflowers was dotted with wrought-iron benches where guests could sit and commune with each other and nature. And at the back of the property a delicate gazebo provided a private, romantic setting for viewing the sweeping, verdant valley and the tan, velveteen hills, lined with rows of dark, gray-green avocado trees in the distance.

Dirk appeared less festive and a lot less elegant than his surroundings, but that was nothing unusual. What *was* unusual was the brown thing sticking out of his mouth.

"What the heck is that you're sucking on there, buddy?" Savannah asked as she walked up to him.

It looked like a rough brown cigarette, but as she got closer, she caught the sweet, fresh scent of cinnamon. Dirk had never smelled so good.

"It's a cinnamon stick," he said, shoving it to the side of his mouth and talking around it, "and I don't want to hear a word about it," he snapped. "Not one word, you hear?"

She chuckled. "Oh yeah," she said. "You're going to walk around with spices sticking out of your face, and you and I aren't going to have a conversation about it? That's going to happen . . . sure." Then it dawned on her and her face softened into a sweet smile. "Oh-h-h. This is a 'quit smoking' thing, right?"

He looked embarrassed. "Can we just not talk about it?"

"After I ask you one question." She reached up and thumped the end of the stick with her finger. "What's wrong with a chocolate lollipop?"

He shrugged. "The guys at the station were calling me Kojak, and it was pissing me off."

"Why? Just because Telly Savalas was bald? I keep telling you, you aren't bald. You're just a wee bit follicularly disadvantaged . . . there on the top. But you comb it pretty good, so—."

"It's not 'cause the dude was bald."

She didn't believe him, but said nothing.

"It's not!" he protested. "It's just because, well, 'cause you and I are old enough to even know who Telly Savalas was."

She nodded and smiled. "Right. Whatever."

"No! Don't you go 'whatevering' me! I hate it when you do that."

She shrugged. "Okay. Whatever." She looked around the empty

yard. "I thought you were interviewing the gardener or somebody like that out here."

"I was. You missed out. He was . . . well . . . I didn't exactly notice, being a guy and all, but you would have thought he was gorgeous."

"Really? I *am* sorry I missed him." She waggled one eyebrow. "Maybe he'll just have to be interviewed all over again."

"Oh, I'm sure you'll work him over sooner or later."

"Anything out of him?"

"Naw, says he hardly knew the vic. Hasn't been working here long—just a couple of months."

"Did you get anything more from Dona this morning?"

"Get anything? Hell, I didn't even see her. She was gone before I even got here at eight o'clock, some sort of meeting in Hollywood."

"Yes, that's what Mary Jo told me."

Dirk made a face. "There's a whack-job for you. Have you read what they say about her?"

"What who says?"

"Magazines. You know . . . in the grocery store."

"You buy that junk? You actually subsidize an industry that destroys people's lives by printing pure lies and—"

"Eh, come on, Van. You know me better than that!" She was surprised that he looked so indignant, so genuinely offended. Until he added, "I don't buy them. I pick them out of my neighbors' garbage cans there at the trailer park."

"You take them out of the garbage? With garbage still on them? And handle them, and take them into your home?"

He shrugged. "Hey, if you lay them out in the sun for a while, the wet coffee grounds dry and you can just brush them off. Good as new."

Savannah rolled her eyes. "Well, duh . . . of course. What was I thinking?" She glanced around to see if they were still alone, then leaned closer to him. "Well? What *do* they say?"

"Oh! *Now* she wants to know! Now she wants to hear all the evil lies and gossip. Well, not from this guy! I don't want to be accused of—"

"Oh, shut up and dish the dirt."

"Okay. They say Mary Jo's a no-talent loser who's been riding Dona's coattails for years, working her with a big guilt trip because Dona made it big and she didn't."

Savannah sniffed. "Big deal. I figured that out after talking to her for two minutes."

"Well, so did *I*. Even airhead Tammy could see that one."

"Speaking of Tammy, and don't call her names, I've got to think of an excuse to get her over here. She's having a conniption sitting there at home, missing all the fun. Especially now that some of my relatives have arrived."

"Oh, no! Which ones?"

"Jesup."

"The wannabe vampire queen, mistress of darkness?"

"Yeah, and her husband of a few hours. A creepo named Milton Pillsbury, thirty-three years old, from Vegas, birth date one-thirteen. Run him for me, would you?"

Dirk laughed. "Come on. How bad can a guy be who's named Milton Pillsbury?"

"Alias, Bleak Manifest."

He nodded. "Vegas, one-thirteen, you say. Got it." He pulled a small notepad from the inside pocket of his bomber jacket and wrote it down. "By the way," he said, "if you're really serious about getting the squirt over here, do it right away. I think she could probably weasel more out of that gardener guy than you or I could. Especially if she's wearing that cute little bluejean minskirt of hers."

Savannah grinned, making a mental note to tell Tammy that

Dirk had noticed she looked cute in her denim skirt, whether he would ever deign to tell her so or not. "Oh, you think he's the sort of guy who would enjoy the sight of Tammy in her mini?"

"He's breathin', ain't he?"

Savannah had done a cursory exam of the house's exterior, checking windows that were surrounded by thick shrubbery, which could provide coverage for an intruder, and upstairs windows that were easily accessed by climbing trees or lattice trellises. And before she went inside to continue the examination, she decided to give Tammy a call on her cell phone.

She sat down on one of the cushioned chaises by the barbecue pit and punched in the number.

Tammy answered after the first buzz and her "Moonlight Magnolia Detective Agency, may I help you?" greeting had a ring of panic in it.

Savannah was afraid to ask. "How's it going?"

In a whisper, Tammy replied, "They're awful! Bleak has already been into our office computer! I caught him going through our crime-scene photos, the ones I've taken with my digital camera that Ryan and John got me for Christmas last year."

Savannah felt a need, a deep and passionate desire, growing in her loins and rising . . . rising—the desperate need to lop off somebody's head, give it a kick and watch it roll, roll, roll into a ditch. Now *that* would be a picture ol' Bleak would like!

"Dirk is running a check on him right now," she told Tammy. "I foresee a ray of sunshine in the kingdom of darkness. Other than that, what's happening?"

"Jesup is trying to get him to go to Disneyland, which he says is lame."

"Eh, they probably wouldn't let him in anyway. His clothes are potentially lethal weapons. And besides, I think they have a 'major weirdo detector' there at the front gate."

"I suggested they go to the old mission and check out the

mass graves of the native Indians buried there . . . you know, the ones that the missionaries forced into slavery to build the place? Bleak perked up at that idea. I think they're going there after lunch."

"Yeah, that sounds more like his cup of tea. Or poison, as the case might be. So, why don't you pack a bag and come over here ASAP? We need you."

There was a moment of stunned silence on the other end. Then, "Really? Really? I get to come there? You *need* me?"

Savannah smiled. It was so fulfilling to give to those who really appreciated a bread crumb when it was thrown their way. "Desperately."

"Why?" Tammy asked. "What do you need me for?"

"Tart bait."

"Yay-y-y!" Savannah could practically see her jumping up and down, ponytail bouncing. "Want me to bring a miniskirt and a tube top?"

"The skirt's a 'yes.' But this is a classy joint; the tube can stay home."

"High-heeled, strappy sandals?"

"The four-inchers." *Hey*, Savannah thought, *somebody has to wear them and better her than me. One advantage of not being in your twenties and thirties anymore.*

"How many nights should I pack for?"

She was giddy to the point of panting and breathless. Savannah was afraid she might hyperventilate and pass out while driving over. "Just for a couple of nights," she said, reining her in just a little.

"Oh?"

The disappointment in that one syllable was too much for Savannah to stand. Better she die of a case of the vapors than a broken heart. "That's all I packed for," she added quickly. "We'll run back to the house to get clean stuff when we need it. Okay?"

"Okay? Okay? Ohmigawd! This is just awesome."

Savannah laughed and was about to say good-bye when a vision of manliness like she hadn't seen in years came around the end of the house and began walking toward her. A young man in his mid- to late twenties, carrying a rake over his shoulder—his extremely broad shoulder—his extremely broad, *tanned and muscular shoulder*—and wearing only a pair of well-worn cutoff jeans shorts, was walking toward her. The mid-morning sunlight was shining on his long dark hair, giving him an almost unearthly beauty. He spotted her sitting on the chaise, and gave her a breathtaking grin that made her knees go weak in an instant.

"Lord have mercy," she whispered, as every "hunky handyman gets handy with the mistress of the house" fantasy she'd ever had came rushing to her mind . . . and other regions of her anatomy.

"What?" Tammy—poor, forgotten Tammy—asked on the other end of the phone. "What did you say?"

Savannah shook her head. "Uh, nothing. Just get over here as soon as you can."

"Thank you," Tammy said. "I owe you one."

"Oh, sugar, you have no idea. No-o-o-o idea!"

A few minutes later, when Savannah passed through the kitchen, scouting out the possibility of a fresh cup of coffee, she heard someone close the front door. The click-click of high heels on the marble tiles announced the arrival of the mistress of the house.

Savannah quickly forgot the coffee and hurried into the entryway. Dona was pulling off a scarf and hat that were the same creamy ivory wool as the impeccable suit she was wearing. Savannah couldn't help noticing that the hat was adorned with one of those deliciously glamorous nets that covered the wearer's eyes. Yes, Dona knew how to do "old Hollywood" to perfection.

She seemed surprised to see Savannah in her home, then a bit irritated. "Oh," she said. "It's you. I forgot you were coming."

"And I didn't realize you were going out," Savannah returned, "without protection."

Dona sighed. She looked weary, her beautiful red eyes swollen, her face puffy, as though she'd spent the night crying. "I have a life to live," she said. "And a very busy schedule. I don't expect you to keep up with me every minute of the day."

"I don't mind. That's what you pay me for. If you'll just let me know, even a little ahead of time, I'll be ready to accompany you anywhere, day or night."

"I don't know if I'm going to want accompaniment day and night."

"That's your choice, certainly," Savannah said softly, "but until Detective Coulter finds out a bit more about what's happened here, it might be a good idea if you had an escort when you go out." She walked over to the alarm-control panel. "And you should keep this system activated when you're here. If it isn't on, it's just an ugly piece of wall décor."

Savannah studied the panel for a moment, then asked, "What is your code?"

Dona had to think for a minute. "If I remember right, it's my birthday. Oh-six-one-five."

"That's pretty predictable. We should change it right away." She punched in the numbers and watched the display come to life with its assorted red, gold, and green lights. "My assistant is very good with these things. I'll have her change it when she gets here."

Dona headed for the library with Savannah only a few steps behind. "When she gets here?" Dona asked, not bothering to hide the irritation in her voice. "Someone else is coming, too?"

"Oh, when you hire me, you get the whole Moonlight Magnolia Detective Agency," Savannah returned brightly.

"Lucky me." Dona sank into a big leather chair behind a heavy mahogany desk and tossed her scarf, hat, and purse onto a nearby side chair.

"Actually, you might be luckier than you think right now," Savannah said, trying not to sound as miffed as she was. "We're pretty darned good at what we do."

"I'm sure you are, Savannah. It's just that . . . well . . . privacy is such a precious commodity in my life. I've always tried to keep my in-house staff and houseguests as few as possible. Otherwise you never have that feeling of . . ."

"Coming home?"

"Exactly. No one wants to be 'on' all day and night."

Savannah nodded. "I can really understand that. I love my assistant but I also look forward to her going home in the evenings and leaving me alone. Unless one of my crazy relatives is visiting. Then there's just no rest for the wicked."

Dona seemed to bristle a bit less, hearing Savannah's words of empathy. She even chuckled a little. "Where are you from? With an accent like that, I'd say Alabama or Georgia."

"McGill, Georgia. Population four thousand, seven hundred and eight-two. And four thousand, seven hundred of them are related to me."

"But apparently you escaped."

"They follow me here. Right now I have one sister and her newlywed husband at my house. They met in Vegas a few days ago, got married lickety-split, and are now honeymooning at my place."

Dona grinned. "No wonder you want to hang out with me night and day."

"Guilty as charged."

Dona began to rummage through some papers on her desk. "Do you really think I need your protection, Ms. Reid? Or is your friend, Detective Coulter, overreacting?"

Savannah considered her answer carefully, then said, "Dirk doesn't usually overreact to anything. In fact, he tends to err on the side of apathy and indifference. Doesn't really give a hoot about much but cold beer and heavyweight boxing. If he says he thinks you need me, you probably do."

"So, he thinks the killer intended to kill me, not Kim. Is that what you're telling me?"

"I'm telling you that it's too early to tell. But if someone is after you, I intend to make it as hard for him to get to you as possible."

"Does that mean you're going to be escorting me everywhere? Are you going to sit on the edge of the tub when I take my bath in a few minutes?"

"No, just right outside your bathroom door."

Dona looked appalled.

"Just kidding," Savannah was quick to add. "As long as you're inside the house and the alarm system is on, I'm not going to worry about you too much." *Just don't stand for long periods of time in front of big windows,* she added silently, but decided to keep it to herself. No point in scaring the daylights out of the woman.

Dona grabbed a note card and began to write on it. "Then you're in luck. I'm in for the rest of the day, so you can spend the afternoon by the pool if you want."

"Actually," Savannah said, her mental wheels turning, "if you're going to be home, I may just leave my assistant, Tammy, here with you, and I may go do some fieldwork with Detective Coulter."

"Fieldwork?"

"Check out what leads we have. Kim's house, friends, family, and neighbors. Your former agent and old boyfriend. That sort of thing."

"Whatever you think best." Suddenly, Dona's already white skin blanched even paler. A sheen of sweat appeared across her upper lip, and her hand was shaking as she laid down her pen.

She stood abruptly and hurried toward a door on the far side of the room. "Excuse me," she said. "I just . . ."

She jerked the door open, hurried into what appeared to be a small powder room and slammed the door closed behind her.

A moment later, Savannah could hear the sound of violent retching.

She wasn't sure what to do. Something told her that Dona Papalardo would *not* welcome any sort of intrusion at a moment like this, even in the form of sympathetic assistance.

But when she heard the woman crying, she couldn't resist at least an offer of help. She walked to the door of the bathroom and said softly, "Dona, are you okay? Can I do anything for you?"

"No, go away," was the curt reply.

Then another round of sickness, and more crying.

Savannah laid her palm on the door, wishing she could help, wondering what was wrong. Could the woman on the other side be pregnant? Food poisoning maybe? It seemed to have come on very quickly. Only a few moments ago, she had seemed tired and sad, but healthy.

"If you need anything, let me know," she said softly. "I have eight younger brothers and sisters. Barfing is nothing to me. Can I get you a glass of water or—"

"You can get the hell away from me and leave me alone," was the sobbing reply.

"Okay. I understand."

Savannah walked away. If she couldn't offer Dona Papalardo help in her time of misery, she could at least give her the one thing she seemed to crave most.

Her privacy.

Chapter 8

As she left the library and passed through the foyer, Savannah found Dirk studying the security system's control panel. "Good," he said. "She's got it turned on now. I warned her last night that she needs to keep it on all the time. But by this morning she'd forgot."

"I engaged it," she said. "How did you get in?"

"I was in the backyard. The maid let me in."

"Well, as soon as Tammy gets here, she's going to reset the code. Right now it's Dona's birthday."

Dirk shook his head. "People think they're being so subtle. Their birthdays and their pets' names . . . real sneaky." He glanced over her shoulder toward the library. "She in there?"

"In the bathroom."

He snickered. "I guess even movie stars have to do it sometimes."

"She's sick," she whispered. "Upchucking."

"Oh, that's nasty. Did you upset her, talking about the killing?"

"Not really. She seemed okay, maybe just a little tired. Then all of a sudden, she's heading for the bathroom."

"Hm-m-m. Well, delayed reaction maybe. It happens even to us cops, let alone the people who know the victims."

Savannah saw a flash of hot pink through the etched glass beside the door, a car pulling into the driveway in front of the house.

"Tammy's VW bug," she said. "The queen of sleuths has arrived."

"Good. Then you'll have help here if you need it. I'm outta here."

"Out of here? Where are you going?"

"To check out Kim Dylan's house. I got the keys from Dr. Liu this morning." He took a key ring with a large, rhinestone-studded *K* on it from his pocket and dangled the keys in front of her face. "Wanna come?"

Her mouth practically watered. "Of course I want to come. You're cruel. You know I have to stay here and 'guard.'"

"Let Nancy Drew guard her. She'd be thrilled to death."

Through the glass, Savannah could see Tammy approaching, miniskirted, as requested, an overnight bag in hand and a water bottle in the other. Her face shone with the light of a thousand suns . . . or a contented heart, doing what it loved best in the world.

Dirk was right. She *would* be thrilled.

"Well," Savannah said. "Dona did say she'd be in all day." She bit her bottom lip, thinking, considering the possibility. "How far away is Kim's house from here?"

"Four minutes. Five, tops."

More lip biting, more soul-searching . . . "Will you wait for me in your car? I'll just show her around and—"

"Sure. Just make it snappy. I don't like to be kept waiting."

She punched him in the arm. "Don't get smart with me, boy. You'll wait and you'll like it."

He gave her a grin and flicked the end of her nose with his finger. “Take your time,” he said with a heavy sigh. “I’ll just be sitting there, feeling sorry for myself . . . chewing on that friggin’ cinnamon stick.”

“I’m very proud of you, you know,” Savannah told him as she rolled down the Buick’s passenger window and allowed the fresh air and California sunshine to fill her senses. “I can’t even imagine how hard it must be to stop smoking.”

“No, you can’t imagine it,” he grumbled. “You don’t have a clue. It’s miserable. I feel like I’m about to explode at the seams.”

“Sorta like I’d be if I swore off chocolate for twenty-four hours?”

“Maybe . . . if you swore off chocolate, ice cream, *and* bubble baths.

“Life wouldn’t be worth living.”

“Exactly.”

“Sorry, buddy. But you know it’s the right thing.”

“Yeah, it’s a matter of life and death.”

Savannah gave him a quick sideways glance. She was shocked by his candor. Heaven knows, she had lectured him for years about the potentially lethal effects of tar and nicotine, but she’d never dreamed that her words had been heeded. She smothered a smile and turned to look out the window to her right.

She was a good person! She *did* deserve her space here on earth! She genuinely *helped* people! She made a difference in the world!

“Yep,” he continued. “I’ve gotta hang in there this time and really quit. Otherwise I’d have to kill myself for throwing my Harley lighter away like that.”

Okay, she thought as her bubble popped, *so much for the power of a woman’s nagging*. Granny Reid had always told her girls: There’s no point in nagging men. In the end they always do exactly what they want to do anyway . . . being the freewilled creatures that God created them to be.

More than once she had said, "You nag a good guy, he just keeps doing whatever he's doing, only he's cranky while he's doing it. And if you nag a bad guy, he'll do whatever it is twice as much . . . and be cranky doing it."

But Savannah couldn't help herself. Gran had forgotten to mention that women simply couldn't stop themselves. Nagging was in the genes, along with chocolate cravings and an illogical obsession with shoes.

"I suppose you ran a check on Kim Dylan," she said, hoping he hadn't so that she could feel at least a little superior for a minute or two.

"Of course, I did. Nothing. Clean as a whistle. Not even the proverbial parking ticket. I never trust anybody *that* clean."

"Or anybody who has a couple of offenses."

He nodded. "True. You just gotta know that a couple of convictions is just the tip of the iceberg."

"Or a rap sheet a mile long."

"Of course not. They're scummers."

Savannah sat, quietly waiting for a ray of self-awareness to shine into the top of his ever-more-balding head.

Nope. Nada. Self-awareness, self-enlightenment, or self-improvement weren't high on Dirk's list of priorities.

He pulled the Buick off the main road and headed down a dirt road through a grove of orange trees.

"Oh, no," she said, "not another nature call. Didn't you go back there before we left?"

"Get off my back, woman. The gal lives down here. Or lived, as the case might be."

"In an orange grove?"

"In a ranch house, they say, at the end down here somewhere."

"Who says?"

"The new chickie-poo at the station desk. She drops a lot of calls and forgets to give you your messages but she's nice."

Translation: Looks good in a sweater, Savannah added mentally. After all these years, she knew how to speak Dirk-ese.

"And you trust her directions?"

"Yeah, she looked it up on the computer and printed it out for me. The house oughta be about . . . right there." He pointed to a clearing down the road and to the right, where a small white cottage sat, surrounded by a picket fence and neatly kept patch of green lawn.

On one side of the yard, a stone wall was partially constructed from a pile of natural stone nearby. A stack of pipes that looked like some sort of irrigation system lay on the other side of the yard.

"Looks like she was in the middle of sprucing the place up a bit," Savannah said as Dirk parked the car in the shade provided by some avocado trees.

They got out of the car and walked toward the house, raising dust with every step as they walked down the dirt road. The midday sun was hot and warmed the orange trees, enhancing their sweet fragrance. Bees buzzed in nearby bottlebrush bushes, and in the distance a dog barked furiously at some intruder, real or imagined.

"I wonder what it would be like to live out here on a ranch like this," Dirk said, a sentimental tone in his voice. "Sometimes I think I'd like to buy a piece of land like this and move my trailer out on it. No neighbors to have to mess with."

"No free coffee-ground–stained tabloids. But you could enjoy the occasional drop-in visit from a coyote or mountain lion."

He shuddered. Dirk wasn't big on four-legged critters period, let alone wild ones. "Well," he said, "it was just a thought."

When they reached the front door of the cottage, he pulled out the key chain with its gaudy *K* and sorted automobile keys from house keys. After two tries, he found the right one and the door opened.

He ushered Savannah inside, and they both entered warily.

While Savannah had never really considered herself a nosy person, she did find the insides of other people's houses interesting. Especially if no one was home. It never failed to amaze her how much you could tell about a person just looking around at their belongings: the never-ending combinations of furnishings and ways to decorate, the items they chose to display prominently, whether the house was clean and tidy or filthy and disorganized. It all said so much about the people who lived within those walls.

But when she looked around Kim Dylan's house, what she saw confused, more than informed, her.

"She was a girlie girl," she said, more to herself than Dirk, as she observed the colorful floral pattern on the living room sofa and love seat, the ruffled tablecloth on a round lamp table, the lacy curtains hanging in the window, gathered back on either side with bouquets of silk roses.

"Hm-m-m," Dirk said, "I see what you mean. But what about that?" He pointed to a large plasma TV that dominated the far wall. "That sucker's gotta be fifty-eight inches and it's high definition. Something like that would set you back between five and six grand!"

Savannah had to admit the monstrosity did stand out—obviously a "boy toy" in a room that was otherwise relatively "sissified."

"It's new, too," she said, as she walked over to a stack of packing materials that had been stashed behind the sofa. Styrofoam, clear plastic wrap, bubble pack, and a stack of manuals and other printed materials announced the fact that the TV was a recent acquisition.

"Either some guy is living here with her," Savannah said, "or she's trying to lure some guy into living here with her."

Dirk chuckled. "You get a fifty-eight inch screen like that one, and *I'll* move in with *you*!"

She shot him a look of pure horror. "Thanks for the warning," she said. "I'll cancel my order."

They passed through the living room, the dining area, and the kitchen. All were relatively "lived-in" but neat. The dishes were done, counters bare. On one counter, an answering machine blinked with two messages.

Dirk pushed the button and the first one began to play. It was a male voice. "Hey," he said, "you there? Pick up. We have to talk. Tonight! Call me back as soon as you get this. We may have some problems. Well . . . *you* may. Call me."

The second call was female and sounded older. "Penny, are you there, honey? It's Mom. I haven't heard from you in a couple of days. Pick up if you're there. Daddy's been sick. I need to talk to you. Call me. Love you."

"Penny? Who the heck is Penny?" Savannah said. "Are you sure the cutie at the front desk gave you the right address?"

"The key opened the door, didn't it?"

"True. Maybe Penny is the not-so-girlie roommate."

They walked into a short hall that led to a tiny bathroom and one bedroom.

Dirk poked his head into the bathroom, opened the medicine cabinet and looked in the cupboard under the sink. "Guy living here," he said. "Or at least staying over. Triple-blade razor, shaving cream, Road Racer deodorant, and condoms."

Savannah was already checking out the bedroom. The bed was made with a comforter fringed with row upon row of eyelet ruffles. And a dozen decorator pillows were carefully arranged in an attractive manner. Some of the linens appeared to be hand-embroidered. On the floor beside the bed lay a pile of plastic bags, labels, and cardboard inserts. Apparently the bedclothes were new, too.

In the closet she found mostly women's clothing, but several men's shirts, jeans, and slacks hung next to the rest and a few pairs of men's shoes jostled for space among the high heels, sandals, and sneakers. Savannah picked up one mud-encrusted men's boot, and looked at the size. Ten. "Common enough," she muttered, replacing it.

"Anything in there?" Dirk called from the bathroom.

"Men's stuff in the closet." She noted the size of the pants and shirts. "He's a bit smaller than you. Better taste in clothes."

"Gr-r-r-r."

She left the closet and walked over to the dresser, which was covered with a long, lacy runner. In the center of the dresser was a modest jewelry chest filled with costume jewelry. But beside it was a small, black, velvet-flocked box. She opened it and saw a pair of diamond earrings winking back at her. Set in white gold, the princess-cut stones had to be at least half a karat each.

More new acquisitions, she thought. *New*, expensive *toys at that. Somebody came into some money recently. Some real money.*

At one end of the dresser, a clear, plastic shoe box caught her eye. She could see through it and tell that it was filled with papers.

Opening it, she found assorted bills and on top of the stack, a checkbook and bank statement.

Her investigator's heart took an extra beat as she reached for the statement. She was happy to see that the envelope had already been opened. It saved her the trouble of having to break the law or wait for Dirk to come into the room and do it.

It was the most recent statement and a stack of canceled checks . . . more than Savannah wrote in an entire year.

She thumbed through them and saw they had been written to everything from nail salons to exclusive women's boutiques, to jewelry shops, to a tire place . . . top-of-the-line steel-belted radials.

"Again," she mumbled. "Somebody must have won the lotto recently. She was wading though this money like it was warm, shallow water."

"What?" Dirk asked as he entered the bedroom.

"She was spending cash like her pocket had a hole in it." Savannah's eye ran down the "credits" column of the statement, seeing only the occasional, modest, deposits that must have been earned from her job at Dona Papalardo's.

Then she found what she was looking for . . . a deposit for $44,000, made about six weeks before. "Hey, take a lookie at this," she said, handing Dirk the statement. "How does a personal assistant come up with a little bonus like that?"

"That's a lot of bucks to drop in out of nowhere. Maybe she settled some sort of lawsuit."

Savannah shrugged. "Oh, sure. There are some perfectly legitimate ways to score a sum like that."

"But a lot more illegitimate ways."

"You're so cynical."

"Practical. Honest. I see things as they are, not through rose-colored sunglasses."

She stuck out her tongue at him, then reached into the box and took out the checkbook that was folded between some of the bills. "When was that deposit?"

"On the fifteenth," he said, "last month."

She thumbed through the checkbook's registry and found the credit noted in a woman's clear, artistic handwriting . . . both the amount and the source of the check she had deposited. "Well now," she said. "Ain't that just interestin' as all git-out?"

"What's that?" He looked over her shoulder.

"We may not know 'why' yet, but we know 'who.'"

"Who?"

"Who paid her all the money she's been spending around here. The forty-four thousand dollars." She stuck the checkbook under his nose and tapped her nail on the entry.

"So, who's that?" he said reading the name. "Who's Miles Thurgood?"

Savannah grinned. "The thlot plickens . . ." she said, ". . . Miles Thurgood is Dona Papalardo's agent. Her former agent. And better yet, the former agent whom she's suing and who's suing her."

"Oh, yeah." Dirk nodded, remembering. "She told me about him. In fact, when I asked her who she thought might want her dead, he was the first one she mentioned, a step ahead of her ex-boyfriend."

"I guess you'd better check him out."

Dirk grinned his "nasty" grin and stuck the checkbook into his inside jacket pocket. "He was next on my list anyway. Now him and me . . . we've got us somethin' to talk about!"

Chapter 9

As Savannah and Dirk left Kim Dylan's house and drove down the dusty road through the orange grove, they discussed their next moves.

"I can't believe we went through the whole house," Savannah said, "and couldn't find one piece of paper with that guy's name on it. His clothes and shoes are in the closet, his underwear in a drawer, but not a piece of mail, a note, nothing with his name. That was just downright aggravating."

"Tell me about it. I'm going to call in," Dirk said, grabbing his cell phone off the dash. "Maybe the new gal's had time to run those names for me."

Savannah couldn't help but notice the sappy little grin that appeared on his puss the moment he mentioned the "new gal." Over the years, she had watched him develop these little crushes from time to time. And while she didn't want to admit for a second that she experienced even a twinge of anything resembling "jealousy," she did feel better somehow when she reminded herself that she had been head-over-knickers in lust with Ryan when she had first met him. And there had been that hunk who modeled for the covers of romance novels—another almost-romance that had lasted no longer than the common cold.

They had reached the end of the dirt road, and as they were pulling onto the main highway, Savannah spotted a small stucco house, nearly hidden in some lemon trees across the road. An elderly lady was trimming rosebushes in the yard.

Her sunbonnet, simple cotton dress with a small floral pattern, and the elbow-high leather gloves reminded Savannah of her grandmother. Her heartstrings twanged, and she reminded herself that she owed Gran a phone call.

"Pull over," she told Dirk. "While you're talking to the front-desk bimbo, I'll do some real work and have a chat with that lady over there."

"About what? Rose pruning?"

She stuck her tongue out at him. "Oh, I'm sure I can think of something other than that. Besides, Granny Reid already taught me all I'll ever need to know about pruning roses. 'Cut 'em short, feed them a banana peel, and don't let 'em bite you.'"

He pulled over to the edge of the road. She opened the door and said, "While you're flirting with cutie buns there, ask her to run ol' Bleak for me."

"How did you know she's got great buns?"

She snorted. "Call it a lucky guess."

She slammed the door and walked over to the woman, who appeared surprised to see her—or anyone for that matter. Savannah got the impression that visitors were few and far between for this lady.

"Hi, my name is Savannah," she said brightly as she approached the woman and her rose garden. "And how are you doin' today?"

"Well, I'm all right, I guess," the woman replied, peering at her suspiciously from under the broad brim of her sunbonnet. "What do *you* want?"

O-o-okay, Savannah thought. *Not all old ladies are as sweet as Gran.*

"I was wondering if I could just talk to you for a minute, if you don't mind."

"I *do* mind. You're tramping down my lawn!"

Savannah looked down at the ground beneath her feet. Bare dirt, a few brown weeds, some rocks and broken glass. "I'm so sorry," she said. She saw a spot with fewer weeds a couple of feet away. She hopped onto that. "There. Is that better?"

"I asked you what you want."

"So you did. Yes, you sure did."

This was going to be tough, Savannah decided then and there. She also decided that maybe there was a perfectly good reason why this lady seldom had company. What did the rest of the world know that she was just now discovering?

"I was wondering about your neighbors, the ones who live down there." Savannah pointed to the dirt road.

"She's dead," the woman snapped, emphasizing her statement by snipping off a particularly thick branch from a rosebush. "Got herself shot right there in front of that place where she works. I read about it in the paper this morning. And it was on the *Los Angeles Wake-up Show*, too."

"Yes." Savannah nodded somberly. "That's true. But I was wondering about him."

"Him?"

"Yes, the guy who's been hanging out there. Her boyfriend," she added, deciding to venture an educated guess. After all, it was a *one*-bedroom apartment and there *were* condoms in the bathroom.

"Oh, *him*!" Another, even more violent snip with the pruning shears. "I can't stand him."

Savannah's heart beat a little faster. "Really? Was he rude to you, or . . . ?"

"Rude to me? He's rude to everybody, riding that noisy motorcycle in and out of here at all hours of the day and night. Rattles my windows! Wakes me up out of a dead sleep at seventy-thirty!"

"That early in the morning?"

"No, seven-thirty at night! I'm dead to the world at that hour!"

"Oh, I see. That's just plumb rude of him!"

"That's what I said when I called the cops on him."

"You called the police? Did they come out and talk to him?"

"They said they would, but they didn't. I sat right there on my porch all day long and watched, but they didn't bother."

"I'm sorry to hear that," Savannah said, and she meant it. If the SCPD had sent someone out, there might be a record with the motorcyclist's name on it. "You wouldn't happen to know what his name is, do you?"

"No. Don't give a tinker's damn either. I just want him to stop riding that infernal thing in the middle of the night."

"What does he look like?" At least she could get a physical description. Not nearly as good as a name, but better than going back to Dirk empty-handed. She had to do at least as well as the bimbo at the station desk.

"I don't know what he looks like."

"You haven't seen him?"

"Of course I've seen him."

"Then . . . ?"

"He's always wearing that big black helmet. And a black leather jacket and jeans. That's not going to tell you much about him, now is it?"

"Uh. No, it's not." Okay, maybe she *could* go back with squat. Lord knows, it had happened before. Maybe the front-desk chickie-poo had struck out, too.

"But I do have his license number. The license plate on the back of his motorcycle. I wrote it down."

"You do? You did!" The sun shone brighter. The birds sang louder. Nearby orange blossoms burst into bloom. "Would you mind terribly giving it to me?"

"Why? I don't even know you. What do you want it for?"

Savannah thought fast, a dozen lies racing through her mind. The truth just seemed so . . . complicated. "I want to make sure he gets what's coming to him," she said.

"For racing through here like a Hell's Angel and waking up an old woman who needs her sleep?"

Savannah nodded. "For that, and for anything else he's done that he oughtn't."

The woman smiled, a big and somewhat unpleasant smile. "You just wait right here," she said, laying her pruning shears and gauntlets on the ground. "I'll be right back!"

Savannah suppressed a chuckle. "And I'll be right here waiting."

"So, there!" Savannah shoved the piece of paper under Dirk's nose the moment she got into the car. "Call your little desk muffin and give her that plate to run, and we'll find out who Kim's mystery man is."

Dirk took the piece of paper, looked at it, then cleared his throat and scowled. "Well, maybe we will and maybe we won't," he grumbled.

"What?"

"The desk gal, Jeanette . . . she looks better than she is."

Savannah was devastated to hear that, but she figured she could get over it. A hot fudge sundae would probably do the trick. "Really? What a shame. She didn't run those names for you?"

"I guess she tried, but she couldn't even find Kim Dylan,

other than this address. And I already had that from the ID in the victim's purse."

"What do you mean, couldn't find her?"

"No record. Not even a Social Security number."

"No Social?"

"Or driver's license in any state."

"It's an alias."

"That's what I'm thinking. That or Jeanette is a lot dumber than she looks." He flipped open his cell phone and punched in a number. As he waited for an answer, he added, "You'll be happy to know, though, that she was able to locate your new brother-in-law. And other than a couple of trespasses on private property last year, he's clean."

"Trespasses?" She'd been hoping for an outstanding warrant for a parole violation. "What sort of trespasses?"

"He broke into a mortuary one time and somebody's crypt another time. Didn't take anything, or hurt anything. So it was just trespassing."

"Oh," she said, sagging deeper into the Buick seat. She should be happy for her sister. She knew it, and she felt guilty for feeling disappointed. But she couldn't believe this slapdash marriage was a good thing. And she was hoping that maybe it could end quickly and cleanly before Jesup got any more deeply involved with this character, while there was still time to just get a nice, easy annulment. Maybe even before Granny Reid or the other relatives back in Georgia had to know about it.

But she couldn't see Jesup leaving her new husband in a huff over some trespassing charges. Heck, Jessie herself had done worse than that. Way worse.

She listened as Dirk read the motorcycle plate number to the woman on the other end. It was pretty obvious from the flat tone of his voice that his infatuation level had plummeted at least seventy degrees. Dirk liked a female who filled out a sweater or a tight skirt nicely, but a woman who couldn't run a good background check wasn't going to be high on his list for long. It might have taken a lot of years for his priorities to rearrange in that order, but he had eventually evolved.

This time Jeanette seemed to have done better. He was actually smiling when he hung up from the call. "Okay," he said, "we've got a name. Not a familiar name, but a name."

"What is it?"

"James Morgan. Ring a bell?"

She shook her head. "Nary a tinkle."

"Me either."

"Did she give you an address?"

"Yeah," he said. "She did." He sighed. "*This* one."

As they pulled back onto the road, Savannah called Tammy on her cell, and Tammy answered right away.

"Hi," Savannah said. "How's it going?"

"Fine. Earlier, I had to run off a batch of reporters who came to the door and were demanding to talk to Ms. Papalardo, but now I'm having a nice cappuccino with Dona's housekeeper. She's very . . . uh . . . friendly."

"Chatty?"

"Yes."

Savannah could practically hear Tammy smiling. "Good girl," she said. "Squeeze everything you can out of her. In fact, ask her right now if she knows a James Morgan."

She heard Tammy ask and the negative response.

"Oh well," Savannah said. "It was worth a try. What's Dona doing?"

"She's upstairs in her bedroom. She's been sick all day. Called down for a glass of water earlier and that's all we've heard out of her."

"Anybody else in the house?"

"Gardener's outside and . . . well . . . everything you said about him . . . it's so true. But he's the only one around, except me and Juanita here."

"Okay, well, Dirk and I are on our way back. We'll be there in a few minutes."

"Take your time," Tammy said. "Really. No hurry."

Savannah could hear it in her voice, the excitement you get when an interview or interrogation is going well and you're actually getting something from your subject. She got the message.

"Okay," she said, "we'll take our time getting back. We don't want to interrupt if you're getting some good stuff there."

"Excellent." She could hear Tammy suppress a giggle. "See you *later*."

When Savannah ended the call, Dirk turned to her and said, "Sounds like the kid is doing okay."

"It sounds to me like she's doing better than okay. She's sharing a cup of java with the maid, and I got the idea it's going well. She all but told me to stay away because she's getting somewhere with her."

"So, how's about we get some lunch before we go back?"

Dirk inviting her to lunch? She turned to him, her mouth hanging open. "Really? You're going to take me to a restaurant for lunch? Why you sweet thing, you."

He looked suddenly quite uncomfortable. "Well . . . I . . ."

I should have known, she thought. *Dirk forking over for a proper meal. Way too good to be true.*

"Okay, okay," she said, "Burger Bonanza's on the way. I'll settle for a burger and a chocolate shake."

She expected him to perk up, but he still looked as though he'd just been told that he was going to have gallbladder surgery.

"What?" she said. "What's with the puss? Where do *you* want to go to eat? You're the one who brought it up, you know."

"Well, I was thinking that your house is right on the way.

Burger Bonanza is a few blocks out of our way and besides, you've probably got some of that fried chicken left over from Ryan's party, right? And you said you'd save me some birthday cake. Besides, I haven't seen your sister, Jesup, since I was in Georgia and that's been years and—"

"Oh shut up, you friggin' mooch. You're not the least bit interested in seeing any of my kinfolk. You just want to sink your chompers into my leftover fried chicken. My *free* leftover chicken."

He shrugged and looked moderately guilty. "Well, hell, Van, you can't blame a guy for that?"

"*Blame* a guy?" she said, "I could *slug* a guy for that. For a lot *less* than that."

He grinned broadly "So, is that a 'yes'?"

She sighed. "Just drive."

Chapter 10

"What the hell do you think you're doing there, boy?" Savannah roared.

She stood in the middle of her living room, hands on her hips, glaring at her new brother-in-law. He and Jesup were sitting at Savannah's desk, staring at the computer in front of them with morbid fascination.

They were so enthralled that they hadn't even noticed when Savannah and Dirk had entered the house.

Both of them jumped at the sound of her voice and whirled around, guilty looks on their faces.

Savannah stomped over to the desk and pushed the power button on the computer. The gory pictures on the screen dissolved to black.

"You'll hurt your computer," Bleak said dryly, "turning it off like that. You're supposed to close down the programs first."

Dirk snickered and shook his head.

Savannah fixed Bleak with a look that could have melted a polar ice cap. "I'll hurt *you* if you ever touch my private property again, bud. Just try me and see if I'm foolin'."

Jesup rolled her eyes. "Oh, Savannah, get over it. Big deal. Just some dead bodies."

"Those are *my* crime-scene photographs, and I wouldn't even have them if they hadn't been important to cases I've worked on. Have a little respect, would you? Those were once living, breathing people, who had a horrific thing happen to them—the worst thing that can happen to anyone. And you two ghouls are going to delight in their misfortune?"

"Oh, come on," Bleak said. "Don't tell me that you don't find dead bodies interesting. The kind of work you do? You have to be into it, too."

"Yes, I'm interested in dead bodies," she replied, her voice low and ominously emotion-free. "I'm interested in what they can tell me about what happened to them, about who took their lives from them. I don't delight in the gruesome aspects of their passings, and you shouldn't either. It's disrespectful to the point of obscene."

Jesup turned to Bleak and made a face. "See, what did I tell you? Savannah's a little weird, but we love her anyway."

Bleak snickered. "Yeah, okay. I've got weird relatives, too, so—"

Savannah reached across him to the computer, pulled the cord out of the back of it and yanked the other end out of the wall. She rolled it up and stuck it in her slacks pocket. "I'm about to make some lunch for Dirk and myself," she said. "Do you two want a plate of cold chicken and potato salad?"

"Sure!" Jesup beamed.

"Don't mind if I do," Bleak replied.

"One plate of chicken," Savannah grumbled as she walked toward the kitchen. "A special order. Raw, bloody, dripping with salmonella and smothered in E. coli. Coming right up."

"See," she heard Jesup say as she left the room, "like I told you, even when Savannah's hoppin' mad at you, she'll still feed you. She just can't help herself."

"Thanks for lunch, Van," Dirk said when he dropped her back at Dona Papalardo's mansion.

She gave him a quick, quizzical look. He rarely remembered to thank her for anything, let alone anything as mundane as food. In an average week, she fed him ten to twelve times, so a cold chicken lunch wasn't something she expected a heartfelt outpouring of gratitude like this one.

"You're welcome," she said.

Granny Reid had always said, "Reward good behavior right away. And with menfolk, faster than right away. They've got the attention span of a gnat."

She grabbed her purse off the floor and unfastened her seat belt. "Where are you off to now?" she asked.

"I thought I'd go get hold of that ex-agent of Dona's," he said. "Maybe find out why he was paying Dona's assistant a bundle of money that would choke a horse."

"Good idea. Also get his side of why he and Dona are suing each other."

"What are you up to now?" He nodded toward the mansion.

"I'm going to find out what Tammy managed to squeeze out of the maid, maybe the gardener, and check on Dona. Tammy said she's been sick, holed up in her bedroom since I left this morning."

"Might be from that crazy weight-loss surgery she had," he suggested. "Or the stress of having someone you're close to die in your arms."

"Or both," Savannah said. "I'd vote for both."

He nodded somberly. "Me, too."

* * *

Savannah knocked at the front door of the mansion, and it was answered by a tiny Hispanic woman with an enormous smile, wearing a pale blue maid's uniform. No sooner had Savannah introduced herself, than the maid hurried her inside with a warm, "Ah, hello, hello, Senora Savannah. Senorita Tammy told me about you. My name is Juanita. Come in!"

"Actually, Juanita, I'm a senorita, too," Savannah told her. "As in, no husband."

The maid gave her a sad smile. "Oh, I'm so sorry."

Savannah chuckled. "Don't be," she said. "I'm not."

Once inside the door, Savannah looked around and said, "Where is Tammy?"

Juanita shrugged. "I don't know. She was in the kitchen before. I've been doing the laundry downstairs, and I haven't seen her."

"And Dona?"

"My lady is resting upstairs," she said. "Sick again. Sick again." She shook her head sadly. "Always so sick."

"Sick in her body?" Savannah asked. "Or in her heart?" She pointed to her chest.

"Both, I think." Juanita paused and looked up the empty staircase. Then she lowered her voice to a whisper. "I cannot say too much about my lady's business, you know. But I do worry. I worry. And then, with that bad, bad thing that happened to Senorita Kim. I'm scared."

"I understand." Savannah laid her hand on the woman's forearm. "Please try not to worry. That's why Tammy and I are here, to keep all of you safe. Just keep the doors and windows closed and locked and the alarm system on at all times. And if you see anything unusual, anything at all, you tell one of us right away. Okay?"

Juanita nodded vigorously. "I promise."

"Good. Thank you."

"May I go back downstairs now and finish the laundry?"

"Of course. Just go on about your duties here as you always do. Try to ignore us, and we'll try to stay out of your way."

With another of her warm, broad smiles, Juanita disappeared down a hallway, leaving Savannah alone in the entryway.

She considered going upstairs to see if Dona was okay and to maybe persuade her to talk a bit. She wanted to ask her if she knew anything about a man in Kim's life. Specifically, one named James Morgan.

But she decided against it. If Dona truly was sick—and she certainly had been earlier—she didn't need to be disturbed.

Deciding that she would go looking for Tammy instead, she headed toward the back of the house and the kitchen. But as she passed the library door, she heard the rustling of papers inside.

Walking softly so as not to be heard, she approached the door carefully and looked into the room. In the dim interior of the library she saw someone standing behind the desk.

Once her eyes adjusted, she realized it was Tammy. She was rummaging through some papers in one of the lower drawers of the desk.

"What are you doing there, girl?" Savannah said.

"Oh!" Tammy jumped, grabbed her chest dramatically and sank down onto the desk chair. "Savannah Marie, you nearly scared me to death!"

Savannah laughed at her. "Eh, it's good for you. Clears out your arteries. And I keep telling you, my middle name isn't Marie."

She giggled. "I know. I call everybody that."

"What were you doing that you weren't supposed to be doing?" She nodded to the stack of papers on the table that looked like cutouts from tabloid newspapers.

"How do you know it's something that I'm not supposed to be doing?"

"Because nobody jumps like that unless they're caught doing something wrong."

"Hey, I'm snooping. And that's what we're getting paid for, right?"

Savannah shrugged. "Well, technically, this time we're being paid to protect and serve. The snooping is just a service we throw in for free . . . generous folks that we are. What did you find there?"

"Well," Tammy gave a quick, cautious glance toward the doorway, "the reason I was looking in here in the first place is because, just before she went upstairs to her bedroom, Dona was looking at these and crying really hard. I wanted to see what it was that would make her cry like that."

"Excellent." Savannah picked up the top cutting off the stack and looked at it. "Let's see what we have here."

"They're about Dona, of course. The nasty articles about her being fat, then more about her getting the gastric bypass. They say she nearly died on the operating table and then again a week later from a post-op infection."

Savannah scanned that article in particular. "Yes, I recall stories about that even in the *Times*. I think she really did have a hard time with her surgery, during and after."

"But I guess it was worth it," Tammy said. "Look at how big she was there," she pointed to one especially unflattering picture of Dona wearing a swimsuit, bent over, dipping her hand into a swimming pool.

"Okay, she's got some extra pounds," Savannah said thoughtfully, "but remember, pictures make you look heavier than you really are. And she doesn't look all that heavy. Not as large as some people who get gastric bypasses. I know you have to be a certain size, a particular body-mass index, before you're even eligible. And she doesn't look all that big to me."

"But she looks great now, so it worked."

"Yes, but they surgically make your stomach smaller so that you can't put as much in it without feeling miserable. And they bypass part of your small intestine so that you won't absorb all of the small amount you do eat. I hear you have to eat only tiny amounts of foods and even then, you have to be sure not to eat anything too rich, too sweet or fatty. And they tell you to get on an exercise plan, too."

"That's what I've heard, too," Tammy agreed.

"Well, let's see now. Small amounts of food, cut out the sweets and fats, exercise . . . gee . . . that sounds a heck of a lot like a *diet* to me!"

"When you put it *that* way. . . ."

"That's what it is, an enforced diet. Sorta like the old-fashioned business of wiring your jaws shut so that you couldn't eat. Only the jaw wiring could be taken out at any time and you would be back to normal. And I doubt that very many of those people died on the operating table."

"Sounds barbaric, unless you take into account that some people need the surgery to save their lives. It's supposed to help people who have diabetes, asthma, sleep apnea, all sorts of life-threatening illnesses."

Savannah shrugged. "If that's the only way to save their lives, more power to them. But looking at this picture, which was supposedly taken a week before Dona had the surgery, I have to wonder if she really met the qualifying criteria."

"You aren't the only one who questioned that," Tammy said. "There are a couple of articles here that quote Dona's girlfriend, Mary Jo, saying exactly the same thing. Apparently, she openly opposed the surgery and even accused Dona of being superficial and vain. She said Dona's surgeon was irresponsible and greedy for performing the surgery on a woman who didn't meet the criteria."

"That must have gone over well with Dona, having a friend

say that about her publicly. Have you seen Mary Jo today, by the way?"

"Just for a moment as she was leaving earlier. I overheard her and Dona arguing and Mary Jo said something about 'getting out of here before I wind up like Kim.'"

"Wow, that's pretty brutal."

Tammy nodded. "There's definitely trouble in paradise around here right now." She pointed to the stack of papers on the desk. "And as if there isn't enough going on in her 'real' world, Dona drags these things out, reads them, and hurts herself all over again. Can you imagine even cutting them out and saving them, let alone dwelling over them like this?"

"No, I can't." Savannah shook her head. "Granny Reid always used to warn us about what she called 'scratching at the wound.' She used to say, 'It's bad enough that you or somebody else caused you a wound. But the worst thing you can do is to keep scratchin' at it, thinkin' about it, talkin' about it, frettin' over it. That only keeps it raw and open and if it ever does finally close over, the scar's gonna be a lot worse. Just leave it alone and let it heal; no point in reinjuring yourself.'"

"That's what Dona was doing today, going through these," Tammy said. "She was reinjuring herself all over again, scratching at old wounds."

"No wonder she's upstairs sick." Savannah began to gather the articles up into a pile. "But maybe you should put these away before somebody comes in here and catches us with them."

She gave the stack to Tammy, who promptly placed them back into the drawer and closed it.

When she was finished, Tammy brushed her hands against each other, dusting her fingers off.

Savannah snickered. "Yeah, right. Like guilt is *that* easily removed."

"Out damned spot and all that."

"Exactly, Lady Tammy Macbeth."

Savannah motioned toward a leather sofa with nail-head trim and ball-and-claw feet. "Sit over here with me and fill me in on what the maid told you," she said.

"She's very sweet and friendly."

"I know. I met her in the foyer earlier."

They took a seat side by side, both keeping an eye on the doorway, in case there were any eavesdroppers lurking nearby.

"She seemed reluctant to talk too much about Dona," Tammy said. "After all, she *is* her employer, and I'm sure celebrities are sensitive about house staff with loose lips."

Savannah ran her palm over the supple smoothness of the sofa's leather cushions and thought that she could probably decorate her entire house for what Dona Papalardo paid for this one couch. "So, if Juanita didn't talk about Dona, what was the juicy stuff that you were getting out of her? I distinctly picked that up on the phone earlier. You got my hopes up."

"Mostly she was talking about Kim. I got the idea that she didn't like her very much. Juanita said Kim bossed her around, talked down to her, disrespected her in general, expected her to do all sorts of personal errands for her. Juanita didn't really seem to be grieving that she was gone. Quite the contrary, in fact."

Savannah processed that for a moment, then said, "When Dirk and I were at Kim's house just now, we found evidence that some guy is living there with her. Maybe named James Morgan. Did she say anything about that?"

"Actually, she did say that this past month or so Kim was in better spirits and easier to get along with. Juanita thought it might be because she had a new boyfriend. And she also seemed to have more money than usual. She was buying new clothes, getting her hair styled at expensive salons and bragging about it."

"Hmm . . . sprucing up can also be a sign of a new boyfriend."

Tammy giggled. "If she was buying new, sexy lingerie, then it would be a sure thing."

"Speaking of sexy things . . . did you get a look at the gardener yet?" Savannah put a hand over her heart and fluttered her eyelashes.

"Just a glance. I went out back to check out the yard area, and he was skimming the pool. He walked away before I had a chance to talk to him." Tammy snickered. "But he did get a look at the miniskirt, and he seemed to approve. *Really* approve."

"Well, now we know that his vision is fine and he's probably not gay. I'd be very interested in getting his take on Kim."

Tammy reached down and ran her fingertips lightly over her left thigh. "I could try again later if you like."

"Eh, don't overdo it. I wouldn't want you to strain anything with all that effort."

Tammy shrugged and laughed. "It's what you pay me for."

"I pay you?"

"You sure do."

"When?"

"Every month, when I pay your bills."

"Do I pay you enough?"

"Not really. I'm thinking of giving myself a raise."

Savannah reached over and tweaked a strand of Tammy's long blond hair that lay on her shoulder. She gave her friend an affectionate, sweet smile. "You do that, honey bunny. You give yourself a great big raise. Okay?"

Tammy's eyes widened. "Really! That's so cool! When?"

"I don't know. You do my books. As soon as you think I can afford it."

"Oh." Her face fell. "That long, huh?"

Chapter 11

The front doorbell rang, and Savannah jumped up from the library sofa. "I'll get it," she told Tammy. "Why don't you go grab a cool drink and sit out back by the pool. Maybe Mr. Gorgeous will show up again."

Savannah made it to the front door at the same time as Juanita. The maid glanced through the glass door panel and told Savannah, "It's Senor Mark. He's my lady's special friend."

Ah, the recently jilted boyfriend, Savannah thought. *Just the guy I want to talk to!*

"I'll let him in," Savannah told him. "Thank you, Juanita."

"Okay. No problem. I'll go tell Miss Dona. I don't think she will want to talk to him, but I should tell her he is here."

The maid hurried up the staircase as Savannah opened the door and greeted the tall, thin, dark-haired man standing there.

"Hello," she said, extending her hand. "I'm Savannah Reid."

She gave him a quick visual check, looking for any lumps or bumps beneath his clothes. But his thin polo shirt and tightly fitted jeans couldn't have concealed much in the way of a weapon.

"Mark Kellerher," he said, taking her hand and giving it a limp shake. "And you're here because . . . ?"

"I'm Ms. Papalardo's new security consultant."

He frowned, his thick black eyebrows nearly meeting in the middle. "Security consultant?"

"Her bodyguard."

"Oh." He looked uncomfortable, shifting from one foot to another as he cleared his throat. "Yeah, I guess she might want one now, after . . . that . . . you know . . . bad thing happened. Yes, of course *you* know. That's probably why she hired you and well, you know . . ." He babbled on until Savannah pulled the door open wider and beckoned him inside.

"Won't you come in? Juanita has gone upstairs to tell Dona that you're here," she told him as she led him inside the foyer.

"She probably won't want to see me," he said, running his fingers though his thick, black hair in a self-conscious gesture. "But I thought I'd at least come by and tell her how sorry I am to hear about Kim."

"You and Kim were close?" Savannah asked. Normally she would have worked up to it more gradually, but she was afraid Dona would come down any minute and then her opportunity to question him would be lost for the moment.

His eyes clouded with tears and his voice shook as he said, "Yes, Kim and I were really good friends. She was a sweet person, smart, and ambitious. And she worked really hard for Dona. Dona's not the easiest person in the world to please."

Savannah glanced toward the staircase, which was still empty. "So I've heard," she said. "In fact, I understand that you and she have . . . um . . . sort of had a parting of the ways."

"After years of being together, she dumped me like a sack of garbage on the side of the road, if that's what you mean." His dark eyes flashed momentarily and it occurred to Savannah that Dona had definitely underestimated this man's capacity for passion. Savannah decided to tell Dirk to take a really close look at him.

"Do you think Kim was killed deliberately?" she asked. "Or do you think someone was trying to murder Dona?"

A look of pain washed over his face, raw and intense. "I'm sure of it," he said. "Nobody would have any reason to kill Kim. She was a really sweet kid."

"And Dona?"

He opened his mouth to speak, closed it, then opened it again and said, "Dona is . . . more . . . controversial."

"What sort of controversies is she involved in?"

"What the hell are you doing in my house?"

Savannah whirled around, looked up and saw Dona Papalardo standing at the top of the staircase. She was wearing a rose velvet dressing gown with a cloud of pink marabou feathers around the collar, framing her face. The effect was soft and feminine, but the expression on that pretty face was anything but soft.

"I said, 'What the hell are you doing in my house?'" she repeated, her voice booming off the foyer's marble surfaces.

Savannah was suddenly aware that the statue of the warrior goddess Diana in the center of the room looked a lot like the fiery mistress of the manor.

"Get out of here before I call the cops!" she screamed. "Now!"

"I just came by to give you my condolences, Dona," Mark said, his voice small and mousy compared to her lion's roar. "You don't have to be so nasty. I only wanted to—"

"Get out of here! Go!" She ran down several steps and nearly tripped on the hem of her gown. "For all I know, you shot Kim, thinking she was me. Get out of my home. I never want to see you again."

She turned on Savannah. "And what kind of bodyguard are you supposed to be, letting him in here like that! Get him out! Out!"

Savannah took Mark's arm. "I think you should leave, Mr. Kellerher. Let me walk you to your car."

She hurried him to the door, opened it and nearly shoved him outside. While Dona Papalardo's tirade didn't faze her, she was eager to get him alone and see if his insult and outrage over Dona's attack would loosen his tongue.

She walked him out to his car, a new black Lexus that was parked a ways down the driveway. On the way they passed the spray-painted marks left on the brick driveway by the CSI techs.

She saw him glance at them as they walked by and again, the stark pain showed on his face. And for a moment she wondered if maybe he and Kim had been closer than close. She looked down at his feet to check his shoe size, but his loafers were a much larger size than the men's shoes she had seen earlier in Kim's closet. He was also much taller than average, at least six feet, two inches, and the clothes had been for a man less than six feet tall.

When they reached his car, he fumbled in his pocket for his keys.

"I'm sorry that happened to you," she told him, trying to get on his good side quickly. "Dona's been under a lot of stress lately. And I don't think she's feeling well at all today."

"She hasn't felt good since she had that damned surgery," he said. "She's been a different person altogether. Dona used to be sweet and funny, bright and charming. But she had that surgery and she nearly died, and now she's like a different woman. I can't believe how much she's changed."

"Pain and depression can do that to you."

"I know, and I've tried to be patient, but I'm not going to keep taking her abuse." He waved an arm toward the house. "Like this. Did you hear her? Accusing me of killing Kim!"

Savannah thought for a moment that he was going to burst into tears. She placed her hand on his shoulder and could feel him shaking violently.

"She's been through a terrible ordeal," she told him. "And stress like she's had doesn't bring the best out in us. Try not to take it too personally."

"But accusing me of killing somebody I care about! That's character assassination. I don't care how bad you're feeling, you don't accuse somebody of murder." He shook his head. "I never want to see her again for as long as I live. And if somebody was trying to kill her instead of Kim . . . I hope that next time, they get it right!"

He shook Savannah's hand off his shoulder, yanked his car door open and got inside. A few seconds later, he was peeling out of Dona's driveway, disappearing in a cloud of stinking smoke.

Savannah watched him until the car was out of sight.

Then she shook her head and walked back to the house, past the crime-scene markings.

No, Mark Kellerher was anything but bland and lackluster. She had seen a dark fire burning in his eyes when he had wished Dona ill. And a flame that hot could scorch you if you were too close when it flared.

The next time Mark came to the house, if he ever did again, she wouldn't be letting him inside.

He might not have tried to kill Dona Papalardo before. But she wouldn't put it past him to try now. And the last thing this palatial property needed was another set of crime-scene marks.

Before she got to the door, she felt her cell phone buzzing in her pocket. Taking it out, she looked at the caller ID and saw that it was Dirk. She decided to speak to him outside the house where she would have more privacy.

"Hey, sugar," she said. "What's shakin'?"

"Got some news for you," he replied.

He sounded moderately pleased. Something fantastic must have occurred.

She grinned. "Okay, shoot."

"They did . . . with a rifle, that is. Dr. Liu dug the slug out of the victim. It was a .270."

"Deer-hunting ammo."

"That's right. And she said there was no powder residue, so it wasn't close range, which you'd figure with a rifle. I'm still thinking he took the shot from up on that hill above the house."

She turned and looked up at the hill in question. A little shiver ran down her back as she imagined someone poised up there with a rifle, likely even a scope, taking bead on an innocent woman in an evening gown and fur coat.

"Did they process that footprint they found up there?" she asked him.

"Yeah, it's a size thirteen, Porter-Marceau hiking boot."

"That's an expensive shoe."

"Four hundred bucks a pair, minimum. And every pair custom made to fit. He doesn't shop where I do, that's for sure."

"Ah-h-h, they might have a pair like that at the mission thrift store."

"Very funny. Size thirteen is larger than the shoes in Kim's closet."

Savannah's eyes narrowed. "Yes, but about the same size as some feet I just saw."

"Huh?"

"Dona's recently dumped boyfriend, Mark Kellerher, just dropped by here to give his condolences to Dona—at least that's why he said he was here—and she tossed him out on his left ear. He's tall and skinny and about a size thirteen."

"Good to know," he said. "And here's something that you might want to know about Kim Dylan. She's a fake."

"What do you mean, a 'fake'?"

"There's no Kim Dylan. It's an alias."

"Get out!"

"Yep. Remember when I said she was clean as a whistle? No record, no nothing. Well, that's because she doesn't exist. At least, not as Kim Dylan. We ran her fingerprints through AFIS. She's Penny Kara Bethany, wanted in Missouri and Indiana for fraud and blackmail."

"No way! That's great!"

"Great? What's great about it?"

"Well, it's interesting, opens up all other sorts of possibilities."

"Like what?"

"Well, hell, Dirk, I don't know off the top of my head. You annoy me to distraction sometimes, you know that?"

She heard him chuckle on the other end.

"What else?" she snapped.

"I couldn't get my hands on that agent of hers. I went to his office there in Hollywood on Sunset, and his secretary said he was out. But I had the feeling she was lying."

"And you didn't storm past her and into his office? You're losing your edge, buddy."

"I was afraid to. I'm so wired from this quitting smoking thing that I'm afraid to get into it with anybody. The way I'm feeling right now, I might spiral out of control. I might kill 'em."

She giggled. "Yeah, yeah, yeah, you need to protect the public at large from those flying fists of fury."

"Laugh it up, chuckles, but you've never seen me really mad before. Boy, when I get really steamed—"

"I've seen you steamed. I've seen you steamed at *me*, and I've survived, so get real. What else do you have for me?"

"Isn't that enough for now?"

"If that's all you've got, I guess it's enough."

"There's one other thing. Penny Kara Bethany had an accomplice in her little blackmail scheme that she perpetrated there in Missouri."

"Really?" A light flashed inside her head. "Let me guess. Somebody named James Morgan?"

"Bingo."

"Got a picture?"

"Sure. It's black and white."

"Well, that'll do."

"It's his fingerprints."

She sighed. "That's peachy. All we have to do is run around asking every male we meet if he'll show us his thumb."

When Savannah entered the kitchen, she found Juanita and Tammy having a discussion about the evening's dinner plans.

"Savannah," Tammy said, "Juanita says she's going to make dinner for us tonight, and I told her we don't expect her to do that." She was perched on a high stool at the center island, her elbows propped on the dark-green marble top. In front of her was a large crystal bowl filled with apples, grapes, and bananas.

Savannah realized it had been a while since lunch and the mention of dinner stirred some appetite pangs.

She walked over to where Juanita was loading dishes into the oversized dishwasher. "Of course you don't need to feed us," she told her. "We work here, too. We're not guests, you know."

Juanita leaned over and adjusted some pans, and when she stood up, her dark eyes were filled with sadness. "I would be happy to cook for you," she said. "It would be like old times here in the house again. We used to have parties all the time, many people, much good food, much laughter. But now we have no parties. We have only tears."

Savannah sat down on one of the stools at the island, next to Tammy. "Dona used to entertain a lot, did she?"

"Oh, all the time! Many famous people came here, movie stars, singers, businesspeople, politicos. They all loved her because she was so funny, so happy. And the food, oh . . . she and I would cook for two, three days before. We would laugh and taste and cook some more. It was wonderful!"

"When did things change?" Tammy asked. "After she had her surgery?"

Juanita cast a wary eye toward the door and lowered her voice a little. "A while before that," she said. "When Senorita Dona got a little bit more big and the newspapers started to make jokes about her. She would read the papers and be sad. She tried to stop eating for days at a time, but she would get so weak. Then she would eat too much and be sick from that, too."

Savannah shook her head, thinking of how many women she knew who were caught in that terrible cycle. "And let me guess," she said, "she did that and got larger and larger."

"Yes. It's true! And the bigger she got, the more they made fun of her and the more she would eat and . . ." She sighed. "And then her agent told her he would no longer have her, you know, as a client, unless she got the surgery."

"That's awful," Tammy said. "For him to give her an ultimatum like that, regarding something having to do with her body and her health!"

"Yeah," Savannah replied, "I would have had to give him an ultimatum—like jump off the end of that dock voluntarily or get thrown off."

"I've seen the pictures of her before the surgery," Tammy said. "She didn't really look all that heavy. I thought you had to be a certain weight before you can even have gastric-bypass surgery."

"She wasn't big enough," Juanita said. "And she went to many doctors. They all told her 'no.' But finally she found one who would do it . . . if she gained another twenty pounds. So, she did. She ate night and day and gained enough."

Tammy gasped. "A doctor recommended that she do that?"

"I don't know if he told her to do it, but he knew she was

doing it. She told him. She would call him and say, 'Ten more pounds, is that enough?' And then call him again, 'Fifteen more. Enough?' And he didn't tell her to stop, so . . ."

"That's criminal," Savannah said. "Who is this guy?"

"His name is Dr. Cahill. His office is in the valley. But you must not tell anyone I told you these things," Juanita said. "I need this job. I feed my mother and my brothers and sisters and my son in Ecuador from my work here."

"No, of course not," Savannah said. "We'll watch out for you. Don't worry about that."

Juanita smiled sweetly. "I can trust you. I can tell. You ladies, you have good hearts. And I want to make a nice dinner for you. I will make you soup. Beautiful soup. You will see. It will be my gift to you. And you will eat it outside on the patio, and I will light some candles, and it will be a little bit like old times here again."

"Well, if you insist," Savannah said. "But only if you let us pay for the ingredients."

"No one is paying for anything they eat in my home," said a voice from the doorway.

All three of them jumped and turned around to see Dona Papalardo standing there, still wearing her marabou-trimmed gown. Savannah worried for a moment that she might have overheard something incriminating, but she had a softer, gentler look on her face than Savannah had seen so far.

She swept into the kitchen with all of the grace and aplomb of a silver-screen goddess. She walked over to a cupboard and took out a fine cut-crystal wineglass, and walked over to the refrigerator.

Savannah noticed that Juanita watched her mistress with a look of concern on her face as she saw Dona pour herself a tiny amount of Chardonnay.

Dona glanced up to see Juanita looking at her, and she gave a wry chuckle. "Ah, Juanita, you have your worried face on. Don't fret. I'll only have a sip every fifteen minutes, okay?"

Juanita didn't reply, but busied herself at the dishwasher again, avoiding eye contact with her lady.

Dona took a tiny taste from the glass and closed her eyes, as though savoring every drop. Then she opened them and gave Savannah a cold, stern look that might have withered a lesser soul. "I have to tell you," she said, "I'm not at all happy with you for allowing that man into my home. I thought you were here to keep me safe."

"I was and I still am. I looked him over good before I let him inside."

"You shouldn't have allowed someone I'm angry with into my home."

Savannah nodded. "I understand your anger, and ordinarily, I might agree with you. But part of me protecting you is also finding out what happened to Kim. The sooner we find her killer, the safer you'll be. And part of conducting an investigation is me talking to everybody I can who knew her, who knows you. I'm sorry if you're upset that Mark was here. And I'll respect your wishes in the future and not allow him in. But—"

The doorbell rang, cutting off her speech. They all stood, frozen, for a moment, then Juanita made a move toward the door.

Savannah held up one hand. "Let me get it." Then to Dona, she said, "Is there anyone else other than Mark and your former agent that you don't want inside your home?"

Dona took another sip as the doorbell sounded again. "There's a list a mile long," she replied, "but for now, the two of them will do."

Savannah hurried into the foyer and looked through the glass at three people—two men and a woman, who were trying hard to appear friendly, open, and charming . . . without looking like reporters. But their perfect hairdos gave them away, not to mention the large video camera the second fellow was trying to hide behind his back.

She yanked the door open and donned her best battle face.

"Ye-e-es?" she asked, as though daring them to identify themselves.

"Hello," the impeccably dressed red-haired woman said, her voice dripping with all of the sexy professionalism that a Los Angeles six-week journalism class could teach a gal. "I'm Candy Diamond, and we're from *News to You* on channel—"

"No, thank you," Savannah said, holding up her hand. "I'm sorry, but no one here has any statement to give you at this time."

"But we just want to ask Ms. Papalardo one or two simple questions," the redhead continued. "I'm sure she will want to go on record with—"

"Stop talking. You need to listen. I understand that you're professionals and only doing your job. I respect that. I really do. Ms. Papalardo is deeply distressed at what happened here yesterday, and she is unavailable for comment."

The redhead turned to the guy behind her with the camera. "Paul, get that." She turned to Savannah. "Say that once more on camera, would you?"

"No, not at all. You have your statement. You need to leave now, because, as of this moment, you are trespassing and subject to being arrested. Good . . . bye."

She shut the door with just enough force to punctuate her statement and yet just short of breaking Dona's fancy etched-glass inserts.

When she turned around, she saw Dona standing just around the corner in the library, watching her, a big grin on her face.

"Okay," Dona said, "That was awesome. I forgive you for Mark. I guess you're not altogether worthless after all."

Savannah locked eyes with her, and for a moment, they were simply two women, connecting and bonding.

"Gee, thanks," Savannah said. "That's mighty big of you."

Dona laughed. "I thought so, too."

Savannah turned back to the door and peered through the glass, just in time to see the white van with the station's logo and call letters on its side disappear down the street.

"They're gone," she told Dona.

"They'll come back. Them or others like them."

"Well, we'll just get rid of them, too."

"Are you that good with termites? Juanita swears she saw some in the pantry the other day."

"Nope, we don't do termites," Savannah replied. "Our specialty is cockroaches . . . of the two-legged variety."

Chapter 12

"Wow," Savannah said after she had tasted the first spoonful of Juanita's soup. "This *is* beautiful. That's the perfect word for it!"

"It's exquisite!" Tammy said. "I've never eaten anything like this in my whole life!"

Savannah and Tammy had been seated at a table beneath an awning, near the back door, and Juanita had placed an arrangement of assorted candles in the center of the table that gave the setting a fanciful glow.

Nearby the pool was lit by floating iridescent orbs that looked like perpetual bubbles, skimming along the surface. The fountain in the center of the pool danced in the blue spotlights trained on it, looking like a million fairy gems spraying into the night sky.

Savannah could smell the sweet fragrance of some nearby jasmine, along with the exotic aroma of the soup set before her. If ever she had been in a fairy land, surely this was it.

Juanita hovered over her two guests, beaming with pleasure at their praise. "I am so glad you like it," she said. "It is my family's favorite. We make it for special holidays in Ecuador."

Savannah pushed the various ingredients around in the white

broth in her bowl. She saw every type of seafood she could imagine: bits of fish, shrimp, scallops, and even a couple of small lobster tails. The broth itself was savory, spiced with chives and black pepper. She guessed it was made with a chicken stock. And yet, there was an exotic sweetness to it that she couldn't quite place.

"What is that strange, wonderful flavor?" she asked. "And what gives the broth its white appearance?"

"Coconut milk," Juanita told her proudly. "Unsweetened coconut milk."

"You never would have told me that you could put coconut milk into a fish soup," Tammy said, "but this really works."

"These are all foods that are found in my country. The place where I lived there, where my family still lives, is much like here, on the ocean, beautiful."

"And what are these things?" Tammy lifted a circular beige object out of the broth with her spoon.

"Plantains," Juanita said.

"What is that?"

"A type of banana," Savannah told Tammy. "They aren't as sweet as the ones we usually eat." She turned to Juanita. "This is just amazing. I've never had anything like this in my life. Thank you for sharing your soup and your culture with us."

"It makes me happy to do so," Juanita said, bowing her head modestly.

Savannah took a piece of bread to soak up some of the broth. She wished that she could share this with Granny Reid. But she couldn't imagine Gran being willing to eat fish with coconut and bananas. Gran was open-minded in most ways, especially for an octogenarian. But Savannah was pretty sure she'd draw a line at bananas and fish.

Savannah was about to take another bite when she saw a movement on the other side of the pool. A movement in the shadows.

Instantly, she stood and put her hand on the butt of the Beretta that was in her holster beneath her sweater.

Tammy jumped to her feet, as well. "What is it?" she asked, breathless.

Juanita took several steps backward toward the house.

"Hey, you over there," Savannah shouted, pulling the weapon and pointing it toward the palms. "Come out of there and let me see your hands! Let me see your hands now!"

A man moved from behind the palm trees into plain view.

Instantly, Savannah recognized him. It was the gardener. His hands were high over his head in full surrender, but he had a cocky grin on his calendar-boy face.

She lifted the end of the Beretta's barrel, but she didn't immediately holster it. "What were you doing back there?" she demanded.

He took several steps toward them, hands still raised. "Don't shoot," he said. "It's me, Jack, the gardener." His voice sounded more mocking than frightened. And that didn't sit well with Savannah. If she pulled a gun on a guy, or a gal either for that matter, she expected a little respect, if not good ol' knee-knocking fear, from them.

He walked right up to them, then slowly lowered his hands. "Really," he said, "everybody knows the gardener's a good guy. It's always the butler who did it, right?"

Savannah gave him a cold, nasty look. In light of the crime that had just been committed on these premises, she didn't find his little joke all that humorous.

She glanced over at Tammy and Juanita and saw that they weren't laughing either.

"I asked you," she said, "what you were doing over there in the dark."

Gingerly, with thumb and forefinger, he reached into the front pocket of his jeans. "I got home and remembered that I'd left my

MP3 player over there in the flower bed next to the palms when I was weeding today. And a guy can't do without his tunes, you know? See?" He pulled out the tiny device and showed it to her, complete with dangling earphones.

She didn't believe him. She was convinced that he was hiding there for the simple reason of eavesdropping on their conversation. At least, that was the most innocent explanation she could come up with.

Slowly, she slipped her gun back into its holster, then she walked back to her chair at the table and sat down. "Join us," she said, pushing out the chair across from her with her foot. "Have something to eat."

"Naw, thanks anyway." He gave her another little smirk that made her want to rearrange his dental work . . . up his nose.

"I insist," she said, pushing the chair out even further. "Really, I do."

He sighed and walked over to the table. Picking up the chair, he spun it around backward and straddled it, laying his thickly muscled arms across the top of the chair's back and resting his chin on his forearms.

Savannah was never fooled by the "pseudo-casual" posture. In her experience, she had seen more guilty guys lean back in chairs and prop their feet on desks than innocent ones. No one was truly at ease after a murder had been committed. And anyone who pretended to be had something to hide.

She glanced over at Tammy and saw that her assistant, in spite of this man's extreme attractiveness, was put off by him. She was giving him as suspicious and nasty a look as Savannah had ever seen her give anyone.

And Juanita seemed just as disapproving. She stood where she was, several steps away from the table, closer to the house, her arms folded across her chest. To say the least, Jack's snooping had put a damper on her party.

"Have some dinner," Savannah said with a less than hospitable tone. "Juanita made us a beautiful dinner, and it's getting cold while we're messing around here with you."

He peered into the soup tureen and made an ugly face. "Ick, what is that stuff? I thought you said Juanita cooked. Where are the tacos and burritos?"

Juanita swelled up and marched over to the table. She snatched the tureen out from under his nose, put the lid on it, and moved it to the opposite side of the table near Savannah. "You," she told him, "are a stupid man. Not every person who speaks español is from Mexico. And not everyone from Mexico eats only tacos and burritos. When you say such things you show how little you know to the world."

"Well said," Tammy added. "You just missed out on an amazing culinary experience."

"I don't eat that stuff anyway," he replied with a slight lift to his chin.

"What stuff?" Tammy asked.

"What you just said. Culin . . . something. I'm a hamburger, hot dog, beer man myself."

"Gee, what a surprise," Savannah mumbled under her breath.

He looked from Savannah to Tammy and back again, flashing the smile that Savannah had previously thought was so very charming, but now seemed more smarmy. Obviously, Jack the gardener figured that he could sail through life, and probably more than his share of women, with a smile and a flex of biceps.

"So, you girls are the security team, bodyguards or whatever, huh?" he said, not even bothering to hide the contempt in his voice.

"Something like that," Savannah replied. "I'm Savannah Reid and this is Tammy Hart. And you are . . . ?"

"Jack."

"I've heard 'Jack' before. Jack what?"

"Roland."

"How long have you been working here, Jack Roland?"

He fixed her with a look that went beyond cocky or rude. She had seen sweeter expressions on felons who had served thirty years of hard time.

"I don't have to answer your questions," he said.

She matched his acid look and cranked it up a notch. "Yes, you do," she said evenly. "Trust me, you do *not* want to get on my bad side. The last thing you should do is come across as a jerk who doesn't care that someone has been murdered here, someone who isn't willing to cooperate in the investigation."

"You're investigators, too?"

"Oh, that's what we do best," Tammy said brightly. A little too brightly. Her mouth was smiling but her eyes were nearly as cold as Savannah's. "We do background checks on people, find out all sorts of things about them. Stuff that goes back, years and years ago. And almost everyone has something if you just dig deep enough. Isn't that true, Savannah?"

"That's right." Savannah nodded. "Remember when you found out that one guy had spit on a girl who lived next door? It was there, right on his police record, plain as day."

"And he'd only been five years old when he did it," Tammy replied solemnly. "You'd be surprised what you can uncover if you just keep digging and digging and—"

"What do you wanna know?" he asked.

"That's better," Savannah said as she continued to eat her soup. "I want you to tell us about Kim."

"What about her?"

"What did you think of her?"

He shrugged. "I didn't think much about her at all. She worked here. She was sort of quiet, a little stuck-up maybe. We didn't talk much."

He reached up and ran his fingers through his thick, long hair.

And Savannah was pretty sure that she saw his hand shaking slightly. Suddenly, he wasn't meeting her eyes and his ever-present, mocking smile was momentarily replaced by something that seemed a little like fear.

What did Pretty Boy Pain in the Hindquarters have to be afraid of?

"Can you think of any reason why anybody would want to kill her?" Savannah asked him.

"Sure, if they thought she was Dona. Dona pisses everybody off lately now that she's lost all that weight and is looking good again. Have you spent any time around *her*? If you have, then I don't have to explain what I'm talking about to you. She's sick all the time, and she takes it out on everybody. Maybe somebody just got fed up and decided to do something about it. And Kim . . . Kim just got in the way." His voice broke and for just a second, Savannah thought she could see the real person behind that irritating facade. She also saw a young man who had more than a casual interest in a victim that he claimed to have barely known.

They sat quietly for a moment as he appeared to struggle with his emotions.

Finally, Savannah said, "Did you see Kim die, Jack? Were you here when she was murdered?"

He laced his fingers together and stared down at his hands. Savannah noticed that his grip was so strong that his fingers were turning white.

"Yeah," he said. "I was."

"Will you tell us what you saw?" she asked gently.

A shudder ran through him and he closed his eyes. Then he said, "I was here in the backyard, testing the pool water and adding the chemicals. I heard a pop. It seemed to come from up there." He nodded toward the hill high above them and to the side of the property. "Then I heard a guy yell."

"What did he yell?" Savannah asked.

"Just a yell, like he was hurt or upset. I found out later it was the limo driver. He'd just seen Kim . . . realized she was down."

"Okay. What happened next?"

"I heard a woman scream. And then another one started, too."

"That was Senorita Dona, and Senorita Mary Jo," Juanita said. "I ran outside, too, and saw her . . . Kim . . . on the road in front of the house. We all started to cry."

Savannah turned back to Jack. "And what did you do then?"

"I could tell that the yelling and crying was coming from the front of the house, so I ran around there to see what was going on. It still hadn't dawned on me that somebody had been shot. The noise, it had sounded like a firecracker, not a gun."

"People often say that gunshots sound like firecrackers," Tammy said.

"So much so, that if you hear what you think are firecrackers in a public place," Savannah said, "you should probably hit the dirt and worry about how stupid you looked later." To Jack she said, "What did you see when you reached the front of the house?"

"I saw Kim on the ground. She was all bloody, and she wasn't moving. And Dona was sitting next to her on the road, holding Kim's head on her lap. She was crying and talking to her. The driver was on his cell phone, calling for an ambulance, I guess." He looked over at Juanita. "I saw you standing in the door. You looked like you were about to faint."

"I was," Juanita said. "I was. I had never seen anything so horrible."

"Believe it or not," Jack continued, "I thought maybe the limousine had run over her or something like that. It wasn't until I knelt down beside her and saw . . ." He gulped. ". . . the hole in her back that I put it together. The popping sound, her wound. She'd been shot. I told everybody to get into the house. To get out of range in case whoever it was took another shot."

"And did you?" Savannah asked Juanita.

"Yes." The maid seemed ashamed as she admitted it. "The driver, and Jack, and myself, we went inside, but Dona stayed there with Kim until the police came—and then the ambulance."

Quietly, Savannah studied the strange young man sitting across the table from her. At first, she had heartily disliked him. She had chalked him up as a self-centered pretty boy who used his looks to get what he wanted in life. Most of it from women, who should know better than to give it to him.

And yet, the person he was now, telling her about what he had witnessed, she could feel an affinity for him.

At least, she could if he hadn't lied to her. She didn't like being lied to. It was about her least favorite thing in the world. And she knew, without a doubt, that he had lied to her about Kim. He *had* cared about her. More than he had originally let on. And she intended to find out why he had felt the need to downplay that.

"Tell me one more thing, if you will, Jack," she said. "And it's very important, so I want you to take your time and think about it. Okay?"

He nodded. "Go ahead."

"When you first heard that popping sound, where exactly did it come from? Your first impression. Your best guess."

He thought for a moment, then turned and decisively pointed to a particular clump of bushes on the hill above them. It was the same area where the CSI team had found the Porter-Marceau hiking boot print in the dirt.

"Okay, thank you," she said. "I'm sure that wasn't easy for you, recalling such an awful memory. But you helped."

"I did?" He looked pleased.

"You did."

"Good." Every trace of a smile dropped from his face and the expression that replaced it frightened Savannah—shaking her to her shoes. And she was seldom shaken by such things. Then he added, "That's good, because whoever did that to Kim, he should have the same damned thing done to him. He should have a hole blown in him and die on the ground like a dog—the way she did."

"Well, I can understand you having that point of view," Savannah told him. "But for right now, let's just see if we can catch him and hope he gets at least twenty-to-life."

Chapter 13

Later that evening, when the Papalardo estate was retiring for the night, Savannah showed Tammy the pink bedroom with its silk-covered walls, canopy bed, and ornate, feminine accessories. As Savannah had predicted, she was enthralled.

"Oh, this is exactly the kind of bedroom I always wanted when I was a kid!" Tammy exclaimed as she walked into the room and looked around. She set down the suitcase that she had stashed earlier behind the sofa in the library, and twirled around and around in the center of the room. "I feel like a princess," she said, "a fairy, ballerina princess!"

"Well, stop that," Savannah told her, laughing. "You're making me dizzy here with all that spinning around. So you like it. I figured you would. That's why I decided to let you sleep in here at night for as long as we have this gig."

Tammy's mouth fell open, and she abruptly halted in mid-pirouette. "No! You can't! I mean, that would be just too sweet!"

"That's me, too sweet. It's all yours. Enjoy."

"But . . . but where are you going to sleep?"

Savannah walked over to the bed, peeled back the moiré comforter and grabbed one of the pillows that was covered with a lace-trimmed and embroidered pillowcase. "I'm going to sleep downstairs," she said, "on the couch in the library."

"No, you can't! You're the boss. You're older. You should sleep up here and let me take the sofa."

"What does age have to do with anything?"

"You get stiff faster if you have to sit or sleep on anything weird. Remember that long layover in Denver we had that time when we flew to Chicago? We had to sit in those hard airport chairs for five hours. You couldn't walk straight for a week."

"Four days, but who was counting?" Savannah walked over to a chaise in the corner and lifted a thick, plush throw from its back. "I'm set," she said. "Believe me, I've slept with a lot worse than an Egyptian-cotton–covered, down pillow and a chenille throw thick enough to make into a fur coat."

But Tammy still wasn't happy. "Stay here and sleep with me," she said. "I mean, if you don't mind."

"Why would I mind sleeping with a girlfriend? I was one of nine kids, raised in a tiny shotgun house in Georgia. Do you think we each got our own bed? It's not that."

"But this bed is big," Tammy protested. "It's at least a queen, and I don't take up a lot of room."

Savannah raised one eyebrow. "Okay, I'm going to pretend that I didn't hear that last bit there."

"I didn't mean that you would—"

"I know you didn't mean a thing. You're a sweetheart. But to be honest, I think it would be better if at least one of us was on the ground floor, at least for tonight. Security reasons, you know."

"Oh, okay. Well, I don't mind being down there myself."

"Sh-h-h. Enjoy this small perk while you've got it. Lord knows, perks have been few and far between for you while in my employ."

"I never complained."

"Because you're kind."

"Because I love what we do."

Savannah gave her friend and assistant a warm smile. "You're the best, Tams. The best. Enjoy your room and sleep tight. You know where I am if you need me."

"Same here."

Savannah leaned over and gave Tammy a peck on the cheek. Then she headed for the door. "And watch out that you don't break anything, especially that lamp over there. It belonged to some old movie star who used to date Howard Hughes or something like that. If you break it, we'll have to steal that silver brush-and-mirror set just to pay for it."

Tammy blew Savannah a kiss as she walked out of the room and closed the door firmly behind her. She could hear Tammy lock it from the inside.

Good girl. All that nagging . . . or training . . . had paid off, after all. Now if she could only paper-train Dirk, all would be right with her world.

She turned and was starting down the hall, toward the staircase, when she saw Mary Jo Livermore coming up the stairs. Unsteady on her feet, the redhead was clinging tightly to the banister rail. At first glance, Savannah thought she might be injured in some way, but a closer look told her that Mary Jo was "in her cups." In fact, she looked like she had partaken of several cups of something highly intoxicating. Recently.

When Mary Jo reached the top of the stairs, she saw Savannah and appeared to realize that her clumsy ascension had been watched.

"Oh, you again," she mumbled as she staggered down the hall toward Savannah. "I forgot you were staying here. We're roommates, huh? Or hall mates, 'cause you're right across the hall from me and . . ."

Savannah had little use for sloppy drunks. Her own mother

had suffered from a severe drinking problem since Savannah could remember. And she wasn't the only one who had suffered from it. All nine of her children had, too. Terribly.

The police chief of her tiny hometown had found Savannah and her young siblings playing among the broken glass and assorted garbage behind the town's main tavern at midnight while their mother drank inside. And as a result, the children—all nine of them—had been removed from her custody and given to Savannah's grandmother.

Granny Reid had done a wonderful job of raising the brood, and Savannah had never regretted, even for a moment, the way things had turned out.

But she still couldn't abide sloppy drunks.

"I won't be sleeping across the hall from you after all," she told Mary Jo as the woman bumped clumsily against her as she passed. "My assistant, Tammy is in that room, and I'll be in the library downstairs if you need me."

"I don't need you," she said as she fumbled with the door, trying to get it open. "I don't need anybody or anything. I just need my own place away from here. Away from *her*!"

"Away from whom?" Savannah asked, though not really expecting a coherent answer.

"You know who," she mumbled. "*Her*. Queen God-Almighty Dona. We are just humble servants, groveling at her feet. She who must be obeyed, that's what we should call her . . ."

Her voice trailed away as she stumbled her way into her bedroom and managed to get the door shut behind her.

"Boy," Savannah mumbled as she made her way down the stairs, her pillow under one arm, her throw tossed over her shoulder, "she gives these people jobs, a roof over their heads and all they've got to say are rotten things about her behind her back."

Then she remembered how Dona had yelled at her earlier

when she had allowed Mark into the house, the fiery light that blazed from those famous, beautiful eyes.

"Yep, the sad part is: all that they're saying, nasty though it may be, appears to be the pure *D* truth. Now ain't that just a cryin' shame?"

As she passed through the dark, silent foyer, she paused for a moment in front of the statue of Diana. The lights had been turned off in the house, but a shaft of particularly brilliant moonlight shone through the etched transom and onto the goddess's face. The silver light gave the statue an unearthly beauty and made her all the more lifelike.

"So, you're the great hunter goddess, guardian of the woodlands, the animals and trees," Savannah whispered to her. "You carry that bow and arrow like you aim to use it on somebody."

As Savannah expected, Diana said nothing, but continued to stare through the window at the full moon. The artist had done a good job of capturing both a feminine softness in her features and a ferocity in her expression that radiated the epitome of female strength.

"Well, I reckon you wouldn't shoot anybody who didn't deserve it," she added, remembering the story of how Diana had shot some fellow who had secretly watched her as she bathed. "And being a goddess, I reckon you'd know who had it coming and who didn't."

Leaving Diana to her moon bathing, Savannah crossed the foyer and passed through the arched doorway into the library.

Although the room was quite dark, she could see well enough to find her way to the sofa. She kicked her shoes off and stretched out on it, tucking the pillow under head and covering herself with the soft chenille throw.

Certainly, it wasn't as comfortable as her bed at home, but it was a lot nicer than lying across the backseat of Dirk's Buick Skylark. And a lot classier, too.

There were no Styrofoam hamburger boxes, empty soda bottles or taco wrappers on the floor.

Her gun holster wasn't particularly comfortable sleepwear, but she wasn't prepared to take it off just yet. What it lacked in physical comfort it made up for in mental consolation.

However, she could do without her cell phone biting into her right side. She was just slipping it off her waistband when it began to buzz.

She answered it. "Hello."

"You busy?" Dirk asked with a curt, unpleasant tone. He sounded tired and cranky. Even more tired and cranky than usual.

"No . . . for the first time all day," she snapped back.

"Sorry," he said with more humility than he hardly ever demonstrated.

Heck, she thought, *he didn't sound that remorseful when he put that long scratch on my coffee table with his Harley boots.*

"You okay, buddy?" she asked.

"Yeah." He thought about it a few seconds. "No."

"What's the matter?"

"This 'no smoking' crap sucks."

Ah, that's my Dirk, she thought. *Articulate, succinct.*

"Sorry, sugar," she said, "But you know it's good for you. You'll feel better, run faster, cough and hack less . . . live longer."

"Not if I drive my car off a cliff and into the ocean."

She grinned. Dirk was never happier than when he was miserable. "Are you behind the wheel right now?"

"Yeah."

"Any cliffs in sight?"

"No."

"Then you're probably okay for the moment." She glanced down at her watch. "It's after eleven. Why aren't you at home in bed? Aren't you about ready to turn into a pumpkin?"

"I can't sleep. I can't stand being awake, because I feel like

I'm jumping out of my skin. But I can't sleep either and get away from the feeling. I'm telling you, this is friggin' awful."

"I'm sorry, honey. I really am. But you're doing so well! I'm very, very proud of you."

"Yeah, yeah, yeah. Enough with the pep talks, Pollyanna. I think I'm going to have just one. A half of one, just to take the edge off."

"You light up, boy, and I swear, I'll rip your right arm off and beat you to death with it."

He chuckled. "Now *that's* the Savannah I know and love."

"Seriously," she said, "why are you out driving around at this time of night?"

"I told you, I can't sleep."

"And there weren't any reruns of *Bonanza* on TV?"

"Nope. No *Gunsmoke* either."

"Poor baby. So, you just went out, got in the car and took a drive?"

He hesitated, then said, "Well, I went out to get a pack, but drove past the Seven-Eleven and didn't stop."

"Good. Really, Dirk. That's good. Where are you now?"

"At the end of the driveway."

"Which driveway?"

"Dona Papalardo's."

She tossed off the chenille throw and walked over to a window that looked out on the front of the property. And sure enough, there at the end of the driveway was Dirk's pale blue jalopy.

The headlights blinked twice.

She laughed. "You wanna come in and keep me company?"

"I could. Or you could come out *here* and keep *me* company. I'll let you pat me down, make sure I'm not carrying any cigs."

"Be still my heart." She stuck out her tongue and gave him a noisy raspberry. Then she said, "Hold onto your breeches. I'll be right out."

* * *

Minutes later, when Savannah climbed into Dirk's passenger seat, she was nearly overcome with the strong smell of cinnamon.

"Good lord, boy, do you have a bakery in here? Smells like the cinnamon bun place at the mall, only stronger."

He sniffed. "You're just never satisfied. You complain about the smoke in my car, or the way the food wrappers in the back smell, and you didn't like my pine tree freshener. You're just a little too—"

"Hey, I wasn't complaining." She held up her hands. "The cinnamon is a definite improvement—especially over that pine tree. I'm good with the cinnamon. Really."

Even in the semidarkness of the car, she could see the cinnamon stick dangling from the corner of his mouth. He looked ridiculous, of course, but he looked pretty dumb when he had smoke rolling out of his nostrils, too. So . . .

"Wanna go for a drive?" he asked.

"Yeah, but I should probably hang out here. Tammy thinks I'm downstairs, and she'd get spooked if she came down there and I was gone. I just wanted to come say 'hi' to you and see if you're surviving your withdrawal symptoms."

"I'm all right. I've been through worse than this. Way worse. Why, back when I was passing those—"

"No! I'm not listening to another kidney stone story rerun. You're not putting me through that ever again. You've gotten enough mileage out of that kidney stone attack to last for the next twenty years."

"It was horrible! You have no idea! My doctor said it was the worst pain any human being on earth has ever felt."

She rolled her eyes. "Considering the Spanish Inquisition, that's doubtful. Ever hear of 'the rack' or the iron maiden? Drawing and quartering?"

He bristled. "Have *you* ever passed something as big as that through something that small?"

"That *small*? Really?" She gave him a sideways look and a smirk.

"Don't be a smart aleck. You know what I mean."

She laughed at him. "Yes, I do. And no, I haven't. Every woman who's ever given birth has, but I can't say that *I* have."

"This was worse than childbirth. My doctor told me so."

"A male doctor?"

"Yeah, what's your point?"

"Who, me?" Her eyes widened with mock innocence. "I have no point. Nope, not me."

She reached over, put her hand on his forearm and squeezed. "I know it was awful for you, buddy, that stone attack. And I'm sure this is terrible, too. But you're doing it, and I can't tell you how strong and totally sexy I think you are for taking this stand and conquering this demon of yours."

He turned toward her on the seat and stared at her, incredulous. "Really?"

"Absolutely." She gave him her most serious, no-nonsense, level look. "You're hot, Dirk. The epitome of a truly manly man."

His chin lifted; his chest swelled visibly. "Wow! Cool! Thanks, Van."

"Just tellin' it like it is, good buddy. Just tellin' it straight."

He sat for a long time in silence, staring out the windshield at the moonlit surroundings. Finally he said, "Wanna go for a walk? Check out that hill where we think the shooter stood?"

"Sure. Let's."

He got out of the car first. She sat there for a moment, shaking her head, snickering. "Men," she whispered. "Tell them a pile of hooey about themselves, they'll believe it every time."

She swung the Buick's door open and stepped out. The fragrant dampness of the evening air surrounded her, and she breathed it in. No cinnamon, but sweet all the same. The full moon overhead lit the Papalardo mansion, coloring it with a silver patina that made it look like something from one of Dona's beloved black-and-white movies.

Being a hopeless romantic herself, Savannah could understand the diva's love affair with the silver screen. The glamour created by those old-time stars and those bigger-than-life sets had no equal in contemporary filmmaking.

"Nice digs, huh?" Dirk said, nodding toward the mansion.

"Eh, put some iron rails on my balconies, my house could be its twin."

They walked slowly, arm in arm, up the steep trail that curved along one side of the property. The path had a relatively steep pitch, and they had to lean into it as they climbed.

"How sure are you that the shooter was up here?" she asked.

"Pretty sure. I questioned the limo driver today. He was actually helping Kim into the vehicle when she was shot. He had hold of her arm."

"Wow, close call for him."

"And he knows it, too. He's really mad and wants us to catch the dude."

"And he was pretty helpful?"

"He was. He was very clear about the position she was in when she was shot. And when Dr. Liu showed me the trajectory of the bullet into the body, it was clear that the shooter was high, shooting from above and behind her. That would have put him up here."

"And," she said, "we had a long talk with Jack the gardener at dinner tonight, and he said he heard the gunshot. He placed it up here, too.

"Any luck on running down that footprint, the hiking boot?"

He shook his head and looked disgusted. "I left it up to that bimbo at the front desk to check it out on the Internet, and she didn't get to first base."

"I'll put Tammy on it tomorrow. She's going to bring her laptop computer here so that she can work from it."

"The kid *is* good at that stuff. Way better than anybody at the station."

"She'll be glad to hear it."

"Don't tell her I said anything good about her. Next thing, she'll want to be my friend or something."

"Not *that*! Lord help us."

"Exactly."

Savannah scanned the thick sagebushes that lined the path on either side. Most of them were low-lying, but one patch, about twenty feet away from her, was slightly taller than her waist. "If I were going to take a shot from up here, I'd do it over there," she told him.

He took a penlight from his pocket, turned it on, and pointed it to the dirt beneath the bushes she had indicated. "Good guess," he said. "That's where they found one of the hiking boot prints. The other one was about thirty feet away."

"This direction, right?" she said.

"Yeah, right over there. Lucky guess."

"*Educated* guess."

"Hey, it's fifty-fifty. This way, down the hill, or that way, up the hill."

She cleared her throat. "Excuse me. If you were the killer, which way would you go to make your exit? Down the hill, where the sagebrush is lower and thinner? In clear view of the house? Where the people you just shot at can get a long, good look at you? I don't think so."

She pointed up the hill. "Or you could go up the hill, under cover of this dense, high sage and disappear on any one of those trails that interlace behind these fancy properties. All you'd need is a trail bike stashed somewhere up there and you could skedaddle before anybody says a 'hi-de-ho' to you."

"Skedaddle? Hi-de-ho?"

"Oh, come on boy. Don't act like you don't understand me. You should speak fluent Southern by now."

But Dirk was already halfway up the hill. Savannah caught up to him just as they crested the top.

In the moonlight, they could see the softly undulating foothills, spread out around them, looking as lush as silver velveteen. This area had burned in a massive brush fire a couple of years before, but nature had replenished the native growth until it was even thicker than before.

Savannah loved these hills. When life's cares overwhelmed her, a hike up here, breathing in the rich aroma of the sage, listening to the wildlife rustling in the underbrush, feeling the Santa Ana breezes hot and dry on her skin, all worked together to restore her soul.

"I like it up here," she said simply. "It's good for me."

"Yeah, well . . . do the nature girl routine some other time. We're workin' a case here."

She turned to him, an instant scowl on her face. "I'm well aware of that, turkey butt," she said. "I was just communing with the universe for a second there. If you'd do a little more of that, you wouldn't have to have a crutch like tobacco to calm your antsy, impatient, nervous self down."

He winced. "That's a low blow to a suffering man."

"Then don't get smart with me when I'm enjoying a spiritual moment here. I'm recharging my batteries. And you'll be one of the first ones to reap the benefits of having a newly energized me."

He sniffed. "Don't think much of ourselves, do we?"

She reached over and snatched the penlight from his hand. "Get out of my way, boy, and lemme show you how it's done."

"How what's done?"

"I don't know yet. But when I've done it, you'll know."

He sighed, crossed his arms over his chest and began to tap his foot.

Ignoring him, she continued up the path, sweeping the penlight from side to side as she went.

The beam was fairly feeble, but combined with the bright light of the full moon, it was enough. Reaching a fork in the path, she chose the one that would lead away from the mansion and turned to the right, going deeper into the foothills.

Dirk lagged behind, then came rushing up behind her, radiating impatience. "The CSI techs already went over this," he told her. "You're just wasting your time."

"How far?"

"How far what?"

"How far did they search along this path?"

He shrugged, thought, then pointed to a curve in the trail ahead. "Maybe up to about there."

"Okay."

She continued to sweep, but more quickly than before, until she reached the curve in the path. Then she slowed her pace and made sure she missed nothing before she took another step.

About thirty feet from the bend in the trail, she saw something and dropped to her knees in the dirt.

Dirk was beside her in an instant. "What is it?" he asked. "What do you see? What did you find?"

"Oh, suddenly he's curious. Suddenly he's no longer bored and grousing."

He knelt in the dirt beside her. "Don't make me have to hurt you, woman," he said.

She gave him a disgusted look. "Oh, right. That just happens all the time."

"What is it?"

"Looks a heck of a lot like a tire print to me," she said, pointing out the lines in the dirt. "A two-wheeler."

He sniffed. "Big friggin' deal. A trail-bike tire print on a trail. Who would have predicted such a thing? Whoopie-do."

She turned and gave him a glare that could have started a fire in a pile of wet straw. "Watch it," she said. "Don't get smart with me, buddy, or I won't tell you why this track is so special."

"Sure you will," he said. "Because you're grinnin' like you do when you've got something really good. And you've never been able to keep it in, not for a minute, when it's good. You're already just bustin' to tell me."

"Oh, shush and ask. Ask me why this simple, routine track is special."

"No, 'cause you'll tell me. You'll tell me because you have no willpower and you can't help yourself."

She stood, dusted the dirt off her knees and reached into her pocket. Pulling out a tissue, she walked over to the side of the path and tied the tissue around the branch of a sturdy bush. "There," she said. "That'll mark the spot."

"What spot?"

"The spot where your evidence is. You can come back tomorrow when it's daylight and if you look hard enough, maybe you'll find it."

With that, she started back down the hill.

He followed at her heels until they were nearly halfway back to the mansion. She suppressed a laugh as she listened to him snort and mumble expletives under his breath.

But as they approached the midway point, he suddenly darted around her and blocked her path.

"Listen, you," he said. "If you think you're going one more

step before you tell me what you saw back there, you're wrong . . . just wrong, wrong, wrong."

She took not only one step, but two, until she was nose to nose with him. "Oh yeah?" she said, grinning at him. Then, in a breathy and bad Marilyn Monroe impression, she said, "Whatcha gonna do to stop me? Huh?" She poked him in the chest with her forefinger. "Whatcha gonna do, you big, bad po-o-lice man?"

He reached out and put his hands on her shoulders, then pulled her against him. She put her hands on his chest to push away, but he held her tight.

For a moment, a fleeting moment, Savannah was acutely aware of the moonlight flowing soft and silvery around them, his face so close to hers that she could smell the cinnamon on his breath, mixed with a hint of his Old Spice shave lotion. With her hands on his chest, she could feel the heat of his body through the thin fabric of his T-shirt. And she was all too aware of how broad and hard his chest felt beneath her palms.

She took half a step back and tried to get away from him, but he only tightened his grasp.

"Let go of me, boy," she said, her voice low and husky.

"Not until you tell me what it was."

"I could get away from you if I really wanted to," she said.

He grinned, and even though she didn't want to even think such things, she remembered what a really sexy smile Dirk had when he was happy—an event that happened only a time or two a year, but it was worth the wait.

"No you couldn't," he said. "You and I have never really gotten into it physically, but if we did, you know I'd win."

She wanted to argue, but there was no point in lying. She was a very sturdy woman and a fierce fighter when she had to be. But she could feel the male power in his arms, hands, and chest. And there was no denying who would win in an all-out affray between the two of them.

"Okay," she said. "You'd win. But you'd be bitten and scratched and kicked and gouged and bloody as hell, boy. It wouldn't be worth it."

He laughed and abruptly let her go. "What was it? What was so special about that stupid trail-bike track back there?"

Slowly, reluctantly, she lowered her hands from his chest. "That track was special," she said, "because of what was beside it."

He was instantly, fully alert. "And that was . . . ?"

"A boot print. A boot print with a PM on the heel."

"A Porter-Marceau hiking boot."

She grinned, stood on tiptoe and gave him a peck on the cheek. "You got it, babycakes, a Porter-Marceau hiking boot."

They continued on down the hill, and as they reached the bottom, Savannah decided to share the rest.

"One more thing," she said. "That print in the dirt didn't look to me like a track from a trail bike."

He looked confused. "Well, it was too thick for any kind of bicycle, like a mountain bike or even a moped."

"That's right. I think it was wider than any of those. I think it's a motorcycle tire. Not a big cycle, but a street bike of some sort."

They stopped in the middle of the path and turned to look at each other.

"Like the one that Kim's mystery man rides?" Savannah said.

"Maybe," he replied. "Just may-be."

"We've just got to lay eyes on that guy. We really do."

"Lay *eyes* on him?" Dirk gave a little growl deep in his throat. "To hell with laying eyes on him. I wanna lay *hands* on him. And I want to lay them on him really, really hard. Several times if necessary. We need some answers here."

"Amen, Brother Dirk. Amen!"

Chapter 14

Savannah knocked softly on Tammy's bedroom door, trying not to disturb Mary Jo Livermore across the hall. A little bit of a drunk Mary Jo went a long way, and Savannah wasn't interested in shooting the breeze with her twice in one evening.

She was about to knock a second time when she heard, "Who is it?"

Good girl, Savannah thought. Caution. An excellent quality in a private detective—or their assistant.

Then she heard the lock turning, and a couple of seconds later the door opened a crack and Tammy peered out, wearing her pink Minnie Mouse pajamas and looking a bit tousled.

"Is everything okay?" Tammy asked, instantly awake and concerned.

"Everything is fine. Just fine." She glanced up and down the hallway, but the rest of the house appeared to be fast asleep. "Let me in for a minute. I've got something to tell you."

"Sure, come on in." She swung the door open wide, and Savannah hurried inside. "Sorry if I woke you."

"You didn't. I was just lying there in that beautiful bed, enjoying the room."

Savannah felt a tiny pang of conscience. "Actually, I was wondering if you'd mind coming downstairs and doing library sofa duty for an hour or so. Dirk's waiting for me outside. We thought we might go back to Kim's house tonight and see if we can catch the guy who's been living with her."

"Tonight? It's after midnight."

"I know. We're thinking if he spends the nights there he might be around."

Tammy nodded, walked over to the foot of the bed and picked up her robe, which was spangled with Tinkerbells. "Could be. But why doesn't Dirk go by himself? Not that I mind coming downstairs, but . . . ?"

"We were walking around outside. We went up the hill and found more of those boot prints, the ones we think the killer left. And right beside another set of them was a motorcycle track."

"Ah, and you think since Kim's live-in rides a bike—"

"You got it."

"And if the guy really is the killer, ol' Dirko could use some backup."

"He'd never admit it in a hundred years, but yes."

Tammy grabbed a scrunchy, spangled with hot pink sparklies off the nightstand and pulled her hair back into a ponytail. Then she slipped on a pair of penguin house slippers. "Should I bring my gun down with me, too?" she asked, reaching for her Dora the Explorer backpack on a nearby chair.

Savannah looked her over from head to toe, shook her head, and said, "Yes, the one that shoots bullets, not the Donald Duck water squirt gun."

"What?"

Sigh. "Never mind."

They walked downstairs and Savannah led her into the library. "I appreciate you doing this," she said. "If the guy's not there, we'll be back directly. And if he is—"

"If he is, none of us are going to mind because the case will probably be solved," Tammy said brightly.

Savannah looked at her with sweet affection for a long moment. "That's right, kiddo. And then it's pop the cork on a bottle of champagne time."

Tammy settled herself on the leather sofa, then carefully laid her weapon, a Glock 9mm, on the coffee table.

Tammy carrying a gun was a new and big event in the Moonlight Magnolia Detective Agency. Previously, all of them, from Savannah and Dirk to Ryan and John, were routinely armed. Their experience in law enforcement caused old habits to die hard, and they all felt safer, considering their line of work if they kept their weapons close by at all times.

But Savannah, like a watchful mother hen, had been reluctant to arm Tammy. And it was only after months of Savannah training her at the local shooting range that the four other members had presented Tammy with her own weapon.

Savannah had given it to her on her birthday, along with a fervent, big-sister wish that she never even had to draw it, let alone fire it.

Savannah stood there, looking down on the weapon and, not for the first time, shuddered at the very thought of Tammy having to use it. But if there was anything worse than being in a situation where you would have to fire a gun, it was being in that same predicament and not having one *to* fire.

"Remember, Tams," she said, nodding toward the pistol. "Don't ever—"

"I know, I know," Tammy interjected. "Don't ever pull your weapon and point it at somebody unless you're willing to shoot them."

"Or else . . . ?" Savannah prompted.

"Or else you're just handing them the means to kill you."

"And if you do shoot?"

Tammy stared Savannah straight in the eye with a look that was far colder and more determined than Miss Minnie Mouse Jammies ever exhibited otherwise. "If you shoot," she said firmly, "aim for center mass. Double tap. Two shots in rapid succession. Then two more if you need to. Then two more—"

"Until?"

"The threat is neutralized."

Savannah nodded somberly, closed her eyes for a second and whispered, "God forbid."

"Well, if this gets any more exciting I just might pee my bloomers." Savannah yawned and sank lower in the passenger seat.

"Oh, stop your griping. If you weren't here with me—"

"I'd be sleeping on a cushy leather sofa in a gorgeous mansion with a down pillow under my head and a soft, luxurious throw over me."

"Yeah, but you wouldn't be with *me*."

"O-o-okay. And your point is?"

He gave her a sideways grin. "And you'd rather be with me than anywhere on earth."

"Uh, we don't think much of ourselves, now do we?"

He shrugged and snickered. "Just telling the truth."

She rolled the window down and stuck her arm out, feeling the moist night air on her skin. They were parked behind an old outbuilding, among some trees and brush. They could see the house well, but wouldn't be obvious to anyone coming down the road.

When they had first arrived, they'd checked the house, but not only was no one there, but the leaf that Dirk had stuck between the door and the jamb was still there. No one had entered since they had left.

After an hour and a half of just sitting there, listening to Dirk suck the daylights out of his cinnamon stick, Savannah was wishing she had brought a bottle of nail polish. She could have at least gotten a manicure out of the deal.

"You're wrong," she said. "As delightful as this outing may be, I'd rather be in my claw-foot antique bathtub at home, basking in a rose-scented bubble bath with a glass of brandy, some really dark chocolate truffles and a hot steamy romance novel with some gorgeous hunk on the cover."

He looked hurt and disappointed for only a heartbeat. Then he shook his head and laughed. "Nope, you'd rather be here with me."

"And you think this is true because . . . ?"

"Because you like the idea that you might get to tackle some bad guy and nail him for murder."

"Oh, I thought you meant it was because I reveled in your scintillating conversation about last night's heavyweight bout and how the Dodgers stunk in that doubleheader on Saturday."

"No, the sports roundup is just the frosting on the cake of this experience."

"Woo-hoo. Lucky me."

She heard a chorus of coyotes begin to yip in the distant hills. "They sound like a bunch of Midwestern farmers at a Vegas floor show when they bring the strippers out," she observed.

That was Dirk's kind of joke. When he didn't laugh, she knew that he, too, was getting bored.

"How much longer do you want to sit here?" she asked.

"I don't know. You?"

She rolled the window up and rubbed her arms. "Well, it's getting a bit airish out here without my jacket on. I didn't think we'd be out here all night or I'd have brought a coat."

"You want mine?" he said, starting to peel off his bomber jacket.

"Naw, thanks." She reached over and pulled it back onto his

shoulders and gave him a pat. "But we could sit here till dawn and still, most likely, come up empty-handed. And then tomorrow neither one of us would be worth shootin'."

"Yeah, you and me, kid, we don't recuperate from these all-nighters as quick as we used to."

She opened her mouth to argue with him, but closed it just as quickly. He was right. Fortysomething felt a lot different from twenty or even thirty. She didn't dare think what eighty might feel like.

"So, this is just going to be a wasted trip," she said, "unless . . ."

She turned on him, suddenly energized. "Do you still have that old fingerprint kit in the trunk?"

"I don't know. I guess so. Why?"

"If the guy's been staying there, he's got to have left some prints. Let's go dust some obvious surfaces and see what we can find."

He looked at her as though she had turned chartreuse. "I haven't lifted prints in ages, and neither have you. That's Liu's department."

"Well, Dr. Liu isn't here, and we are. *I* can still remember how to lift a print even if you can't."

"I could. I just don't wanna."

"Lazy."

"Yep. And proud of it."

She reached over and snatched the keys out of the ignition. "I'm getting that kit, and I'm doing some dusting. You can sit here and commune with the coyotes or howl at the moon if you want to. But I want to catch this guy."

Wearily he hauled himself out of the car and met her by the trunk. "You know," he said as she dug among tools, old clothes, empty beer bottles, and ancient copies of boxing magazines, "even if you lift something, it won't be admissible in court. You're not a cop no more. Any evidence you gather won't count."

"It'll count," she said as she pulled a small black case from under the landfill materials. "Believe me, it'll count."

"How do you figure?"

"If that time comes, you'll get up on that stand, hold your hand up and swear to tell the truth—and then you'll lie through your teeth and take credit for what I did. Men have been taking credit for what women accomplish since the dawn of time," she added with a smirk. "Why should you be any different?"

Two hours later, they left the farmhouse with tired smiles on their faces and twenty-two pieces of lifting tape with fingerprints of varying degrees of quality in an evidence bag.

"I think some of those are his," Savannah said, running her fingers through her hair and sighing as they walked back to the car. "There was a definite size difference. I'm betting the bigger ones are his."

"And that thumbprint you found on the beer bottle in the refrigerator, that one'll be good enough to run through AFIS," he said as he tossed the fingerprint kit back into the trunk. "Maybe we'll even get a mug shot or DMV pic."

They climbed into the car. Dirk handed Savannah the envelope and she locked it into the glove compartment.

"I have to admit," he said as they drove down the dirt road to the house. "That was a pretty good idea."

"And it was a bit like old times, us working a scene on our own like that," she said, grinning at him.

"Yeah." He snickered. "When you were bent over there, dusting the bathroom doorknob, I remembered how cute you used to look in your uniform."

"Hm-m-phf. That was a lot of years and quite a few pounds ago."

"You'd still look good in a uniform, if you was to put one on."

"Well, I'm glad you think so. But then, you have a weakness for big butts."

He laughed. "I do. It's true. No scrawny-assed chicks for this guy."

They pulled onto the main road, and Savannah reached out and grabbed his arm. "Wait," she said. "Look at that."

"Look at what?"

"That old busybody. She's awake. Standing there on the porch, watching us. Pull over."

He did, and she jumped out.

As she ran up to the house, the lady stepped off the porch and met her halfway in the middle of the weed-infested yard.

"Hi!" Savannah called out. "Remember me?"

"Sure I do," she yelled back. "What are you doing out here at this time of night? I was about to call the cops on you."

"Now why would you go and do something like that?" Savannah gave her a smile and in the moonlight she could see the woman's face soften. Since she wasn't wearing her sunbonnet, Savannah could see that she had a beautiful, thick head of silver hair. Again, Savannah thought of Gran and missed her.

"You don't need to call the police," she told the woman. "That guy sitting in the car down there, he's a cop. And we're here to try to catch that guy on the motorcycle who's been such a torment to you."

"You came out here at this time of night just to do that?"

"Absolutely!"

"Well, I do appreciate that."

"We aim to please."

"But you didn't catch him, now did you?"

"No. Appears not."

"Then you're not a whole lot of good to me."

Savannah laughed. Who was more delightfully candid than children at the beginning of their lives or older folks at the end of theirs?

"I'm sorry about that," Savannah said, "but you know what? You could be an enormous help to me. You could help me and that cop over there catch this guy and put an end to his shenanigans."

"How? What do I have to do?"

Savannah reached into her slacks pocket and took out her tiny notebook and pen. She began to write, squinting to see in the pale moonlight. When she was finished, she ripped off the sheet of paper and held it out to the woman.

"You've got sharp eyes, don't you?" she said to the old lady. "You see everything that goes on up and down this road."

The woman gave her a tiny smile. "I don't hear really good anymore—thanks to all that damned motorcycle racket—but there's nothing wrong with my eyes. Not much gets by me."

"I'm sure that's true. So here, take this."

"What it is?" she asked suspiciously.

"It's my cell phone number. I want you to take this into your house and put it right beside your phone. And the second you hear that guy coming, as soon as you know it's him, you give me a call. Day or night."

"So let me get this straight," the old woman said, her small grin widening by the moment. "If I call you at, say, five o'clock in the morning and tell you he just came home . . . you'll come out here and arrest him for disturbing the peace?"

"Lady," Savannah said, "you give me a call at dawn or dead midnight and I'll be here with bells on. And your buddy with the bike will be wearing handcuffs. Is that a deal?"

To her surprise, the old woman held her hand out and gave Savannah's a hearty shake.

"You've got yourself a deal. Hell, I'll sit, eat, and sleep out here on this porch. And if he comes within five miles of here, you'll get a call, so be ready."

"Oh, I'm ready." Savannah thought of the bloodstains on the

driveway at Dona Papalardo's mansion. She thought of the motorcycle tracks on the hill above the estate and the expensive boot print.

She didn't know for sure if the guy who had been staying over at Kim's house before her death was also her killer. But she was more than eager to see him in the police station's interrogation "sweat box" with Dirk firing some questions at him.

"Yes," she told the lady. "I'd say I'm as ready as you are."

The woman nodded her silver head and gave Savannah's hand another hearty shake. "Then let's do it."

Chapter 15

Savannah and Tammy were sitting at the island in Dona Papalardo's kitchen, Savannah downing her morning coffee and Tammy sipping her green tea, when Juanita hurried in and said, "Senorita Savannah, my lady would like to talk to you right away, if you please. She is upstairs in her room."

Setting her mug aside, Savannah jumped off the stool. "Is anything wrong?" she asked.

Juanita shrugged. "With my lady, there is always something wrong these days."

Savannah hurried up the stairs, down the hallway, past the guest bedrooms, and up yet another flight of steep, curving steps to an area of the house that formed a sort of mission bell tower above the rest.

At the top of the steps was a small, open area with windows that provided a panoramic view of the property and the neighboring countryside. Opposite the staircase, a door—a heavy, arched affair with mission-style hardware—was slightly ajar.

Savannah walked over to it, stuck her head inside the room and said, "Hello? Dona? It's Savannah. May I come in?"

"Yeah, come in," was the feeble reply.

Savannah walked in and instantly felt as though she had taken a step back in time. It was as though she had entered a nineteenth-century boudoir. The thick, dark red, velvet drapes were closed and at least a dozen candles gave the room a romantic and yet somehow sinister ambiance.

The air was heavy with the smell of smoke from the candles and Dona Papalardo's custom-blended French perfume.

Gold glinted everywhere on gilded picture and mirror frames, on candlesticks, and in satin brocade fabrics. From the fainting couch, draped with fur throws, to the dressing area separated by a tri-fold screen covered with hand-painted cabbage roses, to the canopy bed with its red velvet curtains and mountains of accent pillows, the room spoke of a gaudy but playful spirit. It looked like a room where a grown-up woman could play "dress up" with Grandma's old clothes and pretend to be a grand lady.

If Granny were an expensive French courtesan.

In the center of the enormous bed, nearly hidden among the pillows, lay Dona Papalardo.

She was wearing a white lace-trimmed corset and bloomers, and a pink silk scarf was tied headband-style around her hair.

But in even in the dim candlelight, Savannah could see how pale Dona's skin looked, and how sunken her eyes were. Her face shone with a fine sheen of sweat, like someone caught in the throes of a terrible fever

The realization struck Savannah, with a force that nearly took her breath away, that Dona Papalardo wasn't long for this world. Whatever was wrong with this woman was more than depressing or challenging; it was life-threatening.

She hurried over to Dona and leaned across the bed to put her hand on her forehead. "Are you all right, sugar?" she asked without considering their employer-employee relationship. "I hate to say it, but you don't look so good."

Dona brushed her hand away. "What are you? My mother?" she asked, irritated, but half-smiling.

Savannah chuckled. "No, too many people's big sister, that's more like it." She sat down on the edge of the bed. "But seriously, you look sick. Can I get you something? Take you to the doctor or . . . ?"

"The doctor? No, thank you. I've already been to the doctor. That's why I'm in this condition in the first place." She reached over, picked up a gold-and-red brocade pillow and hugged it to her belly.

Savannah found the gesture pathetic and telling.

"What did they do to you?" she asked softly.

"Nothing I didn't ask them to do, beg them to do, *demand* that they do," Dona replied. "So I have no one to blame for this but myself."

"I heard you had gastric bypass surgery," Savannah said. "I guess it didn't go so well."

"The whole world knows I had gastric bypass surgery. You can't keep something like that a secret in this industry. And no, it didn't go well. It took me a year to find a surgeon who would perform it for me . . . and this is the result. I'm still sick long past the time when they said my body would adjust. I'm in constant pain, can't eat anything—no matter how small—without suffering for it, and my weight is now actually lower than I ever wanted it to go. Imagine the irony of *that*!"

Savannah was pretty sure she knew the answer, but she asked the question anyway. "Why was it so hard to find a doctor who would perform the surgery for you?"

Dona gave a horrible, dry, ironic laugh. "Because I wasn't fat enough. I didn't meet the body mass index criteria. I had to convince them that I was suffering from a bunch of other nasty symptoms: sleep apnea, diabetes, hypertension."

"But how could you fake those things? It would be hard to fool a doctor."

"Not an unscrupulous doctor who wants to be 'fooled,' who has a fancy car and big house to pay for, not to mention a hefty alimony."

"And apparently you found one of those."

"Eventually I did. One who was willing to ignore certain test results and fudge on others, one who suggested that if I could just pack on another twenty or thirty pounds, he could justify the surgery. 'Don't worry,' he said, 'it'll melt right off you afterward. You'll be surprised and pleased at how quickly.'"

"And were you surprised and pleased?"

"At first I was too sick to care if I lost weight or didn't, or even if I lived or died. I got a post-op infection that nearly killed me. And after I recovered from that, every time I tried to eat anything, I got the condition they call 'dumping.' And even though you're supposed to get over that in time, I still have it."

"I've heard of that," Savannah said. "Vomiting and diarrhea, right?"

"And extreme weakness, dizziness, sweating. I've fainted more than once in public. Boy, that gets the paparazzi swarming like buzzards."

"I'm sure it does." Savannah watched as Dona grimaced and held the pillow tighter against her belly. "Does it hurt all the time?" she asked.

"Yes. I can't sleep, I can't think, I can hardly function. The painkillers make me sick, and now I'm getting ulcers on top of everything."

"Can it be reversed?"

"No. I'm going to be this way for the rest of my life."

Savannah reached over, covered Dona's hand with her own and squeezed it. "I'm so sorry. I had my doubts about gastric bypass surgery, but I had no idea it was this bad."

To Savannah's surprise, Dona squeezed back. "It isn't for everyone," she said. "It truly saves some people's lives. They tolerate the surgery well, they shed enormous amounts of weight, and they thrive afterward. I have friends in the entertainment industry who swear it saved their lives."

"Maybe they had better doctors."

She shrugged. "Maybe. Perhaps a doctor who's willing to bend the rules like mine did shouldn't have been trusted. And maybe it wasn't even his fault. Everyone's body is different. Maybe I'm just one of those who didn't do well for whatever reason. A certain percentage doesn't."

They sat quietly for a few moments, saying nothing. Savannah could feel the waves of depression and despair radiating from the woman lying on her luxurious bed. She felt the cold perspiration on her hand and her trembling. She thought of the pictures of Dona taken just before the surgery. She had been heavy, yes, but beautiful and vibrant and bright-eyed. This woman was an empty, lifeless imitation of her former self.

Well, Savannah thought, *society demanded that she be thin. Okay, now she's thin. And this is supposed to be, somehow, more beautiful?*

"Juanita said you wanted to see me," Savannah said at last. "How can I help you?"

Dona released her hand, fell back onto the cushions, and stared up at the canopy above her. "I was wondering how much longer you and your assistant intend to be here."

"You're the boss. It's your call. But I think it's a good idea if at least one of us is here at all times until we solve this case and have Kim's killer in custody. Don't you?"

"I suppose." She took a deep breath of resignation. "Do you have any idea who it might be?"

"Actually, we do have a possible lead. Do you know anything about Kim's boyfriend?"

"Kim had a boyfriend? Since when?"

"We don't know for sure, but there were men's clothes and toiletries in her house. It appeared that a male at least visited and stayed overnight sometimes."

"Hmm. And she was always complaining that she wasn't getting any. She was actually pretty obnoxious about it. I got tired of hearing it."

"So, you'd have no idea at all who he might be?"

"No. Other than griping about her long bout of celibacy, Kim kept her private life to herself."

"Okay." Savannah swallowed her disappointment and went on to her next question. "Would you mind if my assistant brought a computer here to your house? Juanita said you have an Internet connection in your downstairs office, as well as wireless access."

"Sure. I don't care. Do whatever you want."

"Do you think you'll be going out today or . . . ?"

"I'll be in. I'm far too weak to even think about going anywhere or doing anything other than lie in this bed."

"I'm so sorry."

"It isn't your fault. It's mine. I chose this."

"I don't think you did. I think you tried a desperate move to improve your life, and sadly, it didn't work out. Don't be so hard on yourself."

Dona wouldn't meet her gaze, but Savannah thought she saw tears welling up in those famous green eyes. "Why do you ask about me going out?"

"Oh, that. Well, if you're going to be inside the house all day today, I'd like to go to my house and get Tammy's computer."

"Go, that's fine."

"And . . . also if it's okay with you . . . I'd like to invite two friends over this evening. Ryan Stone and John Gibson. They work with me sometimes on cases, and I'd like to run some of this by them. They're former FBI agents and quite resourceful."

Dona waved a dismissive hand. "Whatever. I don't care. For

the time that you're here, the house is yours. Have a pool party if you want. Heck, somebody should be enjoying it."

"Well, we won't get all that festive, but thank you." Savannah stood. "I guess I'll go then. Are you sure there isn't anything at all that I can do for you? Anything I can get you?"

"My old body back? Fat but happy."

"How about a chocolate raspberry truffle? They aren't very big."

"I'd never keep it down. But thank you." She laid her head back, reached down, and pulled the comforter up around her shoulders. "Close the door on the way out, would you? And tell Juanita I don't want to be disturbed."

As Savannah left the room, her heart ached for the woman who lived behind heavy drapes, blocking out the golden California sunshine, in a room that smelled of candle smoke, Parisian perfume, and desperation.

Dona had everything that people thought they wanted. Beauty, fame, talent, money, the admiration of countless fans. And now she even had the stick-thin body that society adored and demanded.

But none of that matters, Savannah said to herself as she left the room and headed down the stairs, *if the Grim Reaper himself is sitting on your front porch.*

And Savannah had the sinking feeling that no matter what she did to try to protect Dona Papalardo in the next few days or weeks . . . the old fellow and his scythe weren't going to leave until there was yet another harvest.

Chapter 16

When Savannah first entered her house, she thought someone was being slaughtered in her living room. Then she realized it was Jesup and Bleak—or at least a movie they had rented and were watching on her television.

She walked in just in time to see a crazed killer who was chasing a young woman in skimpy lingerie around a dark house.

"Run out the front door, idiot," she said to the screen.

"What?" Jesup wanted to know, pausing the movie.

"I told her, 'run out the front door.' That never seems to occur to those nitwits. They just keep running around the house in their knickers, squealing and waving their arms around all girlie-silly. Sheez, makes you wanna start rooting for the bad guy. Like, if she's that stupid, she deserves to die."

"Whoa," Bleak said, "that's a little brutal."

Savannah thought for a moment. "Yeah, I guess so. But then, it's just a stupid movie, right?"

Savannah bent down and scooped up the two black cats, who had come running out of the kitchen, their tails waving in the air. "Hello, girls," she said, nuzzling their black, silky coats. "Did you miss Momma?"

"I fed them," Jesup said. "Even that stinky mushy crap that you set out."

"Thank you. I really appreciate that." She set the cats back onto the floor and walked over to give her sister a hug. "Have you guys been having a nice honeymoon?"

Bleak didn't stand for a hug, and that was fine with Savannah. He had restarted the movie and was staring, transfixed, at the running, bouncing bimbette on the screen.

"Not particularly," Jesup said, yawning and stretching.

She and Bleak were both still in their sleeping attire, her wearing his Marilyn Manson T-shirt and Grateful Dead boxers, he wearing his own Charles Manson T-shirt and Grateful Dead boxers.

"Actually, it's been pretty boring around here," he said, pausing the movie on a frame where the imperiled chickie-poo had her heinie only inches from the camera. "Hanging out here hasn't been as much fun as we'd hoped it was going to be," he continued. "Jess made it sound like her sister was this big-shot private detective who went around solving murders, and maybe you are, but that doesn't help us a lot if you're not here."

"Well, last time I checked nobody had been murdered here at my house, knock on wood," she said as she walked over to the desk, scooped up the mail and thumbed through it. "Are you two going to spend your whole honeymoon watching the idiot box?"

"What else is there to do around here?" Jesup said, stretching and running her fingers through her gelled hair until it stood on end.

"What are you talking about? You're in southern California, for heaven's sake. There a zillion fun things to do. Go soak up some rays at the beaches, cruise Sunset Strip, gawk at movie stars in Hollywood, go to Disneyland, Six Flags, Knott's Berry Farm, Universal Studios."

She looked up from the mail to see them both giving her slack-jawed, glassy-eyed stares.

"O-o-okay," she said. "Not your speed."

She pulled open a filing cabinet drawer and took out Tammy's laptop computer in its leather case.

"Is that a computer?" Jesup said. "We need to check our mail, our message boards. You took the cord on the other one and by now we're way behind!"

"Sorry," she said, "this one's going with me. We need it for work."

"But what are we going to do-o-o?" Jesup did everything but stamp her foot and start to cry. Savannah was reminded of the sweet, curly-haired child she had been, good-natured enough, but never self-sufficient. Someone had always needed to entertain her. And in a family with nine children, entertainment was a luxury. As a result, Jessie had often been unhappy.

She looked at her sister's new husband and realized that she had married someone who was, if possible, even less motivated than she was. Not something a couple wanted to have in common.

Suddenly, inspiration struck Savannah. "Hey," she said. "You oughta go out to Malevolent Valley and poke around. If you can handle it, that is."

"Malevolent Valley? What's that?" Bleak was all ears.

"It's northeast of here. You pass through it on your way up to Twin Oaks. You might not want to go there, though. It's a . . . darkly spiritual place. The Native Americans considered it an evil place, where restless spirits roamed, waiting to do harm to innocent people who passed through."

Jesup turned to Bleak, her eyes wide. "Wow, cool! Huh, honey?"

"Yeah! Awesome."

"No, it's a really bad place. They say that a bunch of Satanists do devil worship up there, sacrifice goats and all that stuff. You two shouldn't really go there by yourselves. And certainly not today."

"How do we get there?" Bleak was practically jumping out of his boxers. "Which way is it, huh?"

"Well, again, I don't recommend it, but if you take Lockhart Road north out of town, up the coast and then turn inland when you see the signs for Twin Oaks, you'll go through this valley that's dark and shadowy and full of gnarled oak trees. About a mile and a half in, you'll see a wide spot in the road and an old, old sign that says, 'Apple Juice Two Dollars a Gallon.' Pull over and park by the sign and take the path that's there. Go down deeper into the valley. But are you sure you want to do this? I mean, it's—"

"Oh yeah, that sounds so cool!" Jesup grabbed Bleak around the waist and nearly lifted him off the ground. "Let's go now!"

They rushed upstairs to dress, as Savannah put out some extra food for the cats and watered her plants. Then she grabbed some clean underwear and ran into them in the foyer by the front door.

"You two be careful," she said. "There are some swimming holes a ways down that trail. They're filled with water this time of year, but there's a legend that the water turns to blood on summer solstice and Halloween, and the pagans go skinny-dipping in it. So, I don't know if you should actually touch the water or not."

"Oh man! That's just awesome!" Bleak said as they bolted out the door, leaving it wide open.

She watched as they raced to their rental car. "Suckers," she whispered. She shook her head and then started laughing. "Malevolent Valley, my ass." She looked down at the cats at her feet, who looked as amused as she was. "You know, Cleo and Diamante, your Auntie Jessie is a dingbat. And so is your new uncle. But at least they'll get some sunshine and fresh air. And with any luck they'll do a little cavorting au naturel on their honeymoon. And, sadly, that's about the closest thing to *normal* that those two may ever do."

On her way back to the Papalardo mansion, Tammy's laptop computer on the seat next to her, Savannah pulled her cell phone out of her purse and dialed Dr. Liu's office. The medical examiner was seldom at her desk, but she figured it was worth a try.

To her surprise, Dr. Liu answered after the first ring.

"Hi, Dr. Jen. It's Savannah," she said.

"Well, hello there. Are you on your way here with chocolate?"

Savannah laughed. She and Dr. Jennifer Liu had bonded many times over chocolate. In fact, a two-pound box of Godivas seemed to be the price the ME charged to do a special favor for someone who had once been on the SCPD, but was now a private investigator—a civilian.

"No, sorry. Not this time," she said. "But I do have a favor to ask of you. A big one."

"Shoot."

"My sister is here, visiting me with her new husband. They're both into this weird crap, white faces and blood-red lipstick, tattoos of bats and demons, a totally unhealthy obsession with death, blood, and gore."

Savannah could hear Jen laughing on the other end. "I partied with a bunch of people just like them in this underground club in Hollywood last weekend. Creepy but fun crowd. Nobody you'd want to bring home to Momma, though."

"Oh, please, my grandmother is going to die when she meets this guy."

"You want me to tell you how to kill him and get away with it?"

"Oh, honey," Savannah said, "I know how to get rid of him in at least fifty ways and not even you would figure out how I did it."

"I'm sure you could. So, how can I help you?"

"I think a good, nasty dose of reality would just do these two a world of good. Know what I mean?"

"I think I do. How long are they staying?"

"Oh, mercy, I hope not long. Maybe a week."

"So, if I get a good one sometime this week, give you a call?"

"A nice, ripe, juicy one."

"Like the first one you saw?" Dr. Jennifer started guffawing.

Savannah bristled. "That was a really bad one, you have to admit. He'd been outside for days in the summer sun."

"He wasn't that bad. All in a day's work for me."

"Yeah, yeah. He was extra bad, and you just won't admit it. But if you get another one like him, be sure to call me. I'll bring them over and let them watch. That should cure them for a while anyway."

"Should I offer them face masks smeared with Vicks?"

Savannah nearly gagged as the memory came flooding back. "That is *not* funny, Jen."

"I guess not. Didn't really help *you* that much, did it?" She was laughing so hard she could barely breathe, let alone talk. "You went running out of there, hand over your mouth, gagging like—"

"Okay, this conversation is over."

"Good-bye, Savannah. Nice talking to you."

"Hurrumph."

Savannah lifted her wineglass and looked over its rim at one of her favorite sights in the world—Ryan Stone's face. "Here's to the two of you," she said to him and John, who was sitting beside him. "Not only are you guys the perfect dinner guests, but you bring the perfect dinner with you. It just doesn't get better than that."

"Here, here," Tammy said as she toasted the men, as well. "I can't believe you got Antoine to put together a take-out dinner. That just has to go against every principle he holds dear."

"Antoine is a dear friend of ours," John said, clinking his glass against Tammy's. "And besides that, he's madly in love with Savannah. He said as much when we popped by his establishment to pick up the meal tonight."

"Eh, Antoine isn't in love with me. He's in lust with that blue silk dress of mine—the wraparound that shows off my womanly wiles to their best advantage. But he has the fanciest restaurant in town and this salmon mousse is to die for."

Juanita walked out on the patio where they were eating by candlelight once again. "Do you need anything?" she asked. "If not, I will be leaving for tonight."

"Thanks for asking, but we're fine," Savannah said. "Is Ms. Papalardo still in her room?"

"Sí, she has been there all day. I just checked on her, and she is asleep. She took her pill. I think she will sleep all night now."

"Then why don't you go on home? We'll clean up here when we're finished." Savannah gave her a warm smile and the maid returned one just as friendly.

"Thank you. I will. Good night."

When she had disappeared into the house, Ryan leaned closer to Savannah and said, "Is that true? Dona has been in bed all day?"

Savannah nodded. "Today and most of yesterday, too."

"Is she sick?"

"Very. In mind, body, and spirit, I would say. I'm very worried about her."

"What a terrible shame," John said. "I recall seeing her perform for the first time at the Palladium. She played Sally Bowles in *Cabaret* and did a fine job of it, too, I must say. A truly talented woman who appeared to thoroughly enjoy her craft. A real actor."

"She was wonderful on-screen, too," Ryan said. "She was the most sultry Stella I've ever seen in that television remake of *Streetcar Named Desire*. That's when I knew she was something very special."

"Why did she disappear from the public eye for so long?" John asked. "One moment, she was the toast of the town, and the next, she was gone."

Savannah shook her head sadly. "I hear it was because she gained some weight. She's in her mid-thirties. It isn't at all unusual for a woman to 'blossom' at that stage of her life."

John lifted his glass again. "Here's to ladies in full bloom."

"Hear, hear," Ryan said.

"Does that mean I haven't . . . uh . . . flowered yet?" Tammy asked, pretending to pout.

"Don't worry, sugar," Savannah told her. "You will."

"Especially if you eat Savannah's good cooking," Ryan added.

"But who would mind if Ms. Papalardo gained a bit of weight?" John continued. "Surely there are roles for women who are more zaftig, both on screen and the stage. Especially for an actress of her caliber."

"I don't know if it was because the roles weren't available," Savannah replied, "or because she was hiding here in her own fantasy world." She waved her hand, indicating the mansion and its lush grounds.

Ryan offered Savannah more wine, but she shook her head. "No thanks. On duty and all that, you know."

He nodded. "Very conscientious of you. But back to Ms. Papalardo and the decline of her career. You don't have to be gone from Hollywood long for them to forget you exist."

"I understand that her agent wasn't a lot of help either," Savannah said. "He was too busy berating her for gaining weight to put any effort into her career."

Tammy jumped in. "That's right. That's what Juanita told me.

And she also said that Dona fired him. They had a big, big fight about it here at the house, and she fired him. Now he's suing her, and she has a countersuit against him. Apparently, there's a lot of money involved."

Ryan and John were suddenly all ears.

"Oh, that sounds like a red flag to me," Ryan said. "Have you or Dirk checked him out to see if he has an alibi for the time of the shooting here?"

"We've been trying," Savannah said. "Dirk drove into Hollywood yesterday to talk to him. His secretary said he's out of town, has been for the past week. But Dirk didn't believe her, said she was way too nervous to be telling the truth."

"Dirk has good instincts when it comes to that sort of thing," John said. Then with a grin he added, "You know, an instinctual cunning that comes natural to the low-born rabble."

Tammy giggled and hid her face behind her napkin.

"Now, now," Savannah told John. "I don't let him potty talk about you, so you can't about him either. Besides, I was going to ask if the two of you might follow up on that agent for us. You're the best when it comes to finding someone who doesn't want to be found."

"We'd be happy to," John said. "We'll find out if he's sunning himself in Cancún or hiding out in his basement, shooting darts to pass the time until this investigation cools off a bit."

"Just give us everything you've got on him before we leave tonight," Ryan said, "and we'll get on it first thing tomorrow morning."

They heard voices behind them, and they turned to see Mary Jo Livermore coming out of the house and walking toward them. Someone was behind her.

"No one else answered the door," she said, "so I let him in." She was a bit unsteady on her feet. Apparently, she was drinking rather heavily tonight as well.

They had invited her to join them for dinner, but she had declined in a less than gracious manner. It seemed that alcohol hadn't improved her disposition any.

Dirk stepped from behind her, a scowl on his face that matched hers. "What are you doing, eating out here?" he snapped when he saw the table and its bounty.

"Having a beautiful dinner," Savannah said. "Come sit down and have some, too, unless you're still in grouch mode, in which case, you can go sit in a corner somewhere and sulk properly." She turned to John and Ryan. "Dirk is quitting smoking . . . again . . . and we don't like him much these days."

"Not a lot of love lost in days of yore either," John mumbled under his moustache.

"I came by to see if you want to go over the case some more," Dirk said, "but I see you've got company, so I'll leave. But I gotta tell you, I think you're all nuts to be eating out here. Somebody got killed while hanging around outside on this property and here you are, wining and dining out in the open."

Savannah stood, walked over to him and laced her arm through his. "Now stop your frettin', darlin'," she said. "If you'll just look a little closer, you'll see that we set the table up here so that it's situated very nicely behind the cover of the pool house and that fence there. If our buddy was up there on the hill again, he couldn't possibly get a shot off that would hit anything in this area. So why don't you just sit a spell and have a bit of some of this good food that Ryan and John brought us from Antoine's?"

He looked eager for a second at the mention of free food, but then he grimaced. "Antoine's? That's that fancy place where they took me that time and told me I was eating buffalo wings when it was frog legs. No way. I'm not falling for *that* again. I felt sick to my stomach for weeks after that. No, thank you!"

"Don't be silly," Savannah told him. "Surely you can tell the difference in frog legs and chocolate cake. At least have some dessert with us and a cup of co—"

The tones of a cell phone playing "Hotel California" sounded from among the dishes on the table.

"That's mine," Savannah said as she grabbed for it. She didn't recognize the number on the caller ID but it was a San Carmelita prefix. "Hello."

The voice on the other end was an elderly lady's voice that reminded her of Granny Reid. But the language wasn't any that Gran would use.

"He's here! That no-good son of a bitch just came barreling down our road at seventy-five miles an hour and headed down to that house where the gal that got herself killed lived."

"Wait a minute," Savannah said. "Are you the rose lady who I gave my number to and—"

"Well, of course I am. Are you going to come out here and arrest this freakin' maniac or am I going to have to take matters into my own hands? I've got a bunch of boards with nails that I drove into them, and if I have to, I'll lay them out there in the road right now. I swear I will! Or better yet, I'll just go on down to the house and bash him in the head with one of them. Or maybe I'll take my pruning shears to him and see what I can snip off, if you catch my drift. I'm telling you, I'm fed up with this crap!"

"No, no, don't do that. You just sit tight. We're on our way. We're on our way right now. Don't you move. We'll be there in five minutes."

She hung up and looked at Dirk. "Let's go."

"Where?" he asked.

"Out to Kim's house. The guy on the motorcycle is there, and Granny Goodin' is threatening to brain him with a board with nails on it or circumcise him with her rose-pruning shears."

Every man present winced and said, "Owww!"

"Exactly," she said. "Coulter, let's make tracks."

Chapter 17

When Savannah and Dirk drove down the road, past their elderly informant's house, they saw her standing on the porch, waving what appeared to be a dish towel at them.

"Boy, she's loaded for bear, isn't she?" Dirk said.

"No kidding. I think if we do anything short of execute him on her front lawn, she's going to be furious with us."

Dirk turned onto the dirt road and turned off his headlights. "No point in announcing our arrival," he said. "In fact, I'm going to stop right here. We can walk the rest of the way."

"Sneak and creep the rest of the way, you mean."

"On tippy toes. I want to see what this guy is doing in that house before he knows he's got visitors."

"Sounds good to me."

He parked the car, and they both climbed out, their weapons and flashlights ready.

As they approached the house, they saw a motorcycle parked near the front door, just outside the picket fence.

"Could he take that thing up into the hills behind Dona's place?" Savannah asked him. Dirk was the motorcycle enthusiast in the family.

"Sure," he said. "Those trails are fairly smooth and that's a Juergin Orlet. It's small enough to maneuver on the trails and yet it's street-worthy."

"You think that bike left those tracks we saw?"

"It could have, can't rule it out. But there's no way I can say for sure till I have a closer look."

"You can look at bike tires if you want to," she said, "but right now I'm more interested in getting a look at James Morgan."

The moon wasn't up yet, so they crept slowly across the property, using their flashlights to pick their way through farm equipment, rusty car parts, falling-down fences, and the occasional broken-down pieces of furniture that looked like they had become disoriented on their way to the city dump.

But once they stepped over the picket fence, the rustic chaos gave way to urban perfection. The newly laid sod was as pristine as the grass surrounding Dona Papalardo's mansion. Kim had obviously been in the process of changing her surroundings for the better, and the project appeared to be as dead as the property's owner.

Dirk went straight to the bike, and Savannah headed for the living room window. While he shone his flashlight on the bike, specifically the tires, she squatted down in front of the window.

Slowly, she rose, inch by inch, until she could see through the lace curtains to the inside. But, even though she craned her neck first one way, then the other, stood up, and even pressed her nose to the glass, she couldn't see a soul inside.

Leaving Dirk to peruse the bike, she sneaked around to the side of the house. From a window there, she could see both the kitchen and the dining area.

On the table she saw a black helmet and hanging on the back of one of the table chairs was a black leather jacket.

Granny Grump with the roses was right, she thought. *Evel Knievel's home.*

At least they hadn't driven out this time for nothing.

She worked her way around the house, being sure she didn't trip over any garden hoses or irrigation pipes—more evidence of the recent renovation.

And as she neared the back of the house, she heard a strange noise that sounded like an animal whimpering.

Slowly, she crawled beneath the bedroom window and raised herself, bit by bit, until she could see inside.

The young man lay in the middle of the bed, curled into a fetal position, sobbing hysterically. He had a nightgown clutched to his face, a pink satin and lace gown that Savannah remembered seeing hanging on the back of the bathroom door when she and Dirk had been there before.

She felt someone brush her shoulder. Turning, she saw Dirk was right behind her, also watching the solitary drama being played inside.

"I knew there was more to him than he let on," Dirk said.

"Yeah, gardener, my butt. What else is he?"

"Well, most upstanding citizens don't feel the need to have an alias like Mr. James Morgan here. Him *and* his dead girlfriend, that is."

They watched him cry for a while longer, then they backed away from the window.

"What do you want to do now?" Savannah asked him. "Are you going to take him to the station house and question him? You can at least arrest him on that outstanding warrant."

"Let's go back to the car," he said, "and we'll talk about it."

They returned to the Buick and got inside, all the time keeping a close watch on the house.

"He's really broken up about her death," Savannah said when they were settled. "Doesn't look like a killer, lying there, crying, and hugging her nightgown."

"Eh, that doesn't mean a thing. I've seen guys who just cut their family into little tiny pieces bawl their eyes out."

"That's because you just beat the crap out of them."

He didn't bother to deny her charges. "Sometimes," he said matter-of-factly. "But not always. Sometimes people just go off and then they regret it a second later."

"Whoever took a bike up that hill, took aim and fired on Kim—that person wasn't somebody who just 'went off' in a moment of passion. They thought about it."

"Speaking of bikes," Dirk said, "that one ain't it."

"What?"

"That bike over there didn't leave the tracks that we saw up there on the hill. Not unless he put on different tires since the shooting. And those that are on there are pretty ragged. I'd say they're original, and that's an old bike."

They sat in depressed silence for a few moments.

"I can't imagine Jack the gardener wearing a four-hundred-dollar pair of hiking boots. Or a four-hundred-dollar anything for that matter," she said. "The other day, I noticed his flip-flops were held together with a piece of duct tape. And you could read the *Los Angeles Times* through those cutoffs of his, they were so threadbare—especially on the seat."

"Sounds like you tried." He sounded grumpy. She laughed.

"Oh, yeah. You didn't try to get the 'lay of the land' on that new gal at the station desk."

"Boys are supposed to ogle. Girls aren't."

"Says who? We're just more discreet about it. We don't actually allow our tongues to hang out onto our chins."

"Do you gals compare notes? Do you talk to other women about guys' butts, stuff like that?"

"Sometimes."

He rubbed his hand over his face and shook his head. "Oh,

god, I didn't want to know that. I really did not want to know that."

"Don't worry. When we yak about you, we talk about how totally hot you are."

He cheered up instantly. "Really? You do?"

"Eh, get over yourself. What are you going to do about that guy in there who's crying about his dead girlfriend?"

"I don't know. What do you think I oughtta do?"

"Like I said, you could, and probably should, arrest him on that outstanding warrant. Then you could question him about Kim."

"You think he killed her?"

"No evidence that he did. None at all. You couldn't even get a search warrant for his house or car . . . if he has a house or car."

He reached over to the dash and picked up a cinnamon stick. "I'd like to watch him for a day or two, see what he's going to do if anything," he said as he poked the stick into his mouth. "You'll see him there at the house, doing his gardening crap, and you can keep an eye on him."

"But what about the outstanding warrant?"

"Hey, Missouri's had all this time to find him, and they haven't. I care more about solving my murder than arresting their fraud escapee. He doesn't know that we're onto him. Maybe he didn't do it, but had somebody else do it. Or maybe he knows who did. I'd rather just watch him for a few days before I scoop him up."

She nodded thoughtfully. "I hear you," she said. "If he was going to split, he probably would have right after the murder, so I'll fill Tammy in, and we'll keep an eye on him for you."

With the lights still off, Dirk backed his way out of the dirt road.

It wasn't until they reached the main road that Savannah had a horrible thought.

"Oh, no!"

"What?" he said. "What's wrong?"

"Granny Grump is going to be furious with us!"

He shrugged. "Oh, well. That's the breaks," he said. "She's got *your* phone number, not mine."

As Dirk drove down the street in front of the Papalardo mansion, Savannah saw something that made her reach for his arm. "Wait!" she said. "Don't pull in the driveway. Look, there by the front door."

He slowed down and headed toward the side of the street, but he didn't turn into the brick drive as he had intended. "What is it?" he said, looking where she was pointing.

"That couple standing there by the doorway, making out."

He looked with a bit more enthusiasm than before. "Where? Oh, I see them. There behind the Lexus."

Savannah squinted, cursing her own vanity for not getting glasses when she knew she needed them. Faraway objects just kept getting fuzzier and fuzzier. And if she admitted it, the print on bottles and in the phone book was getting smaller and smaller.

The couple in the mansion's doorway was just a blur, until she recognized the distinctive pale blond hair on the woman.

"Lordy be!" she said. "That's Dona! And I recognize the car. It's her ex-boyfriend, Mark Kellerher."

Dirk cleared his throat. "Uh . . . judging from where he's got his hands right now, I'd say he's not an 'ex' anymore."

Savannah lifted one eyebrow. "Well, she's got a lot of nerve, that one!"

"What? Making up with her old boyfriend is a bad thing?"

"Yes, it is. She yelled at me for letting him in the door and now . . ."

"And now she's letting him cop a feel."

"Precisely. She needs to make up her mind and not go around spouting her mouth off until she does."

"He's leaving," Dirk said, taking a long draw on his cinnamon stick. "If I'd got that far with a dame, I'd have finagled an invitation into her bedroom."

"Yes, but the last time you 'got that far' with a woman, females were still called *dames,* and a lot's happened since then—what with the dinosaurs becoming extinct and all."

They watched him get into his car and drive toward them as Dona vigorously waved good-bye.

"Besides," Savannah said, "for all you know, he's coming from her bedroom right now. Although, when I saw her earlier, I wouldn't have figured she had enough energy for a rendezvous."

The Lexus pulled out of the driveway and disappeared down the street. Dona had turned and was heading back to the door.

"Okay," she said. "Take me on up. I want to catch her before she goes back upstairs."

"You're not going to tell her what we know about her gardener, are you?"

Savannah thought about it as they headed up the driveway. "I really should. I mean, I work for her as an investigator and now we know that a person she employs is an escaped felon. I sorta owe it to her to tell her."

"I don't want you to. Not yet."

"Okay. For how long?

"Twenty-four hours. I'm going to go back there right now, and I'm going to watch him for as long as I can keep my eyes open."

They pulled up in front of the door just as Dona was about to disappear inside. "Keep me posted," Savannah said as she bailed out of the Buick and slammed the door behind her. "Oh, Dona. Yoo-hoo! Wait for me!"

Dona paused, the door half open, looking irritated.

"Was that Mark I just saw leaving?" Savannah asked as she

squeezed through the door after her. There was no point in pretending she hadn't seen. Not when confronting her would be infinitely more satisfying. "Looks like you two have made up."

Dona gave her a withering look that only a diva could manage to such perfection. "I beg your pardon, but my personal affairs are none of your business."

Savannah chuckled. "You're absolutely right. All I have to know is that he's . . . well . . . off the list of people that I need to shoot on sight."

"Very funny." She turned and headed toward the staircase, her pink chiffon peignoir swirling around her with each movement. "I'm going back to bed. And I'm not to be disturbed, by you or anyone."

"Good night," Savannah called gaily after her. "Sleep tight. Don't let the bedbugs bite."

Once Dona was upstairs, Savannah decided to go to the kitchen to get herself something to drink. It was probably too much to hope that Dona had the makings of a cup of cocoa laced with Bailey's, but it was worth a try. Then she would hunt Tammy down and fill her in on the evening's latest gossip.

But as she neared the kitchen, she heard Tammy's voice and another woman's, as well.

She entered the room and found Tammy and Mary Jo sitting at the island. Tammy had a glass of herb tea in front of her, and Mary Jo had a Cosmopolitan martini.

"It just . . . ma-makes me sh-hick!" Mary Jo was saying, her voice slurring so badly she could hardly be understood. Tears were streaming down her face, dripping onto her chin and into her martini. "Ma-a-rk," she said, "he's a good . . . a . . . man. And Dona just doesn't, you know, appre-e-echiate him like she sh-sh-should. And he loves her so-o-o mutch that he comes running uh . . . back . . . you know . . . to her every, every time. It's just so, um, sad."

Tammy nodded to Dona, "I know. I know." She gave Savannah a half-smile as she walked in.

"Are you talking about Mark and Dona getting back together?" Savannah asked.

"Yes," Tammy said softly. "He came by here earlier, and I refused to let him in, as Ms. Papalardo required. But she came downstairs and invited him to come up to her room. They were up there quite a while. And when they came down . . ." She glanced over at Mary Jo. ". . . it was obvious that they had made up."

"I shaw them," Mary Jo said. She took a deep gulp of the martini. "I shaw them there. On the po-o-orch. They were al-l-l over each other. It's just dish-gusting."

Tammy said, "Mary Jo here was just telling me that she doesn't approve of Dona's and Mark's relationship because she feels that Dona takes advantage of Mark. Isn't that right, Mary Jo?"

Mary Jo nodded, but she seemed to be sliding lower on her stool, losing the battle against her intoxication.

Savannah walked over and slipped her hands under Mary Jo's armpits. "I think we'd better get you upstairs," she said. "You look very, very . . . tired. Tammy, you wanna help me here?"

Tammy jumped off her stool and hurried to assist.

With Savannah on one side and Tammy on the other, they managed to get the highly unsteady Mary Jo up the stairs and to her room.

They even led her inside and over to her bed.

Tammy yanked the covers back, baring the sheets.

The room was similar to the one Tammy was staying in, but instead of pink, it was a delicate powder blue. This bed was also canopied and strewn with a dozen accent pillows.

They sat Mary Jo on the side of the bed. Savannah took off her slippers as Tammy slid her sweater off her shoulders.

Then Savannah turned her around and laid her back on the

bed, fluffing some pillows for under her head. She didn't feel she knew Mary Jo Livermore quite well enough to peel her slacks off, too. She could just sleep in them.

Savannah had a feeling that Mary Jo had slept in her clothes on far more than one occasion.

Covering her with the heavy comforter, Savannah said, "Good night, Mary Jo. You'll feel better tomorrow morning."

"That was her fifth martini," Tammy whispered, "that I know of."

Savannah looked back at Mary Jo, whose mouth was wide open. She was already snoring very loudly.

"Five martinis, huh?" she said. "Well, then maybe you won't feel better tomorrow morning. Maybe not a bit better."

Chapter 18

The next morning, the atmosphere in the Papalardo household was strained at best. Savannah had seen happier, more cheerful faces on cops who were conducting full-body searches on transvestite prostitutes.

Mary Jo had stumbled downstairs around eleven o'clock in search of a glass of orange juice and some aspirin. She and Dona had run into each other in the foyer, and Savannah and Tammy eavesdropped from the kitchen as the two woman had a heated argument about Mark Kellerher.

The dispute ended with Mary Jo threatening to move out rather than observe this "emotional abuse of a fine man." Dona offered to help her—by hurling her things out the window and onto the front lawn and then calling the badly abused Mark and telling him how much Mary Jo seemed to want him.

"Your typical girlfriend fight over boys," Tammy told Savannah once the fur was no longer flying and both women had retired to their rooms upstairs.

"Oh yeah? Well, you and I don't fight over Dirk like that," Savannah said.

"And we never ever will." Tammy shuddered. "Never, never. God forbid."

At noon Savannah and Tammy were on the patio, stretched out in chaise lounges, eating chicken, tomato, and avocado sandwiches that Juanita had prepared for them. The maid lingered nearby, making sure that their tea glasses were full and engaging them in friendly chitchat.

But although they ate the sandwiches and tried to give the appearance that they were relaxing and enjoying the lush backyard and maid service, they were keeping a close eye on Jack, who was puttering around the yard, weeding flower beds, and trimming hedges.

He was wearing the same thin cutoffs, so the task wasn't entirely onerous.

Savannah had informed Tammy of the former evening's developments, so Tammy was watching him as closely from behind her Nicole Miller cat-eye sunglasses as Savannah was from behind her mirrored SCPD-issue shades.

They were sitting near the house, under an awning, where they could keep tabs on Jack and watch anything going on in the kitchen. They could also see through to the foyer in case anyone came or went through the front door.

"His eyes are swollen, and his face is puffy today," Tammy whispered, nodding slightly toward Jack, who was planting a bed of petunias.

"Yeah, well, if you'd seen him last night, you'd know why. I'm surprised he's even at work today considering the state he was in."

They dropped the topic as Juanita appeared at the kitchen door with two dishes of something that looked like sherbet and a large glass of lemonade.

"You like?" she asked, showing them the tray. "Raspberry sorbet. It used to be Senorita Dona's favorite with these . . ." She produced a small plate with some delicate chocolate cookies arranged on it in a circle with some fresh raspberries and whipped cream in the center.

Juanita picked up the glass of lemonade from the tray. "And this is for Senor Jack. He has been working very hard all morning. It is hot out here."

"You know, Juanita, you're way nicer than you need to be," Savannah said as she reached eagerly for the dessert. "We're just employees, like you are, and you don't have to wait on us hand and foot."

"But you are my friends," Juanita said with a pretty smile. "I am happy when I give food to my friends."

"Savannah knows all about that." Tammy laughed. "She's never happier than when she's shoving food into somebody's face. Fattening food."

"There are worse pastimes," Savannah snapped.

"Not for the waistline." Tammy took the sorbet but waved away the cookies.

Savannah grabbed the plate and put it on an end table beside her chair.

Catching a movement from the corner of her eye, Savannah turned to see Dona passing through the kitchen on her way toward them. She had a glass of wine in her hand and a disapproving scowl on her face.

Savannah half-expected to hear a complaint about how they were lounging on the job, but Dona marched past them and around the swimming pool, over to where Jack was kneeling in the flower bed.

"What are you doing?" she barked at him. "Why on earth are you putting those there?"

Jack looked up at her, his face blank. He shook his head. "What?"

"I've never had petunias next to the pool. Are you crazy? Are you a complete idiot? Do you see any blooming plants in this area?"

Jack swept his hand across his face, leaving a dirty smudge on his forehead. "I'm sorry," he said with a meeker spirit than Savannah would have shown, considering the vehemence of Dona's attack.

Savannah gave Tammy a sideways glance and saw that her mouth was open. Even Juanita seemed transfixed as she stood there with Jack's glass of lemonade in her hand.

Dona leaned down, her face near Jack's, and she pulled one of the petunias out of the soil. She flung it onto the deck, slinging some of the dirt into the crystalline pool water.

"Hey," he said, finally rousing, "you don't need to do that. I'll take them out, but—"

She leaned down by him again, reaching for another. He pushed her hand away.

"Knock it off!" he shouted, still on his knees in the dirt. "I told you, you don't need to do that! I'll take them back out if that's what you want, but stop it!"

"Don't you talk to me like that!" she said, her nose only inches from his. "*You* work for *me*, you little bastard."

Dona straightened up, and the second she did, Savannah heard it.

A loud crack.

A sharp, popping sound that echoed down the hill and across the yard.

"Gun!" Savannah leaped off the chaise and reached for her weapon in one movement.

Tammy sprang to her feet, too. But Savannah waved her back. "Get down," she yelled. "In the house!" She gave Juanita a hard push toward the door.

Juanita dropped the glass of lemonade. It shattered on the patio bricks.

Savannah ran out from under the awning and looked up the hill toward the place where they believed the shooter had stood before. But she saw no one.

Less than a second later, she was across the patio and had thrown Dona to the ground. She fell across her, covering the woman's body with her own.

"Down! Get down!" she shouted to Jack.

She turned her head in his direction.

Jack was already down.

He lay in the dirt, facing her, a terrible wound in his throat.

"No!" Savannah didn't hear the word, let alone know that she had screamed it.

She rolled off Dona.

"Get in the house!" she told her. "Run! Go! Go! Call nine-one-one!"

Dona scrambled to her feet and raced around the side of the pool. She slipped and fell hard. Then she jumped to her feet and ran on into the house.

A moment later, Savannah was aware of Tammy standing over her as she knelt beside Jack.

"Watch the hill!" she told Tammy. "Watch for the shooter! Stay down!"

Instantly, Tammy dropped to one knee and ducked her head.

Savannah reached for Jack and realized that she was still holding her weapon. She shoved it into Tammy's hand.

From her kneeling position, Tammy held the Beretta in one hand, her other cupping the gun's butt. She swept the barrel back and forth as she scanned the hill. "I don't see anybody," she said. Casting a quick, sideways glance at Jack, she said, "How is he?"

Savannah pressed her hand tight against the wound in his neck, but blood was pouring between her fingertips at an impossible rate. In her fingertips she could feel a rapid fluttering, but it wasn't anything that could be called a true pulse.

His eyes stared up at her, but were seeing beyond her.

Far beyond.

"He's going," she said as she listened to the terrible liquid sounds of his body's final attempts to breathe.

She glanced up at the hill.

The shooter was gone. She was sure of it. He had taken his one deadly shot, just like before, and by now would be long gone.

"Go get me my phone," she said. "It's there on that table by where I was sitting."

She waited as Tammy scrambled to do her bidding.

Jack's bleeding, along with the rapid, irregular pulse and labored breathing, was slowing with each passing moment.

The glazed look in his unblinking eyes told her Jack . . . or James . . . or whatever his name was . . . was all but gone.

Tammy returned and held the phone out to her.

She reached for it with her left hand, still maintaining pressure with her right.

In some disinterested part of her mind, she realized she was getting Jack's blood all over her cell phone, but she gave it no more consideration.

That was even less important than the fact that she was allowing someone's blood to come in contact with her bare hands.

Some things couldn't be helped.

"What do you want me to do?" Tammy asked.

Savannah looked up and saw that her friend's big eyes were filled with tears.

Tammy held out a trembling hand toward the gardener. "What should we do for him?"

"There's nothing we can do for him," Savannah said. She lifted her hand just a second to show Tammy the entrance wound.

She was grateful her sensitive assistant would never see the devastating exit wound on the back of his neck—the one that she could see from her point of view and, no doubt would continue to see in her nightmares for months to come.

Even her act of applying pressure was pointless, and she knew it.

"Go inside," Savannah told Tammy. "Try to comfort Dona and Juanita. Make sure they aren't hurt."

"Do you want me to call nine-one-one? In case they haven't already, that is?"

"Sure. Go ahead. Tell them it's a code three."

Who are you kidding? Savannah's inner voice asked. It wasn't a code 3, a lights-and-siren emergency. It wasn't even an 11-8, a person down. It was a DB.

Jack the gardener was a DB.

A dead body.

It might not be official until some medical expert pronounced him, but it was a fact nevertheless.

And he had become a dead body on her watch.

Savannah felt a constriction in her own throat, and for a moment she thought she was going to be sick, there in the dirt beside the victim. But she fought it down and flipped her cell phone open.

She had to call Dirk. He had to know about this as soon as possible.

But before she even began to punch in his number, the cell went off in her hand, playing its little tune. The song, "Hotel California," didn't seem as funny as when she had programmed it in.

"Hello," she said.

It was Dirk. "AFIS came through with those prints we lifted in Kim Dylan's apartment," he said without even his usual grunt of a greeting. "And we've got a picture, here, too. This dude, James Morgan, he's your gardener there for sure."

"I see," Savannah replied, her voice sounding small and shaky even to her.

"I'm thinking I'm going to come over there and pick him up this afternoon," he continued, oblivious. "This isn't just your ordinary fraud. He and this gal Kim . . . or Penny . . . as they know her in Missouri . . . they've bilked a lot of people out of a lot of money. They ruined some little old ladies, got them to turn over their retirement money and took off with it. And there's something about a country singer in Branson."

"Okay," Savannah said, staring down at the man who was no longer showing any vital signs at all.

"So, I'm on my way there right now," Dirk said.

"Good. That's good."

"You okay, Van?" he asked. "You sound a little funny."

"He's gone," she said. "Jack's gone."

"I told you to keep on eye on him, to let me know if he looked like he was leaving." He gave a big, weary sigh. "Dammit, Savannah, now I'm going to have to chase him down, and I have a lot I need to do today and—"

"Shut up, Dirk," she said without passion. "You don't know what you're talking about. You're not going to have to chase him down. He's dead."

"Dead? How? When?"

"He just got shot here in the yard, like Kim Dylan. I'm sitting here with his body now." She could hear sirens in the distance, drawing closer. "The ambulance is about here."

"Oh, shit, Savannah, I'm so sorry. Are you all right? Are you safe?"

She looked up and scanned the hills again. "Yeah. I don't see anybody. I'm sure the shooter's gone by now."

"I'll be there in less than five. You hang in there, honey."

Suddenly, she felt the need to have him there. It flooded over her, warm and sweet, making her knees even weaker than they were.

"Hurry," she told him.

"I will, babe," he said. "I will."

Chapter 19

Dirk arrived at the Papalardo mansion even a minute sooner than he said he would. Savannah and Tammy were waiting for him in the driveway in front of the house. Several patrol cars had arrived, but the CSI team and Dr. Liu were still en route.

A couple of officers were in the backyard, draping the yellow crime-scene tape around the patio and pool area.

Dirk climbed out of the Buick, took a quick look up the hill, then ran over to the women.

He scooped one into each arm and held them close, saying nothing at first. Then he held them at arm's length, checking them over for injuries.

"Are you sure you're okay, Van?" he said, looking down at the blood on the front of her sweater and slacks.

"Yeah," she said. "This is all his, not mine."

Dirk gave her a squeeze and a kiss on the forehead. Then he turned to Tammy, "And how about you, kiddo? Are you okay?"

Tammy's eyes were big and full of fear, but her smile was brave. "Yes. I'm all right."

"Good." He let out a long breath. "I want my girls to be okay. My girls have to be okay."

"I'm glad you're here, buddy," Savannah said. "I really am."

"Tell me what you need from me. What can I do?"

She looked up in her old friend's face and soaked in his concern and strength. Throughout the years they had taken turns being strong, and that was one of the best perks of their partnership.

It was his turn.

"Take care of this mess for me now," she said. "I need to just go sit down somewhere and . . . just sit."

He turned and stared up at the hill above them for a moment. A look of grim determination came over his face and he nodded. "Oh, you've got it," he said. "You two go find a hole somewhere and crawl into it and rest, regroup. I'll come get you if I need you."

Savannah could feel an enormous weight shift from her shoulders to his broad ones, even though she knew it would only be a temporary reprieve. In the end, everyone had to carry their own burdens. But for the moment she was happy to hand the whole, sad mess over to him and find refuge somewhere.

That "somewhere" turned out to be the library, with Tammy and Juanita.

Savannah and Tammy sat on the leather sofa. Juanita was in a wing-backed chair across from them, quietly sobbing into a handful of tissues.

Savannah lost track of time as they sat there, watching the parade of law enforcement personnel that came and went through the marble foyer, past the statue of Diana and the curving wrought-iron staircase.

Dr. Liu and her white-coated team trooped in and out for what seemed like forever, until finally, the scene was processed. Through the library's doorway, they watched the gurney, bearing yet another locked body bag, being wheeled through the foyer and out the front door.

"Well, I guess Jack wasn't our killer, after all," Tammy said once the coroner's team was gone.

"Gee, you think?" Savannah snapped. Then she shook her head and reached out for Tammy's hand. "I'm sorry, sugar. That wasn't nice. I'm sorry."

"It's all right. I understand," Tammy replied. "That was the worst thing I've ever seen happen in my whole life."

"It was right up there in my top ten, too." Savannah leaned her head back on the sofa and slid down in the seat. Suddenly, she was beyond tired. She was deeply exhausted in body and spirit.

Having someone murdered in front of you can do that to you, she thought. *Especially when you're in charge of keeping people safe.*

"I blew it," she said, more to herself than the others. "I really, really blew it."

"What are you talking about?" Tammy asked. "You didn't blow anything. You couldn't have known that the killer was up there, ready to take another shot."

"I should have kept Dona inside," Savannah said. "It's obvious now that she's the intended victim. Kim was killed because she was dressed like her and looked like her from a distance. Jack, or James, or whatever his name was, got shot because she moved at the last moment. If she hadn't stood upright at that second, she would have taken the bullet, as, I'm sure, the killer intended her to. I never should have let her walk out there in the open like that."

Juanita dabbed at her eyes with the tissue. "You could not have stopped her, Senorita Savannah. My lady has a temper, a strong mind of her own, as you say. When she is angry like she was today, she listens to no one."

"I need to go up and talk to her," Savannah said. "I have to know that she's okay."

"I took her some hot tea with whiskey in it, the way she likes," Juanita told her. "She was crying and in her bed. But I think she is all right."

Savannah gave a wry chuckle. "I meant, make sure she's okay physically. I landed on her like a duck on a june bug out there. And I'm no lightweight. Maybe she should go to the hospital and get checked—make sure that I didn't squash anything important."

Tammy giggled through her tears. "If she's got breast implants, they might have popped, but other than that, she's probably okay."

They heard someone enter the front door of the mansion that had been left ajar by the CSI techs, and Savannah sat up to attention. But at the sight of Ryan and John, she nearly melted.

She and Tammy jumped up from the sofa and rushed into the foyer to greet them.

"Savannah, Tammy, dear girls," John gushed as he scooped Savannah into his arms. "We heard on the radio that there was a second shooting over here, and we rushed over straight away! What the devil happened here anyway?"

Tammy threw herself into Ryan's embrace and clung to him like a lost schoolgirl who had found her father. "It was awful, Ryan," she said, starting to sob anew against the front of his linen dress shirt. "We were all in the backyard and Dona had just come outside to yell at the gardener about some flowers he was planting when—boom! Someone shot him."

"Shot the gardener?" John said. "Why would anyone want to shoot that chap?"

"We're pretty sure that the killer was shooting at Dona. Only a second before she had been leaning down, her head close to his. She stood up and . . . that's when it happened."

"Wasn't the gardener your prime suspect?" Ryan asked. "At least, that was the last I had heard."

"Yes, he was," Savannah said as she detached herself from John and herded them all toward the library where they weren't so likely to be overheard. "So, needless to say we're now back to square one with no suspect."

When they entered the library, Juanita stood, offering Ryan the chair she had been sitting on. "I'm going to go check on my lady," she said, "and see if your police friends need me. Please ask if I can do anything for you, anything at all."

"Thank you, Juanita," Savannah said before she and Tammy returned to their seats on the sofa.

Ryan sat down between them and draped his arms over both of their shoulders. "Actually," he said, "speaking of suspects. John and I were on our way here when we heard the news on the radio about the shooting. We have a lead for you. Not much of one maybe, but . . ."

"I'll take anything you've got for me," Savannah said. "We have to catch this guy. Apparently, he's going to keep trying until he kills Dona. And she can't be a prisoner in her own home. As it stands now, she can't even risk sticking her head out the door, even with a hired bodyguard within feet of her."

Savannah shuddered and closed her eyes, seeing the aftermath of the crime, a beautiful young man dying in front of her. "I really blew it today."

Tammy leaned across Ryan and took Savannah's hand. "You were strong and capable," she said, "and you took charge of the situation. I was very impressed. You protected your charge. For all you know, if you hadn't thrown Dona down and covered her like that, he might have gotten off a second shot at her. He might have killed her. He could have killed any one of us out there."

Ryan gave Savannah an affectionate squeeze. "Don't beat yourself up about it. All the bodyguards in the world can't save a target if somebody's determined to take them out. If the Secret Service can't even keep the presidents safe . . ."

"I know. I know," she said. "But it's going to haunt me a long time, replaying it in my mind, wondering what I could have done differently."

"You can't do anything to help the young fellow who lost his life today, Savannah, love," John said. "The only thing you *can* do is find the killer and bring him to justice. And we'll do anything we can to help you."

"Which reminds me," Ryan said. "Do you want to hear what we have for you?"

"Absolutely." Savannah cheered a bit. "What is it?"

John gave her a mischievous smile. "We found that fellow you asked us to locate. Ms. Papalardo's former agent, Miles Thurgood."

"Really? And is he out of town, like his secretary said?" Savannah wanted to know.

"Nope." Ryan smiled. "Your hunch was right. She was lying for him. He's been in the area all along. Since the night that Kim was shot, he's been staying at that new hotel on the beach in Malibu, the Casa Del Sol."

"Maybe he's just vacationing locally," Tammy said. "Some people do that."

John nodded thoughtfully, "True, that's true. Some do. But most people who are on holiday check into their hotels under their own names."

Savannah raised one eyebrow. "And he didn't?"

"No, he didn't." Ryan said. "Your buddy checked in under the name of Lester Freeman."

"Are you sure it's him?" Tammy asked.

"Absolutely," John said. "We make certain our information is good before we pass it along to our favorite ladies."

"What John is trying to say, but spreading on the bs a little thick . . ." Ryan reached into his shirt pocket and pulled out a piece of paper. ". . . is that we have his driver's license picture right here. And we saw him, less than an hour ago, soaking up some sun beside the hotel's pool."

"And he's wearing a thong swimsuit," John added with disgust, "that should be a fashion felony in all fifty states, at least on a man of his age and build."

"I'll go tell Dirk." Savannah took the paper from Ryan. She looked down at the man who, according to the license, was sixty-four years old, five feet, five inches tall, and weighed over two hundred and twenty-five pounds.

She had rested and regrouped as Dirk had suggested. Her batteries were recharged, at least enough for now, and she was raring to go. "Oh, yes," she said. "Miles Thurgood needs to be dealt with. If he's wearing a teeny-weeny thong in public, he really *is* a danger to society."

Savannah went upstairs to see if she could comfort Dona before she left the mansion. But Dona didn't answer when she knocked repeatedly on her door, so Savannah decided not to press the issue.

Perhaps she just needed some privacy.

After searching high and low, Savannah finally found Dirk. He was on the hill again, studying yet another set of boot and motorcycle tracks. Fresh tracks.

She explained to him about Miles Thurgood and told him that she was going to go question the agent herself.

"Are you sure you're up to that?" he asked her. "If you want to hang out another hour or two, I'll be done here and I'll go, or we can go together."

"No," she said. "If I don't do something now, I'm going to explode."

"I understand," he told her, "but you be careful, you hear?"

She smiled up at him. Reached up and stroked his cheek. "That's my line," she said.

"Good," he replied. "Then you won't have any problem remembering it."

Before going to Casa Del Sol to question Miles Thurgood, Savannah stopped by her house. She had to change out of her bloody clothes before being seen anywhere in public.

She entered the house and found Bleak and Jesup exactly where she had found them before, sitting on her sofa in their underwear, watching yet another horror movie. This one seemed to involve a chain saw . . . and another scantily clad bimbo running around and screaming inside a big, dark house.

Jesup took one look at the front of Savannah's clothes and jumped up from the sofa, a look of alarm on her face. "Oh, mercy! Savannah, you're hurt! Were you in a car wreck? Oh, Bleak, come here and help her out! Call for an ambulance!"

Savannah held up both hands. "I'm okay," she said. "I didn't have a wreck and I don't need an ambulance."

"Then what . . . ?" Jesup pointed to her clothes.

"One of the people who works at the mansion—the gardener—was shot. Actually, he was killed."

"Oh my god! That's awful!" Jesup ran over to Savannah and put her arms around her waist.

But Bleak looked like he'd just rubbed off a winner on a scratch-off lotto ticket. "Really! Wow! And you were there? You saw it? Where did he get shot? In the head, the body?"

Savannah stared at him for a long, tense moment as the stress of the day rose inside her, hot and explosive. "Get away from me," she said in an ominously low voice. "I mean it, boy."

Jesup took a step backward, looking from her older sister's face to her husband's. "Uh, Bleak. We should just watch our movie," she said. "I think Savannah's having a rough day, and you're aggravatin' her something fierce."

"You better take your wife's advice, you mangy, maggot-infested, piece-of-crap buzzard," Savannah said through gritted teeth, "and back off before I bite your head off and spit it at you."

With that she whirled around and stomped upstairs to change her clothes.

She was halfway up the staircase when she heard her brother-in-law say, "I'll bet it was a head shot, Jes. I think I saw a little bit of brain matter there on the front of her shirt, didn't you? Did you see it, too, Jes?"

Chapter 20

Savannah had never understood why properties that were built on the beach had swimming pools. She was sure there was a good reason, but since she would probably never, never have the money to have even a small swimming pool installed in her backyard, she felt the need to condemn those who did so frivolously.

And Casa Del Sol had a gorgeous big pool within a stone's throw of the Pacific Ocean. Olympic-sized. A three-meter diving board. Two whirlpools.

They just plain ol' bite.

That was her evaluation of the whole establishment, as she pulled her Mustang into the parking lot and got out. And her opinion didn't change when she saw half a dozen gals in no-larger-than-size-two bikinis chasing each other around, squealing and splashing water.

Just wasn't her sort of place.

But she did perk up considerably when she spotted a guy with strawberry blond hair, sunburned, freckled skin, and a jelly-belly roll that lapped over his lime-green thong swimsuit. He wore matching green flip-flops that she noticed couldn't possibly be larger than a size six or seven.

He was lying on a chaise, a tabloid magazine in one hand and what looked like a margarita in the other.

As Savannah approached him, she wondered what hairdresser had told him that he could handle that shade of red at his age.

Probably the same person who had recommended that thong.

She shuddered, reminding herself that once this case was solved and she was officially "off duty" she deserved a stiff drink just for having to see this.

Her eyes might never recover.

"Miles!" she said as she walked up to him. "Long time no see!"

He whipped off the girl-watcher sunglasses he was wearing and peered at her.

"What?" he said. "Do I know you?"

He looked her up and down and grinned, as though he would like to know her better.

The thought made her feel the need for a long, hot shower and a strong soap. Like lye.

"Sure you know me," she said as she pulled up a stool and sat down on it, next to his chaise. "You met me once before. I was with Kim. You know, Kim Dylan."

He sat up so quickly that he dropped both his tabloid and his sunglasses.

She reached down and scooped up the glasses from the cement. "Something I said?" she asked, holding them out to him.

He snatched them out of her hand. "Who are you, and what do you want?"

"My name is Savannah Reid," she said. "I'm a private investigator. And what do I want? I want to figure out who killed Kim Dylan. I want that really, really badly."

"Who are you working for?" He scratched his belly, leaving white marks on his peeling, sunburned skin.

"That doesn't matter," she said. "Who are you hiding from?"

"Who said I'm hiding from anybody?" He sat up straight and kicked at the newspaper at his feet.

"You aren't Lester. So, unless you checked in with a dude named Lester, you're lying. And that sort of lie usually means you're hiding."

"You've got a lot of nerve, walking up to me and saying a thing like that," he snapped.

"Why, thank you." She batted her eyelashes at him. Then she dropped the niceties and fixed him with a level stare. "I have a police detective who's a very good friend of mine," she told him. "And he offered to come over here and question you today. But I talked him out of it. He had a lot to do, and I really wanted to meet you. But I can tell you one thing, Miles. I'm a lot nicer than he is. And better looking, too. You really should talk to me."

He thought it over for a moment, then said, "Okay. What do you want to know?"

"I want you to tell me all you know about Kim Dylan."

"She was Dona Papalardo's personal assistant."

Savannah sighed. "Now, Miles, don't go tellin' me things that I already know, or I'm gonna get al-l-l upset with you."

"She seemed like a nice girl," he said, "you know, when I talked to her on the phone . . . when I'd call Dona for something."

"Why did you pay her a dump truck full of money last month?"

His mouth dropped open, and his face turned redder than his sunburned belly. He stared at her, saying nothing.

"Well?" she said. "There's no point in denying it. It's a matter of record. The police have already seen the bank statements. You're either going to have to tell them or me."

Suddenly, Miles Thurgood looked scared. Very scared. "That's confidential," he said. "I represented Kim in a business deal, honestly and legally. But I can't talk about it."

"Why not, if it was all legal? Why would you have to hide it from the police?"

"The police aren't the only ones you have to hide things from, you know."

"No, I don't know," she told him. "But if you're afraid of someone, maybe I can help you."

Yes, Miles Thurgood was frightened. His hands were shaking as he reached for a towel and threw it around his neck.

"I'm not going to say anything more to you. I'm not interested in ending up dead like Kim."

"Why would you? What do you and Kim have in common? Is someone upset with the two of you?"

He just shook his head and said, "No. That's it. I'm done talking."

Scared people were more likely to tell you things than calm, confident people. So Savannah decided to ratchet up his tension a little. "Do you know that there was another murder at Dona Papalardo's today?"

For a moment, she thought he might be having a heart attack. He clutched his chest and began to breathe heavy. Sweat seemed to pop out instantly on his forehead and upper lip.

"Who?" he asked, nearly strangling on the word. "Who was killed?"

"Jack, the gardener. Someone was aiming at Dona and got him instead. He died there in her backyard."

He looked as though she had just slapped him hard across the face. He sprang to his feet, clutching the towel around his shoulders. "You get away from me," he said, "and don't come back here. You're going to get me killed."

And with that, Miles Thurgood, his sunburn, his towel, his lime-green swimsuit and matching flip-flops made a swift exit across the pool area and into the hotel.

As Savannah watched him, she decided two things: One—she was very glad she had come to see Mr. Thurgood. She wasn't sure exactly what she had just learned from him, but she was sure it was quite meaningful to the case.

And two—she never, never again, for the rest of her life, wanted to watch Miles Thurgood walk away from her, wearing a lime-green thong. Once in a lifetime was way more than enough.

When Savannah returned to the Papalardo mansion, it was dinnertime, but she had no appetite. All she wanted was a long, hot, bubble bath and a strong, steaming Irish coffee.

But she saw neither one in her future.

Working detectives who hadn't solved their cases didn't get to take rose-scented bubble baths.

She wasn't sure if she had been actually taught that in the police academy, but it was some sort of rule, nevertheless.

Tammy answered the door and let her inside.

"How did it go?" Tammy wanted to know the moment she stepped over the threshold.

"Interesting," Savannah replied. "He's not hiding from the law, like we figured. He's afraid he's going to be the next one popped."

"Why?"

"He wouldn't say, but that was the definite take I had on him." She glanced into the empty kitchen. "Where's Dirk?"

"He left. Said he wanted to go to the crime lab and see those casts that they made up on the hill today, make sure they match. He also said he'd go by the morgue and watch Dr. Liu do the autopsy on Jack . . . or James."

Savannah felt mildly disappointed that he wasn't there. But she understood his need to take care of business. They had to get this case wrapped up before yet another body was added to what was becoming a stack in the morgue.

"Ryan and John are still here, though," Tammy said. "They

said they'd stay with me until you got back. Juanita gave us dinner earlier. We saved you a plateful in the kitchen."

"I'm not hungry, but thank you."

Tammy gave Savannah an incredulous look that made her laugh. "Yes, once every ten years or so I do miss a meal. Believe it or not." She glanced up the stairs. "Has Dona been down?"

"Just long enough to get a glass of wine and tell everybody to leave her the hell alone for the rest of the night."

Savannah shrugged. "Okay. Her wish is our command. That's easy enough."

She followed Tammy into the library where, just as she'd said, Ryan and John waited patiently. John was thumbing through some of Dona's coffee-table art books, while Ryan was sending messages on his PDA.

They both looked delighted and relieved to see her.

"We were starting to worry about you," Ryan said, scooting over so that she could join him on the sofa.

"Any luck finding Mr. Thurgood?" John asked.

She made a bad face. "Yes, I found him right where you said he'd be, wearing what you said he'd be wearing. I'm scarred for life."

John chuckled. "Don't say you weren't forewarned, dear."

"In this case the warning didn't help. Some things—no amount of warning can prepare you."

"True," Ryan said, "but we may have come up with some stuff that will help you. We spent the afternoon on the phone here, and I've sent some messages and gotten some replies." He held up his PDA. "And I think you're going to like what you hear."

Savannah perked up instantly. "Really? What have you got for me?"

"That hiking boot, the Porter-Marceau, that left the tracks up on the hill," John said. "That's an exclusive boot. Every pair is custom fit to the fellow who buys them. There were only twenty-seven pairs sold in the entire Los Angeles area this past year. And we know the boot was sold this year because its track shows that it's their latest model, released this past March."

"Twenty-seven pairs . . . that's not such a long list," Tammy said, sounding hopeful.

"And," Ryan added, "of those . . . only three pair were a size thirteen."

"Three! Three pairs! That's all?" Savannah could see sunlight shining, even there in the dark interior of the library. Somewhere in her head church bells chimed. Some bluebirds sang, *Zippidee-doodah!*

"That's right." John smiled, his silver moustache turning up at the ends. "Now ask us if we have the names and addresses of those three chaps."

Savannah turned and gave Ryan a hearty hug and kiss on the cheek. "I love you two. I am madly, wildly, hopelessly in love with you both."

"Me, too!" Tammy said.

"Likewise, to be sure," John added.

"How did you find this out?" Savannah said. "We were only talking about it and here you have it already."

"Like we told you, the Internet," John told her. "What a handy tool that has become in investigations. One can accomplish so much and never even leave the comfort of one's home."

"Or even change out of one's silk pajamas," Ryan said, grinning at John. "You wouldn't believe how productive this guy can be without even bothering to get dressed in the morning."

John blushed, but he didn't deny it.

Suddenly, Tammy stood, walked over to a desk in the corner of the room, and picked up her laptop computer that was sitting there. "That reminds me," she said. "I sent out some e-mails myself late last night. As of this morning I hadn't gotten any responses yet. But let me check now."

She sat back down on the sofa, opened the computer and signed on.

"Wireless access?" Ryan asked.

"Yes," she said. "They have a modem in the basement office downstairs. But it picks up from here." She studied her screen, typed a bit, then exclaimed, "Hey, I got a reply!"

"From whom?" John asked.

"From a motorbike club here in the area. Yesterday, I sent them a copy of the digital picture of the tire track that the lab gave Dirk. I asked them if they recognized the tread. And one of the guys there wrote me, saying it looked like the kind that's on an expensive German bike, a Kusher nine-fifty. So, I wrote him and asked him if he knows anyone in the area who rides that kind of bike. He's sent me four names here."

Ryan reached into his shirt pocket and brought out a sheet of paper. "Okay," he said. "Let's do a cross-reference here and see if we can find a match."

Savannah leaned over his shoulder and quickly scanned the names on his list, then on Tammy's.

It took only a couple of seconds for her to find the common name. And Tammy and Ryan, too.

"Cameron Field," they said in unison.

Savannah looked at Tammy, then they both looked at the guys.

Then Savannah said what was on all of their minds. "Who do you suppose Cameron Field is, and what the hell does he have to do with any of this?"

Chapter 21

Cameron Field's house was less than a mile away, so Savannah was nearly there when her cell phone rang. She reached for her purse, which was lying on the Mustang's passenger seat, and fumbled inside it until she found the phone.

A glance at the caller ID told her it was Dirk.

She wasn't surprised. Tammy had taken a little longer than normal to rat her out. But then, it had been a hard day for everyone, Tammy included. And she would have had quite a bit to tell him.

"Hello, Dirk," she said. "I hear you have Dr. Liu working after hours for you there. How is the autopsy going?"

"Don't you 'how's it going' me! Tammy just filled me in on everything."

"I'm sure she did. Tammy is thorough, if nothing. Especially when she's being a tattletale."

"It's one thing," he said, "for you to go running off on your own to talk to that agent dude, but now you've got a solid lead on a guy who really may be our killer, and you're going over there without backup?"

"You're busy."

"Tammy was there with you when you left. She could have gone."

"She needed to stay with Dona and watch the house."

"And Ryan and John?"

"Boy, Tammy *was* thorough." She sighed and turned off the major road onto a side street that headed up the hill, into an exclusive area of San Carmelita where only those who were fiscally privileged could afford to live. Panoramic views of the Pacific Ocean didn't come cheap. Neither did the luxury of having one's house slide down the hill onto one's neighbor's house when storm after springtime storm rolled in off that not so pacific sea.

"What's wrong with you, Van?" Dirk was asking her. "This isn't like you. You know the rules. You don't go to interview a suspect like that one without backup. If he'd pick innocent people off with a rifle from a hillside, think what he'd do to you if he could."

"I'm not going to give him the chance to do a damned thing to me," she said, feeling a steely coldness in her chest that was unusual in its intensity, but not unwelcome. It felt good. Strong. Hard. And that was just what she needed right now.

"Van, I'm on my way," he said. "Tammy gave me the address. I'm leaving the morgue right now and—"

"No! Stay where you are, Dirk! I'm not kidding, boy. I mean it."

"You aren't thinking straight, Savannah. And I know why you're doing it. You feel bad about that boy, seeing him die right in front of you. You blame yourself and now you're being reckless. You know how that works. You've seen it before with other cops. And it's dangerous."

Somewhere in the recesses of her mind, she recognized his good sense and solid advice. She knew that if Jack hadn't died that day on her watch, she'd have taken Ryan or John with her on this run, or waited for Dirk to join her.

She heard him, and yet she couldn't back down. At least, not all the way.

"I won't make contact," she said. "I'm just going to go look. I want to see his place, maybe look in a window. That's all."

"I don't like that either."

"That's my final offer. Take it or leave it."

"I can be there in fifteen minutes."

"But I'm going to be there in thirty seconds."

There was a long, tense silence on the other end. "No contact. Promise?"

"I promise. You know how good I am at sneaking around and peeking into windows. Don't worry. And don't you come over here. You stay there with Dr. Liu and get all you can from her. This is nothing."

"Yeah, yeah." He sounded anything but convinced. "Call me."

"As soon as I have something, you'll be the first to know."

She hung up and slowed the Mustang at the entrance to Field's cul-de-sac. It was a short road, only a block long, with only three houses. His was the one on the right—with the breathtaking view of the city below and the ocean beyond.

It was a white, modern, boxy affair with odd angles and lots of skylights. The grounds were austere, more cement than vegetation. In fact, the only greenery she saw was a large lemon tree to the left of the front door.

She could see into the backyard well enough to know he had an infinity pool. And for half a second she experienced a pang of jealousy. How nice would it be every evening to sit and watch the sun slide into the sea with your own infinity pool pulling your spirit over the edge and into the world's largest pool of peace?

Maybe money *could* buy happiness, or at least a moment of it, here and there.

She didn't dare pull into the cul-de-sac. Her Mustang was far too conspicuous. If Field was, indeed, the killer, he may very well have seen it parked in Dona Papalardo's driveway. So, she drove several blocks away and pulled into yet another cul-de-sac where there were plenty of trees and shrubbery.

The sun had been down for half an hour and, fortunately for her, darkness was quickly enveloping this area that had no street-lights.

She took her time, strolling back to his street, trying to look like an ordinary woman from the neighborhood, out for her evening after-dinner walk.

As she approached the entrance to his cul-de-sac, she slowed even more, taking a long look at the house. The windows in the front were lit, the back dark.

The other two houses were completely dark. *All the better*, she thought. The fewer people at home, the less chance she'd be observed lurking around.

She was just about to turn down the street when the lights in the front windows of the house went off, and a few moments later, she heard a loud, whirring sound.

Field's garage door was opening.

"Holy crap!" she whispered, as she looked around for a place to duck out of sight. One of his neighbor's poinsettia bushes provided the cover she needed.

She jumped behind it and watched from among the plant's branches as a big, black Dodge Magnum pulled out of the garage and headed toward her, the door closing behind it.

In the darkness she didn't get a good look at the driver, but her limited view gave her the impression that he was a large Caucasian, maybe in his mid-thirties.

Ah . . . his house all to myself, she thought as she meandered on down the street. *And just the way Dirk wants it—no contact.*

She didn't mind. For now she was content to gather what she

could from his surroundings. Long ago, she had realized the value of a simple "break and enter" to a nosy gal who knew what to look for and where to find it.

She glanced around one more time to make sure she was alone, and from what she could tell, she had the cul-de-sac to herself.

Ducking between the houses, she made her way quickly to the back of his house. It took her only two minutes to find a waist-high, sliding window that wasn't locked.

And less than a minute later, she had the screen off, the window open, and she was stepping through it into what appeared to be a guest bedroom.

Once inside, she stood very still and listened. More than once she had entered a house only to find that, although the owner was gone, the owner's Rottweiler or Doberman was still home and on patrol.

She frequently carried some chicken livers in a plastic bag in her pocket for Rottie and Dobie bribing, but tonight she was liver-free, so she had to be extra careful.

She walked across the dark, sparsely furnished room, past the twin bed that had only a bare mattress and TV tray next to it with a simple gooseneck lamp.

Opening the door, she paused and listened again for any occupants, human or canine, but heard nothing. She flipped on her penlight that she always had attached to her key ring, and used it to light her way as she passed through a hallway and into the living room.

In this part of the house she didn't even need her penlight. The recessed overhead lighting had been turned off, but several lamps had been left on a low setting, and their light was enough for her to see by.

For a moment, she felt as though she had stepped into some sort of black-and-white photograph. The walls were a light dove gray and all of the contemporary furniture was in white, tones of gray, and black.

She recognized fine leather when she saw it, and realized Field had spent a fortune on the sleek sofa and accent chairs, though the cushion on one end of the sofa was depressed in the form of a human's rear end, detracting from the overall look. Apparently, Cameron Field was a bit of a couch potato and a pretty heavy guy, considering the depth of the indentation.

On the walls was a series of black-and-white photographs, beautifully framed, of different types of seashells: conches, sand dollars, starfish, displayed on sandy beaches with sea foam sudsing around them.

The chrome-framed, glass coffee table was spotless, as was the entertainment center. Not a speck of dust or a casually tossed magazine gave a hint that anybody actually live here—other than the dent in the cushion.

Cameron Field might be a murderer, and might not play well with others, but he got an *A* for neatness.

She turned from the living room and started to walk into the dining area, a loud barking sound caused her to jump, reach for her gun, and nearly faint—all at the same time.

Her mind couldn't quite process the strange sound. It wasn't exactly a dog and yet it was alive. No doubt about that!

Her Beretta drawn, she whirled around, and looked behind her.

Along the other side of the room, beyond the chrome-and-glass dining set, was a large terrarium. And inside it, lit with a full-spectrum lamp, was a dark gray lizard with reddish spots.

The animal was only about a foot long, but it had a fierce expression on its face and obviously didn't like the fact that she was there. It blinked at her several times, its tongue lolling in and out of its toothy mouth. Then it barked at her again, making a noise that sounded like "too-kay, too-kay."

Savannah recognized it as a Tokay gecko from its distinctive coloring and strange cry. Years ago, she and Dirk had run across one of these while raiding the home of an organized crime figure in Los Angeles. Dirk had made the mistake of sticking his hand in its terrarium and still had the scars to prove it. He had learned later that the Tokay was the pit bull of gecko-dom. Once they had a bite, they didn't turn loose until they were good and ready.

It barked at her again, and she said, "Eh, shut your trap. I already met one of your cousins, and I didn't like him either. Mess with me and I'll make a purse and a sandwich out of you. You'd probably taste like chicken."

As if it understood her, the thing scurried behind some plants and peeked out at her between the leaves.

"That's better," she said as she continued on to the kitchen, which was equally spotless as the living room. Other than a bowl of green apples on the counter, there was no sign that anyone actually ate or drank there.

She walked back down the hallway, past the guest bedroom where she had entered the house, and into a master suite.

The room was massive, as large as the living room. With ceilings that soared at least thirteen feet high and windows that overlooked the town that twinkled with night lights, the room was a place that she could have stayed for days at a time.

Or at least, she thought so, at first.

But when she dared to turn on the light, using the dimmer switch to keep it as low as possible and still be able to see, she changed her mind.

The furnishings here were like those in the rest of the house, contemporary and sparse. There was only a bed with a charcoal gray comforter that was neatly tucked in all the way around the bottom of the mattress. And two black pillows with white piping.

Other than two nightstands on either side of the bed and one bureau, the enormous room was empty.

Except for the Dalí.

On second glance, Savannah realized that the painting on the wall just around the corner from the door wasn't really a Dalí, but the artist who had done it must have been an enormous fan of Salvador's.

The work was a nature scene, a field of green grass where red and yellow flowers dripped and ran into each other, then morphed into other blossoms that waved in the wind before dissolving into puddles of their own.

Savannah couldn't take her eyes off it. She turned the light up a tiny bit more so that she could get the full effect. She studied each flower up close, then slowly walked backward, taking in the painting as a whole.

It was when she was about ten feet away from the painting that she saw it. Collectively, the yellow flowers formed a much larger shape—that of a woman sprawled on her back in the grass, one arm twisted cruelly behind her, her right leg at an awkward angle that indicated it could even be broken.

The red flowers joined to create a horror of their own, a river of blood flowing from her throat and spilling across the grass.

And in the lower right corner of the painting were the initials, bright and bold, signed by the proud artist: CF.

"Cameron, you sick bastard," she whispered.

A cold sense of knowing swept through her. If she hadn't known for sure before, she did now. Cameron Field was a psychopath. And he was the killer they had been looking for.

She had no idea why he would want to murder Dona Papalardo, but now that she knew who he was, she would find out. One way or the other.

Turning the light off in the room, she reached into her pocket and pulled out her cell phone. She dialed Dirk as she made her way back to the guest room and the open window.

He answered after only one ring. "Yes?"

"It's him."

"You sure?"

"Yeah."

"How do you know?"

"I saw him leave as soon as I got here, so I had the house to myself. He lives alone, he's insanely clean, and he has this sick painting of a dead, bleeding woman in his bedroom."

Dirk was quiet as he processed that. Then he said, "Well, the clean part is highly suspicious, him being a bachelor, but I don't know if that nails the case."

"He keeps an ugly pet lizard just like the one that nearly bit your pinkie off."

"It's him! I'll put an APB out on him. We'll get him into the station, and I'll lean on him so hard that—"

"Dirk, Dirk, hold on," she told him as she straddled the windowsill on her way out of the house. "I've got another call coming through. It's Tammy. Hold on."

She pushed the flash button. "Yes, sugar. What's up?"

"Savannah! We've got somebody in the house! Dona just called downstairs on the house phone and said she heard somebody in the room below her. And there's not supposed to be anybody here but her and me!"

Savannah's heart started pounding so hard she could hear her own pulse in her ears. "Where are you?"

"I'm downstairs. I'm headed up there now. I've got my gun and—"

"Wait!" Her mind raced. She couldn't bear the thought of Tammy facing an intruder alone.

The image of Cameron Field's beefy face passed before her. She thought of Tammy's petite form and—

"Just wait!" she said as calmly as she could. "Go into the library and turn the lights off. Get into the corner to the left as you go into the room, behind that bookcase. Take the safety off your weapon, and have it ready, but don't put your finger on the trigger. Do you hear me?"

"Yeah." Tammy was breathing hard, and Savannah could hear the trembling in her voice, but she sounded alert and in control. "Okay, I'm there. But shouldn't I go upstairs in case Dona needs me?"

"No! I don't want you to move from that spot." Savannah left the window open and the screen off and raced down the road toward her Mustang, still talking as she ran. "I want you to stay right where you are, Tammy. I mean it! Do *not* move from that position! I'm going to hang up now. I've got Dirk on the other line. I'm going to tell him what's going on. As soon as you and I hang up, call nine-one-one. I'll be there in three minutes, four tops. You be ready to let me in the front door, okay?"

"Okay."

"And as soon as you're finished with nine-one-one, you call me back. I'm getting into my car and I'm coming."

She switched back to Dirk as she jumped into the Mustang. "Tammy's got an intruder. I think it's Field."

"Did she call for assistance?"

"She's doing it now. I'm on my way. I'll probably beat them there."

"I'm headed there now. Be careful."

"Yeah. Later."

Savannah tossed the phone onto the seat and started the Ford. She was grateful for an old muscle car like the Mustang as she peeled away from the curb and began wringing out the curves on her way to the main road that would lead to the Papalardo estate.

"Let her be okay, Lord. Keep her safe till I get there," she prayed. "Keep them both safe and I'll owe you so-o-o big!"

She knew she was doing wrong.

Her agency had been paid to protect Dona Papalardo. And good bodyguards thought of their clients' safety first and their own second.

If Savannah had been there, she would be running up the stairs right now, gun drawn, prepared to sacrifice her own life, if need be, to save Dona's.

But she wasn't prepared to sacrifice Tammy's.

It wasn't right, but she couldn't help it. The big sister in her, who helped her grandmother raise eight younger siblings, simply wouldn't allow it.

Tammy was a woman, not a child, and she was as well-trained as the other seasoned members of the Moonlight Magnolia Detective Agency could train her. But she was still a civilian.

And even though Savannah was, too, she had once been a law enforcement officer and in her mind, there was a difference.

The phone rang again.

She snatched it up. "Yes?"

"It's me," Tammy whispered.

"Did you call nine-one-one?"

"Yes, but they said they won't be here for at least five minutes. They don't have any units in the area."

"That's okay. I'm almost there."

"Dona called downstairs again just now on the house phone. I answered it here on the desk next to me."

"What did she say?"

"She said someone was jiggling her doorknob."

"Is her door locked?"

"Yes. I told her to hide in her closet, under some clothes."

"Good girl."

"It's him, isn't it?"

Savannah could hear the raw terror in her friend's voice. She was tempted to comfort her with empty consolations, but she didn't dare. "I think so," she told her. "Yes, it's probably him."

"Good. That means we'll get him this time."

Savannah laughed in spite of her own fear. Leave it to Tammy to look on the bright side. Even at a time like this.

"I'm coming down the block right now," Savannah said. "I can see the end of the driveway."

"Oh! Savannah! Oh, god!"

"What? Tammy! What is it?"

"I hear a big bang. I think he's crashing down her door right now!"

"I'm here. In front of the house. Open the door and let me in!"

Chapter 22

Savannah raced through the front door and up the stairs, her weapon in her hand, and Tammy right behind her. They ran down the hall to the second set of stairs leading to Dona Papalardo's private suite.

Pausing for a couple of seconds, Savannah turned to Tammy and said, "I want you behind me, and when we get to the top, I'll enter first. Keep your finger off that trigger unless you have to take a shot. And for heaven's sake, don't shoot me."

Tammy nodded, her eyes wide, but she seemed remarkably calm, considering the circumstances.

Together they hurried up the winding stairs, but as they approached the top, Savannah paused again, listening.

She could hear Dona speaking—she sounded distressed—and a man's voice, angry and demanding. But she couldn't make out their words.

At the top of the stairs, the door leading to Dona's rooms was wide open.

Savannah climbed the remaining steps, quickly but silently. Tammy followed.

Her gun in both hands, she nodded toward the right side of the door. Tammy understood and positioned herself there.

Savannah stood on the left, her pistol pointed to the ceiling.

Inside the room the vocal exchange seemed to be escalating, more angry, more emotional by the second.

Savannah took a deep breath, nodded to Tammy, and ducked her head around the door for one quick look.

The room was dim, lit by Dona's usual clusters of candles. But Savannah had seen enough.

At the other end of the room, Dona Papalardo lay back on her fainting couch, her hands held out in front of her.

And Cameron Field was standing to the right of her, pointing a large revolver at her.

Savannah swung around into the doorway, her own weapon straight out in front of her.

"Freeze!" she shouted. "Freeze!"

He didn't even flinch. At first he didn't even look her way. He just kept staring at Dona.

"I said, 'Freeze,' you bastard. If you move I'll shoot you dead." She hurried a few steps toward him.

In her peripheral vision she could see Tammy standing beside and slightly behind her. She, too, had her weapon trained on him.

"Put the gun down," Savannah said, "slowly. Take your finger off the trigger and put it down."

He didn't comply. She could sense him evaluating, deciding.

"Don't even think about it," she said, stepping closer. "I'll kill you. I swear I will. Put it down! Put it down now!"

"Shoot him, Savannah!" Dona said, holding her hands up in front of her face in a pathetically pointless gesture.

Savannah was close enough now to see his weapon. It was a Ruger .38 special.

Hands would never stop a bullet fired from a gun that size.

"Savannah, shoot him!" Dona screamed. "Do it now."

He stared down at Dona with a look of bitter hatred. "You bitch," he said with cold fury, "you fucking bitch."

"Cameron," Savannah said, "take your finger off the trigger and put the gun down now." She heard sirens in the distance, approaching fast. "The police are on their way," she said. "They know who you are. Don't make things worse for yourself. Put the gun down. Don't make me shoot you."

She watched his eyes. His hands. His body. And she saw the moment he made his decision.

His eyes hardened. His body tensed. He swung around toward her. He swung the Ruger toward her.

She dropped to one knee, ducked her head and fired.

Tap tap . . . tap tap.

The words flashed through her head as the gun exploded four times in her hand.

Center mass

Neutralize. Neutralize the target.

The target was still standing. Fire flew from the end of the Ruger's barrel.

Tap tap.

Her weapon erupted again, spewing its own fire. The air filled with choking, acrid smoke.

His arm dropped to his side and the Ruger fell to the floor.

Cameron Field shuddered once, violently. Then he fell, too.

Target neutralized.

Savannah waited one second, two, three, four. Then she rushed to him and kicked the pistol beyond his reach.

But Field wasn't reaching. He wasn't even trying to reach.

On his chest, several red spots were blooming, like the morbid red flowers in his bedroom painting. And like those blossoms they were stretching, puddling down onto the thick oriental rug beneath him.

Center mass.

"Is he dead?" asked a small, quiet voice behind her.

She turned and saw Tammy standing there, her gun still pointing straight ahead of her, tears streaming down her face.

Savannah stood, walked over to her and took the gun from her hand. Then she folded her friend into her arms. "Yes, sweetie. He's gone."

"Good." Dona stood up from the fainting couch and brushed her hair back from her face. "He was going to kill me, just like he killed Kim and Jack. If you hadn't stopped him, I'd be dead right now. Wow, that was a close one."

Savannah reached over and picked up the Ruger. She swung out the cylinder. He had fired one round in their direction.

She glanced down the length of her body. Then she looked Tammy up and down.

Apparently, luckily, he had missed.

Kneeling beside his body, she saw five distinct bullet holes in his chest. A cold voice that sounded a lot like her weapons instructor at the police academy said, *Five out of six, over eighty percent. Not bad.*

She heard running feet pounding up the steps. A moment later, two young uniformed policemen charged into the room.

"Is everything all right in here?" one of them asked.

"No," Savannah said. "We had an armed intruder. He threatened Ms. Papalardo. I instructed him to lay down his weapon. He turned on me and I had to take him out." She moved aside so that they could see the body on the floor.

"Shit!" the second policeman said. "You sure did. You shot him all to hell and back. Are you a cop?"

Am I a cop? she asked herself. *Good question.*

Savannah could still smell the smoke of her weapon in the room. Her ears were still ringing from the shots. Her target lay dead on the floor. But everyone else in the room was alive and whole, herself included.

She had done what she had to do, and she had done it well. By the books, using her training, her courage, and her innate skill.

Technically, it was a "good" shooting.

"Tonight I was," she said, more to herself than to them. "Tonight—when I really needed to be—I was a cop again."

She looked around for a door that might lead to a bathroom. She saw one on the other side of the room and beyond it, a sink and toilet. "Now, if you'll excuse me," she said calmly, matter-of-factly, "I have to go. I think I'm going to be sick."

Savannah and Tammy were sitting at the island in the kitchen, sipping glasses of water, when they head Dirk charge into the foyer.

"What the hell's going on here?" he roared.

"A shooting. Body's upstairs," said one of the two newest policemen to arrive on the scene. Two more units with two uniforms each had responded. And Savannah and Tammy had been waiting for Dirk, settling their nerves in the kitchen.

"A body? Whose body?" He sounded more than alarmed. He sounded like he was about to start shooting people himself if he didn't get an answer.

Savannah left her stool and hurried through the kitchen to the foyer. "Hey, Coulter," she shouted at him. "Over here."

The instant he saw her, his face dissolved into a sappy, but terribly endearing, expression of relief and pure joy. "Thank god," he said as he ran over to her, grabbed her around the waist and lifted her against him.

Before she knew what he was doing, he had planted a big, warm, hard kiss on her lips.

The two young policemen standing in the doorway looked away, as though embarrassed by this unexpected display of affection by one of the ranking members of their force who was known far more for offending all members of the fairer sex than for hugging and kissing them.

But Dirk was oblivious. And to Savannah's surprise, he gave her a second, even harder and longer kiss.

She pulled back and looked up at him to see if he had lost his mind, but he just smiled down on her with such a pure joy that she had to laugh.

"This has to stop," she said. "This is the second time today that you've come back here after a shooting and hugged the tarnation out of me. And now you're kissing me? I don't like the way this is headed."

"Are you all right?" he asked. Then, he suddenly looked horrified. "Tammy?"

"She's fine, too."

"The corpse?"

"He's not so fine. He's dead."

"Cameron Field?"

"Yeah. I'm having a glass of water there in the kitchen. Come in here with me, and we'll fill you in."

He released her from the hug, but held her hand tightly as they walked back into the kitchen. "Hi, kid," he told Tammy. "Glad you're okay . . . again."

"Thanks to Savannah," she said, tears brimming in her eyes.

Savannah sat back down on her stool, glad to have something more solid than her own legs beneath her. The adrenaline that was still coursing through her body had left her completely drained and as weak as a runner after a marathon.

"So, you took him out yourself?" he asked Savannah. "None of these cops were here yet?"

"No, they arrived right afterward."

"Where did it happen?"

"Upstairs in Dona's bedroom. He broke it down just before I

got here. When Tammy and I ran up there, we found him holding Dona at gunpoint. I told him repeatedly to drop his weapon, but he didn't. And when he turned it toward me, I fired."

"Where were you, Tammy?" he asked.

When Tammy didn't answer, Savannah said, "She was right behind me, backing me up all the way."

"That's such a lie." Tammy crossed her arms on the counter in front of her, laid her face on them and began to sob.

Savannah leaned over and put her arm around her shoulders. "Honey, why are you crying? What's the matter?"

"I didn't back you up, and you know it," she said, her face still buried in her arms. "I let you down so bad."

Savannah looked over at Dirk. He gave her a questioning look.

She reached out and took a strand of Tammy's long blond hair and let it slip slowly through her fingers. "That isn't true, sweetie. You didn't let me down. Why do you think you did?"

"Because . . . because . . . be . . . cause," she sobbed, unable to get the words out.

Then it dawned on Savannah. "You aren't feeling bad because you didn't fire your weapon, are you?"

Tammy said nothing, but she nodded.

Savannah looked across the counter at Dirk, who had a serious and sad expression on his face.

She replayed the shooting in her mind, step by step. And she realized—Tammy was right.

Tammy should have fired, too.

A murder suspect was threatening an innocent person with deadly force. He had been warned repeatedly, and he was turning to fire at Tammy's partner.

She should have fired.

Savannah reached under Tammy's face, cupped her chin and forced her to look up. "What happened, honey? Why didn't you take a shot? Were you afraid? Did you freeze?"

She shook her head. Her eyes filled with regret and guilt. "It wasn't that. I was afraid, but it wasn't fear. It's just that I saw him standing there, alive, breathing . . . a living, breathing person. I couldn't shoot another human being. I just couldn't do it."

"That's okay," Savannah told her, stroking her hair. "Really it is. A lot of people couldn't take another life, and that's all right. It's nothing to be ashamed of, truly."

"But if you hadn't been there," she said, "he would have killed me. I'd be dead right now. He's still be alive and breathing, but I'd be the one dead up there."

Reluctantly, Savannah nodded and said, "That's probably true."

"You know it's true," Dirk said.

"Sh-h-h." Savannah pressed her finger to her lips and gave him a warning frown. To Tammy she said, "But you don't have to think about what might have been. What happened is all that matters. And if someone had to die, at least this time, it was the bad guy."

"But it does matter," Tammy said, hiccuping with sobs. "It matters a lot because next time you might not be there. And you've told me over and over, don't ever pull a gun on someone unless you absolutely know that you can use it. Well, now I know. I can't use it."

She reached to the back of the stool and took her backpack off it. Reaching into the pack, she pulled out her new gun and laid it on the counter in front of Savannah. "There," she said. "I don't want to carry that anymore. And after today, after seeing what a gun can do to a human being's body, I don't even want to touch one ever again."

After a couple of strained moments, Dirk reached over, picked up the gun and emptied it of its ammunition. Then he stuck it in his jacket pocket. "I think that's a wise decision, kiddo," he told her, his voice soft with compassion. "And Savannah's right. Not everyone should carry a gun. Not at all. There's no shame in being a person who feels the way you do. Hell, more likely you should be proud of yourself."

She sniffed, wiped her eyes and gave him a half smile of gratitude. "Thanks, Dirko," she said. Then she turned to Savannah. "But," she said, "as long as there are bad guys in the world who are carrying guns, we'd better be glad we've got somebody like Savannah here who doesn't feel the way I do."

"Hey," Savannah said, leaning over and kissing her on the forehead. "It's a big, big world. There's just gotta be a place for all kinds of us in it."

Chapter 23

One of Savannah's least favorite places in the world was the San Carmelita morgue, or as it was more cheerfully called, the Medical Examiner's Forensic Sciences Laboratory.

She had nothing against dead people. Most dead people hadn't chosen to be so, so how could you blame them?

But she had witnessed too many truly heart-wrenching scenes inside that building to feel warm and fuzzy when she was walking up the sidewalk to the front door.

Normally, she found the whole experience beyond depressing, and this morning, her mood was even less festive than normal. She was going to see the body of the man she had killed the night before.

Not her idea of a good time.

And things got only worse when she walked through the front door and saw that her least favorite desk officer was on duty, Kenny Bates.

Someday, she thought, *someone will murder Officer Bates, and I'll take the stand in their defense and say something like, "Ladies and gentlemen of the jury, if you'd only known Bates . . . if you'd spent one moment in his presence . . . you'd not only release the defendant but give him/her a slap on the back, a 'fare-thee-well,' and the Nobel Peace Prize.*"

She had rehearsed her testimony many times, as well as her own defense. "But your honor, he breathed egg salad and nacho cheese chip breath on me, and then suggested I come to his house and watch his new porn DVDs with him. I had to beat him to death with his own sign-in clipboard. I had to. Being a woman, your honor, I'm sure you understand."

When she walked through the door, he looked up at her and his face split into a big, stupid, leering smile. "Savannah! Hey, baby, what's cookin'?"

"Your head in my soup pot if you even so much as take a step this direction," she snapped. "I ain't in the mood, Bates. I am so-o-o not in the mood. So just back the hell off."

She grabbed the sign-in sheet and scrawled "F. Quew" in the signature column beside her entry time.

"Hey, I hear they've got a guy back there that you shot!" he yelled after her as she headed down the hall toward the autopsy suite. "Is that true? You shot him?"

"Yeah, and I didn't even *know* him, and I shot him five times! I *hate* you, Bates. *Hate*. Live in fear."

At the end of the long hallway was a pair of stainless steel doors. The door on the right was propped open, so she stepped inside.

"Dr. Liu?" she called out. "Jen, are you here?"

Before her was the large, stainless steel table with its scales, the trays of surgical tools, all covered with sterile cloths, the bright lights and the microphone suspended overhead, the pedal on the floor for the ME to turn the microphone on and off as she dictated her findings into it.

And sinks. Everywhere there were sinks and waste bins marked *Hazard—Biological Waste*.

But no Dr. Liu.

Savannah knew the suite well. The doors to the left were the refrigeration units, each of which could hold four bodies. To the right a door led to a small room where bodies were laid out so that they could be identified by loved ones. The room had a window that opened onto the hall and a shade. Savannah had stood in that hallway many times with the next of kin and watched as they dissolved into tears upon seeing their loved one beyond the glass.

That was another reason why she hated this place. She could literally feel the sorrow, like energy stored in a battery, which had seeped into these walls. She didn't know how Dr. Liu could bear to work here, but thankfully, she did.

Someone needed to.

"Dr. Jen?" she called out, louder than before.

The door to her right opened, and Dr. Liu stuck her head out. "Oh, hi, Savannah. I'm in here, getting him ready. His mother is supposed to be by in a few minutes."

His mother. Oh, god, Savannah thought. *This just gets worse by the minute.*

"Then let me look at him and go," she said. "This is one ID I'd just as soon miss if I can."

Dr. Liu looked at her with deep compassion showing in her dark brown eyes. "Yes, that's one you should avoid. Come on it."

Savannah walked into the small room, which held only the two women and a gurney with a body on it, which was shrouded from head to toe with a green surgical cloth. Even though he was completely covered, Savannah was struck by what a large man Cameron Field was. He had to be well over six feet and considerably more than two hundred pounds.

Dr. Liu said, "Are you sure you want to do this, Savannah? You don't have to."

"Yes, I do," she replied. "The room was dark. I didn't even get that good a look at him. I have to know what he looks like or this ghostly, featureless face is going to haunt me forever."

"This could make it worse."

"It could. But it's a chance I have to take."

"Okay." Dr. Liu pulled the sheet back, exposing him to the waist.

Savannah felt her knees nearly buckle beneath her.

"Are you okay?" the ME asked. "I'll bring you a chair if you feel like you need to sit down. Or a glass of water?"

"Thanks, but that's not necessary. I'm okay. But could you leave me alone with him? Just for a couple of minutes."

She hesitated. "Well, I'm not really supposed to, but . . . since it's you . . ."

"Thank you."

Dr. Liu slipped silently from the room and closed the door behind her.

Savannah stared down at the still, white face for a long time, taking in every feature. He had a broad, almost pudgy face, a fair complexion and a small cleft in his chin. Faded acne scars showed on his clean-shaven cheeks. His dark hair was slightly wavy and slicked back.

He wasn't what most people would call attractive in any way. But hardly anyone on the streets would have pegged him for a ruthless killer, either. Quite the contrary. He looked soft, maybe lazy . . . not someone you would give a second thought to if you stood behind him in line at the grocery store.

He was wearing a black sweat suit. The front of the shirt was crusted with his dried blood and five neat holes were burned into the fabric.

Savannah knew Dr. Liu would cover his chest area with the sheet before showing him to his mother.

Around his neck was a small gold chain and on it hung a gold charm in the shape of an anchor.

She noticed a rip in the sleeve of his shirt. A small tear with something that looked like a thorn caught in the fabric beside it. Savannah recognized the bit of vegetation instantly. She had a pair of bougainvillea on either side of her front door. And for all of their lush green leaves and beautiful red blossoms, she knew all too well how badly those thorns bit if you got too familiar with them. This was a bougainvillea thorn that had ripped his sleeve. She filed that bit of information away for later consideration.

She closed her eyes for a moment, and saw this man as he had been last night, staring at her down the barrel of his revolver. If she had taken half a second longer than she had, she'd be the one on this gurney right now, waiting for Dirk or Tammy or Ryan or John to identify her remains.

"Why didn't you just put down the gun?" she asked him. "You'd have wound up in prison, but you would have been alive. And your mother could have written you letters and talked to you on the phone."

Then she thought of Jack and Kim. They'd been given no choice. This man had taken their lives from them with no warning at all.

She had given him a chance to live.

And that was a hell of a lot more than he had given his victims.

"It's on you," she told him. "It's on you, not me. You carry it into eternity with you. And I'm going to sleep a lot better tonight than I did last night. You got what you asked for, you son of a bitch."

She turned and walked out the door. "Okay, I'm done," she said.

Then she realized that Dr. Liu wasn't alone.

The ME was standing in the middle of the room, talking to a

petite brunette who looked to be in her mid-fifties. She was simply but nicely dressed in a navy suit, a pretty woman in a plain sort of way.

She had a heart-shaped face and large eyes, though it was obvious she had been crying profusely. In her hand she clutched a bunch of tissues.

"The investigation is ongoing," Dr. Liu was saying, "but it appears that he was involved in a home invasion of some sort."

"Someone broke into his house? Why? To rob him?"

Dr. Liu glanced quickly at Savannah who had frozen by the doorway, unable to move.

"Uh, no," the doctor said, hesitating, as though choosing her words carefully. "I'm sorry to have to tell you this, but in fact, it appears that it was your son who was the intruder. From what I understand at this point, the police believe he was threatening the movie star, Dona Papalardo with a gun. Her bodyguard was forced to shoot him to save Ms. Papalardo's life."

Don't tell her it's me, Savannah thought, trying to send her wishes telepathically to Dr. Liu. *For god's sake, please just let me get out of here without her knowing it was me.*

The lady gasped and brought the tissues up to her face. "Oh no, I was afraid of something like that. My son was a good boy, but he kept things from me, you know. A mother can tell things sometimes."

Again, Dr. Liu shot Savannah a look. Savannah would have liked nothing better, under normal circumstances, than to question the mother further about her maternal suspicions. But if she ever did find out that Savannah was the one who had killed her son, and she probably would, she would have resented being questioned without being fully informed of Savannah's role in her son's death.

"So," Dr. Liu said, "you aren't entirely surprised that your son may have been involved in . . . some illegal activities?"

"Sad, but not surprised," she said, wiping her eyes. "He was always such a good little boy. He and his father were very close. They both loved the ocean. We had a cottage in Pelican Cove, and they hunted for shells there on the beach day after day. They even photographed the shells they found. Cam got really good with a camera even as a little boy. But his dad died when he was only ten. And he was never the same after that."

Savannah felt like someone had just reached into her chest and squeezed her heart with a tight fist. She didn't want to hear this, but she couldn't bring herself to walk away.

"I had to work all the time to support the two of us," his mother was saying. "And I left Cam alone a lot. He never had many friends his own age, so he was alone for hours every day. I've wondered sometimes if—"

She broke down completely, and Dr. Liu put her arms around her, patting her back. "There, there," she said. "I'm sure you did the best you could. And I'm sure your son knew you did, too. Kids just don't always turn out the way we'd like them to. We can't blame ourselves for the choices they make as adults."

She continued to comfort the woman until she managed to regain her composure.

Then Dr. Liu said, "Is there anything I can do for you, Mrs. Field? I'll prepare your son's body for you to view it. That will only take a couple minutes, and then it will all be over, but is there anything else we can do to help you?"

She nodded, "Actually, there is one thing. Cam always wore a gold chain with an anchor on it. It was his father's. I gave it to him on the day of his dad's funeral, and it hasn't been off his neck since."

"Yes," Dr. Liu said, "it's on him now."

"May I have that? I want to wear it now myself. I need it . . . to feel close to them both."

The fist that was squeezing in Savannah's chest clamped down until she was sure she would never breathe again.

The room around her began to spin.

"I have to go," she said as she hurried past the two women toward the door. "Thank you, Dr. Liu, but I have to—"

"Are you all right?" Dr. Liu called to her as she exited the door and hurried out a rear emergency door. "Savannah, are you . . . ?"

Savannah ran across the parking lot and got into her Mustang. She sat there, gulping in deep breaths of air until her head stopped spinning.

Around her time seemed to slow. The morning sun was streaming through her window, warming her face. A nearby palm tree swayed in the breeze, making its dry, swishing sound. Seagulls overhead swirled, dipped and cawed at each other.

Life continued.

But not for Cameron Field.

And to a certain extent, not for his mother.

Savannah had heard, years ago, an old proverb that said, "When you take a life, you lose a part of your own."

She looked into the rearview mirror and saw the blue eyes of the woman looking back at her.

"Did part of you die last night, Savannah?" she asked the woman in the mirror. "And if so, what part?"

Time will tell, was the answer that came back, whispering its quiet wisdom to her heart. *Time will tell.*

Chapter 24

Savannah wanted nothing more in the world than to go home, take a hot bath, crawl into bed with her two kitties, and sleep for days. But only if she had some sort of guarantee that she wouldn't dream. The few hours she had grabbed the night before had been more stressful than just staying awake all night. Nightmares, featuring dark figures in dark rooms with dark agendas, woke her over and over again, until she had decided to stay awake the few remaining hours until dawn and read.

Anything to keep the demons from bedeviling her.

She had already decided that a good strong sleeping pill or a potent Irish toddy was going to be her pre-bedtime snack tonight.

Unfortunately, it was barely noon. And she had a bit of business to finish before she was officially off-duty.

She headed the Mustang toward the hills and the Papalardo estate.

Nothing would have made her happier than to never return to that place again, but she owed it to Dona to at least check on her and make sure that she was recovering from her trauma.

But when she arrived at the mansion, she couldn't park within a quarter mile of the place. Reporters' vehicles lined both sides of the street, and throngs of people milled about in the driveway and on the front lawn.

The crowds were bad when Kim was shot, but this was far, far worse.

Savannah parked where she could and then hiked to the mansion, ducking and dodging her way through the crowd, until she finally reached the front door.

After several knocks and thumb punches at the doorbell, Juanita answered. Her face was lit with genuine delight to see Savannah. But when she looked beyond her to the mob that was charging toward them, she grabbed Savannah's arm, pulled her inside, and slammed it behind her.

"All night and all day, they do that," she said, shaking her head. "The phone, she doesn't stop ringing, and the people, they don't stop knocking! Ugh!"

As though materializing out of her words, a phone in the library began to ring and someone pounded on the door.

"You see! I do not lie. *Es muy loco!*"

"I'm sorry, Juanita," Savannah said. "Things will probably quiet down in a few days. You'll just have to ride it out. How is Ms. Papalardo?"

Juanita smiled. "Ah, she is good. Much better. She is happy now. Today she told me how happy she is that she is alive. It is a gift to be alive."

"I can't say that hasn't occurred to me a few times today myself," Savannah said. "It was a close call last night. Be glad that you weren't here, that you'd gone home already."

"Oh, I am glad. I mean, I'm sorry it happened to you and Senorita Tammy and Senorita Dona, but I think I would have died, I would have been so scared!"

Savannah thought of Juanita's gentle strength when Jack had been killed and she said, "I don't think so. I think you would have been as strong, even stronger, than the rest of us."

"Savannah! Just the person I wanted to see!"

Savannah looked up at the top of the stairs and saw Dona Papalardo standing there in a black suit with red fox trim around the collar and cuffs. While Savannah thought it gaudy and, where the fox was concerned, a sad waste, she had to admit that Dona looked quite glamorous.

She floated down the stairs on four-inch heels, adjusting a satin pillbox hat, complete with short French veil in the front. Her makeup was perfect, and for the first time since Savannah had met her, she had color in her cheeks and a sparkle in her eyes.

She hurried over to Savannah and, to Savannah's surprise, embraced her heartily. "I'm so glad you came by to see me," she said. "With the police here last night, questioning everyone and processing my bedroom, I didn't get a chance to tell you how grateful I am to you for saving my life!"

Savannah shrugged. "You're welcome, but I was just doing what you pay me to do."

"And that reminds me. I must pay you—pay you for a job well done. Come into the library with me, and we'll take care of that right now." She turned to her maid. "Juanita, get us each a glass of Chardonnay."

Savannah held up one hand. "Uh, I really don't—"

"Oh, don't be silly. We need to celebrate a little, celebrate life, celebrate the end of this terrible ordeal."

Savannah followed her into the library, but she found it difficult to raise her mood to match Dona's. "I'm sorry," she said. "But I just came from the morgue, where Field's mother had come to identify his body. Understandably, she was very upset. It was difficult for me to see that."

Dona stopped abruptly, and she turned around to look at Savannah, her smile evaporating. "Oh, dear. I never thought about . . . I mean . . . I guess he does have some relatives, a mother, someone who would grieve him. He was just so awful that I didn't think of him as being someone's son."

"Everyone has a mother. And no matter what you've done in your life, most mothers will love you anyway . . . and grieve terribly if you pass on before them."

Dona placed a gloved hand on Savannah's forearm. "I'm really sorry, Savannah, that you had to go through that. And that's another price you've paid for me. I don't know how I'm ever going to thank you."

She slid behind her desk and sat down, waving an arm in the direction of a nearby chair. "Please, have a seat. I don't have long to talk. I'm on my way to an interview. *America Tonight* wants to do an entire show about what's happened here. We're taping it today, and it'll air tomorrow night."

Pulling a large leather checkbook from the desk drawer, she said, "I have to tell you—and I feel guilty even thinking it, let alone saying it, considering the fact that both Jack and Kim lost their lives—but I've never felt so alive as I do today. Just having something so terrible happen, having that maniac waving a gun in my face, telling me that he was going to kill me, and then having bullets flying around my bedroom like that! I tell you, it reminds you of how precious life is and how quickly you can lose it!"

Savannah nodded. "A brush with death frequently leaves people feeling like that."

"Do you feel that way today? As though the world is somehow lighter? Brighter?"

"No, I can't honestly say that I do. But maybe after a good night's sleep." She thought for a moment. "Where did *you* sleep last night after the police left?"

"Well, of course, after all that happened in my bedroom, I certainly couldn't sleep in there. Besides, your detective friend said he wasn't ready to release it yet. It's still officially a crime scene. I had to call him earlier today and ask for permission to go in there and get my clothes. I slept downstairs, in Mary Jo's room."

"Oh?" For a moment Savannah thought she might have missed a potentially important element in the Dona–Mary Jo relationship.

But then Dona added, "Mary Jo left yesterday morning, long before the trouble started around here. She said she was going to Encino to stay with her mother for a while. She and I had a bit of a falling-out about Mark. Not the first time either, I might add. Mary Jo is never happy unless she has what I have. Which, of course, means she's never going to be happy."

She scribbled some figures on a check and with dramatic flourish, tore it out of the checkbook and handed it to Savannah. "There you go," she said with a bright smile. "A little something to show how much I appreciate you saving my life last night. I'll never forget you for it."

And Savannah knew that she would never forget this moment. As she looked at the exorbitant amount written on the check, she nearly fainted. Normally, she would do well to make that much in a year. A really good year.

"Ms. Papalardo!" she said. "I think you've made a mistake here. This is far, far more than we originally agreed on."

"And as it turned out, you had to do far more than we had ever expected."

"But that goes with the territory. When I take the job of guarding someone, I know it may be necessary for me to use deadly force to do so."

"Still, it would make me feel better. Take it. I want you to have it."

Savannah stared down at the check in her hand and thought of all the places it could go. Her house was in desperate need of some repairs, as well as her car. And she could give Tammy the big bonus that she had deserved for so long.

When she looked up at Dona, she saw the actress's green eyes were alight with humor and affection. "Savannah, this isn't the time to be proud," she said. "You probably need the money, and I don't mean to brag, but I can easily afford it, so stick the check in your purse and spend it in good health."

"Okay, if you put it that way." Savannah folded the check and slipped it into her pocketbook. "Thank you very much."

Dona flipped the checkbook closed and tossed it back into the drawer.

Juanita entered the room, a pair of wineglasses on a tray. She handed one to Dona and the other to Savannah.

"Here's to the end of a terrible time," Dona said, lifting her glass to Savannah, "and the beginning of good ones."

Savannah raised her glass, but even as she sipped the cold, white wine, she felt the nettling of unsettled questions working on her subconscious.

"Dona," she said, "did you know Cameron Field? Had you ever seen him before last night?"

"No, I hadn't. Why do you ask?"

"I was just wondering why he was so determined to kill you. Do you have any idea?"

Dona looked confused at the question. "Now that you mention it, I wondered that myself. I suppose he was some sort of obsessed fan."

"Why would you think that?"

"I guess because of what he said last night."

"Before we came into your room?"

"Yes. He told me that he'd loved me for years, and that he knew we were meant to be together. When I told him that I had a boyfriend, he threatened to kill Mark, too. He said he's watched from the hill the other night when we were kissing by the front door."

Savannah nodded. "That certainly does sound like a stalker all right. Classic, in fact. But how do you suppose he got into the house?"

"Oh, the police figured that out last night. They said he climbed a tree up to the balcony of Mary Jo's bedroom. She had forgotten to close the sliding door and it's one of the few doors we don't have a sensor on."

"Is there a bougainvillea bush around there?"

"Yes, at the base of the tree. Why?"

"He had some thorns caught in his clothes. I saw them just now when I viewed his body at the morgue."

"Ah, well, then the police were right."

"One other thing," Savannah said, "When Tammy and I were outside your door, about to come in, I thought I heard the two of you arguing."

"Oh, we were! He was telling me that it was *my* fault that he killed Kim and Jack. And even though he was pointing that gun at me, I couldn't let him say that and get away with it. I told him that their deaths were on him, not me. He chose to do what he did, and that was his fault, not mine. That's when you came in."

Savannah took a sip of her wine and thought that one over. "Yes," she said, "I'll bet you that when Dirk searches his apartment, he'll probably find pictures and news articles about you, CDs of all of your movies, stuff like that. An obsessed fan with a criminal streak, not what a celebrity needs."

"A criminal streak?"

"Yes, his own mother admitted today that she worried about him being on the wrong side of the law sometimes."

"Well, there you go. What can you expect from a guy whose own mother thinks he's bad?"

Dona took a tiny sip from her glass, then stood. "I really hate to cut our visit short, Savannah, but I have to be on time for this taping in the valley, and it's going to take me a while to fight my way through those reporters out there."

"Why don't you have your driver pull into your garage and you can get into the car there?"

Dona grinned and the brightness of her smile reminded Savannah of why she was a world-famous star. "Now where would be the fun in that?" she said.

"Then at least let me walk out with you. Considering the bonus you just threw my way, I can work a few minutes of overtime for you."

Both women stood. Dona walked around the desk and laced her arm through Savannah's. "Then let's go, bodyguard. We'll walk out together. I'll look glamorous and you can beat them over the heads with their own cameras."

"'Twill be my pleasure, ma'am. My pleasure, indeed."

Chapter 25

When Savannah arrived back at her own house, her first clue that all wasn't well on the home front was Tammy sitting on the front porch, a miserable look on her face.

Savannah got out of the Mustang and walked up the steps, dreading anything that might even smell like bad news.

Where was that delicious, peaceful feeling of "homecoming?" Where was the serene sense of returning to one's haven from the world's raging madness?

"I hate you, hate you, hate you! I never should have married you! You just suck!"

"Yeah? Well, well . . . well, you do, too! You suck worse!"

"No, you suck worser than I ever did!"

The screams echoed from the interior of Savannah's haven of refuge and drifted out across her lawn to pollute the serenity of her neighborhood, as well. From the corner of her eye, Savannah could see Mr. Viola washing his car, a less-than-cheerful look on his face. And next door, Mrs. McDermott was weeding her flower bed and shooting Savannah looks of disapproval.

Yes, the world's raging madness had come home to roost right there in her own little henhouse.

"Trouble in honeymooner paradise?" she asked Tammy as she climbed the steps onto the porch.

Tammy was sitting on the porch itself—no chair, cushion, or blanket beneath her—leaning against the wall. She was wearing shorts and a T-shirt and had her hair pulled up in a ponytail, but from the spreadsheet on the computer's screen, Savannah could see that she was working on their accounts. Tammy sighed, readjusted the computer on her lap and grimaced as she stretched her long legs out before her.

"Oh, it's nasty in there," she said. "They've been going at it all morning. I had to come outside just so that I could think."

"Why aren't you in the backyard, sitting in a comfortable chair, sipping some lemonade while you do that?"

"I was. But they were going back and forth from the house to the backyard and back to the house. I figured it would be easier to just—"

Another volley sounded from inside. "I can't believe I married a sucky guy like you! What was I thinking?"

"What were *you* thinking? What was *I* thinking? I can't believe I married you either!"

Tammy shook her head. "It's not that they're arguing. That could even be entertaining, but they're just so . . . so . . . inarticulate and redundant. It stopped being interesting two hours ago."

Savannah glanced back one more time at her neighbors. She could tell that her status on the street was plummeting by the moment. Any minute now she and her unruly clan would be classified officially as "white trash."

And no granddaughter of Granny Reid of McGill, Georgia could abide that!

She charged into the house, threw her purse onto the side table in the hallway, and stomped into the living room where her sister and brother-in-law were standing nose to nose in the middle of the room, still debating who sucked the most, longest, and worst.

"That's enough!" she roared. "In fact, that's way more than enough. Have you two just gone plumb crazy?"

"He started it! He said that I—!"

"It's your sister here who's crazy! All I said was—!"

"Shut up, both of you! I will not have this low-class screeching and carryin' on in my house. You two either make up right this minute or get out of my house. I mean it. Decide what you're gonna do right now."

Jesup and Bleak glared at each other, eye to baleful eye.

Savannah glanced toward the sofa and saw two long black tails sticking out from beneath the pillows. "Now look at that," she said. "You've scared my cats half to death. And they live with *me*; they're not all that easily scared. You oughta be ashamed of yourselves, frightening the pee-diddle out of innocent creatures like that."

She walked over to the sofa and uncovered Diamante and Cleopatra, who looked up at her with nervous, blinking eyes. Scooping one under each arm, she carried them into the kitchen, where she dumped some of their favorite treats into their bowls.

When she returned to the living room, Jesup and her husband were each sitting on opposite ends of the sofa, arms crossed over their chests.

Marital bliss at its best, Savannah thought. She walked over, sat down in her comfy chair and propped her feet up on her cushy footstool. Ah, the comforts of home, or at least, it would be without the spitting cobras in her living room.

She wondered if they had any idea how ridiculous they looked, dressed and made up like demons from the bowels of hell—with their bottom lips stuck out like those of pouting two-year-olds.

"Just out of curiosity," she said, "how long does it take you two to put all that crap on your faces and hair every morning? Most days, I don't even have time to swipe on some lipstick before I'm out the door."

Bleak lifted his chin—his chin that had a lightning bolt painted on it today—and said, "You take time for what's important to you in life. And personal adornment and unique self-expression are high on my list of priorities."

Savannah shook her head and thought, *This from a guy who can't think of anything better to say in the middle of a domestic dispute than, "You suck worser."*

"Wow, that's deep," she said with a sniff.

He nodded somberly. "Thank you."

"Now that we've all settled down a bit, do you want to tell me what started this little affray today? Jessie, you go first."

"I made him breakfast, and I even brought it to him in bed, but do you think he appreciated it? No-o-o! He—"

"It was toast!" Bleak interjected. "It wasn't breakfast, it was friggin' toast! That's all you know how to cook. Am I supposed to eat toast three times a day for the rest of my life? You never told me that you didn't know how to cook!"

"Yeah, well, you never told me that you don't have a friggin' job! How are we even going to afford bread for toast if you don't work?"

"Okay, okay!" Savannah held up one hand. "So it appears that maybe you two didn't know each other as well as you thought you did. I mean, a day or two at Blood-Fest-Whatever-the-Hell, might not be enough to truly figure out whether or not you're compatible enough for a lifelong commitment."

"But, but . . ." Jesup started to cry, causing her thick eyeliner to streak black lines down her white cheeks. ". . . but we're soul mates."

"Even soul mates have to work at being married, Jes," Savannah said. "Even if the Universe or whatever puts you together, you still have to work like the dickens to stay together."

"But I don't want to stay with him! He sucks!"

"So I've heard. Recently. Repeatedly. And apparently, he's decided that you do, too."

Jesup looked at her new husband with resentment and disappointment. "I don't think this is going to work out. I think we should go back to Vegas right now and get divorced and forget this whole thing ever happened."

"Good idea." He jumped to his feet. "I'm going to go pack my stuff, and I'm outta here!"

He headed for the stairs, but Jesup was right behind him. "What do you mean *you're* going to Vegas?"

"I'm going to go back home—by myself—and the first thing I'm going to do is divorce you."

"And what am *I* supposed to be doing while you're divorcing me?" she asked as she tramped up the stairs after him.

"Stay here with your sister. Go back to Georgia. I don't care as long as I don't have to be around you anymore."

"You can't divorce me! I'm going to divorce you. You suck!"

"No, *you* do!"

"No, *you*!"

Savannah sighed, closed her eyes, and leaned her head back on the chair. "I've got news for you," she mumbled. "You both do."

When Savannah finally opened her eyes, Tammy was standing nearby, watching her with a sympathetic look on her face. "You look exhausted," she said. "Can I get you something, do anything for you?"

Savannah looked at her usually perky friend and noticed dark circles under her eyes, not to mention the marked lack of exuberance that she normally radiated in irritating proportions. "You look a little droopy yourself, darlin'," she said. "Why don't you sit a spell and tell me what's going on with you?"

Tammy sat on the end of the sofa and laid her computer on the coffee table. "I guess I'm just feeling the aftermath of seeing those two shootings. One would have been enough, but two like that, right together. I think my circuits were overloaded."

"I'm sure they were. Mine, too."

"Then it's not just me? I'm not just . . ." She blinked back some tears and her lip trembled. ". . . just weak?"

Savannah reached over and patted her hand that lay on the arm of the sofa. "You? Weak? Not at all, honey. You aren't a weak person. I've never, never thought of you that way."

Tammy didn't say anything, but her tears began to flow in earnest.

Savannah squeezed her hand. "Tammy, there are all kinds of strength in this world. The ability to pull a trigger and take a life in the defense of other lives . . . that's just one kind of strength. You're strong in your own way."

"What way? How am I strong?"

"In so many ways! Tammy, you amaze me with the intensity of your own personal power."

"I do?"

"Absolutely. You manage to see the sunshine in the middle of the darkest day, every day of your life." Savannah laughed. "I used to think you were a bimbo who just didn't notice that it was cloudy and raining, but now I know you better. And I understand that you see the rain, you see the evil all around, the misery of the human condition, but you make a conscious effort to concentrate on the good, the love, the beauty that's around you. I *try* to do that, but you actually *do* it. That takes a kind of strength that I don't have."

Tammy's tears came even faster, and Savannah handed her a bunch of tissues from the box on the side table.

"Tammy, you're my rock. You're always here, ready and eager to help any way you can and for nothing but the pennies I throw your way when I can. You could have left here ages ago, got a real job, and bought yourself that little house on the beach that you want so badly. But you keep living in that apartment of yours, scrounging and saving, and for what? So that you can come here every day and do my books and search the Internet for ideas about how we can stay in business? That kind of dedication and daily discipline takes strength."

Tammy sniffed and wiped her eyes and nose with the tissues. "I do it because I love the work."

"I know you do."

"And because I love you, Savannah. I love all of you guys. You're like my family."

"And you're mine, too, honey. Don't you ever forget that."

Savannah leaned over to hug her, but someone pounded hard on the front door. A distinctive, all-too-male knock.

They looked at each other.

"Speaking of family members who we love but don't always like," Tammy said. "That's gotta be Dirko."

Savannah got up and let him in. But the moment he stepped through her door, she said, "Lord have mercy, boy. You reek to high heaven!"

"Well, nice to see you, too," he snapped.

"No really. You smell like Gran's hound dog when he's been rolling in something rotten. Oh, no . . . a DB?"

"Yeah, a dead body, but not connected to this case." He walked on through the living room, giving Tammy a concerned, but quick, glance. In the kitchen, he opened Savannah's refrigerator and pulled out a can of soda. "Man, what I wouldn't give for one of those beers in there," he said. "They sent me up into the hills this morning on a suicide case. Some guy shot himself in his pickup there in the boonies, and he'd been there for days in the heat. Shit, that was an ugly one! Major insect infestation and—"

"All right, all right. Enough already. But since you handled the body maybe you should go shower and change clothes before you rejoin the land of the living."

"I didn't touch him, I swear! I smell this bad just from being in Dr. Liu's wagon with him. I'm telling you, on a scale of one to ten for wicked nasty, that one's a twenty."

"Well, either way, why don't you let me throw those clothes into the washer. I can have them washed and dried in less than an hour. You can shower and—"

"Stop with the hygiene nagging, woman. I just dropped by to tell you a couple things and then I'll be out of here, okay?"

"Yeah, I reckon. But let's go sit out in the backyard."

He looked hurt. "Really? I'm that ripe?"

"Oh, sugar, my hair is curlin', just standing next to you. Bring that soda pop out here in the fresh air, and Tammy and I will sit downwind of you."

Once settled under her wisteria arbor, Savannah could stand to be close to Dirk, as long as she breathed through her ears. She noticed that Tammy was leaning as far away from him as possible.

But once he started to deliver his news, both girls temporarily forgot all about the stench of death.

"We found a rifle when we searched Field's house this morning," he said. "A really nice one, a Weatherby Magnum. The lab is checking it now against the slug that we dug out of the dirt there in Papalardo's backyard, the through-and-through that killed the gardener. It was still in pretty good shape, so they should be able to tell if it was from that gun."

"Chances are good it will be," Savannah said.

"Yeah, the ammo that was in it was the same as the slug from the dirt. You'll never guess where we found the rifle."

"Where?" Tammy asked.

"Hidden in a tray underneath that damned lizard's cage."

"Oh, I always keep my gun in my cats' litter box," Savannah said. "Doesn't everyone?"

"Only people who are trying to hide something would choose a place like that," Tammy said. "The top of the bedroom closet wasn't good enough for him, I guess."

"The more I check into this guy, the more I don't think he's ordinary at all," Dirk said.

"Really? How?"

"For one thing, he lived really well in that fancy house of his with the great view. That property's pretty expensive for a guy who hasn't had a job of any kind for the past five years."

"Maybe his parents are rich," Tammy suggested.

"No." Savannah shook her head. "I saw his mother at the morgue, and she didn't strike me as somebody who had more than a couple of shekels to rub together. And she said she had to work hard to support herself and Cameron after his dad died years ago."

"Well, he's making good money someway. And we found something else under the lizard's cage besides just the rifle. Over fifty grand in cash, all bundled up with rubber bands in five batches of ten thou each."

"I must admit that's a bit unusual," Savannah said. "I'm fond of my kitties, but I don't put bundles of cash in their litter box. When I have a little extra cash and can't get to the bank, I stick it in the freezer with my two favorite guys, Ben and Jerry."

She was about to tell them about the bonus that Dona had given her, but Jesup and Bleak came spilling though the back door into the yard. Bleak had an oversized duffel bag in one hand and a black, plastic garbage bag in the other.

"He's leaving me," Jesup yelled as she hurried over to Savannah and grabbed her arm. "My husband is leaving me, and it's all your fault."

"My fault?" Savannah pushed her hand away. "Now wait a cotton-pickin' minute here. I've been blamed for a lot of things in my life, and I was guilty of most of them. But this? Are you kidding me?"

Jesup stomped her foot and shook her fist like a homicidal kindergartner. "No, I'm not. We could have gone anywhere for our honeymoon. We could have gone and seen the Charles Manson family ranch. We could have gone to New Orleans and seen Anne Rice's house and the voodoo queen's tomb. We could have gone to New York and seen the Amityville horror house, but no-o-o, we had to come see *you*."

"Yeah," Bleak chimed in. "'Come meet my sister!' Jes said. 'She's this famous homicide detective. She'll let us tag along while she's solving her cases. We'll get the inside scoop.' But you were too busy to even hang with us."

"And now look at us," Jesup said, starting to cry. "We're breaking up. Our marriage is over!"

Savannah stood there, looking at her sister, then her brother-in-law, then back at Jesup. "Let me get this straight," she said. "You two nitwits get hitched as soon as you meet. You drop in on me from out of the blue. And then, when I have to work—yes, some of us actually do work—you complain that I'm not entertaining you. And you blame me for the two of you breaking up . . . because of *boredom*?"

Jesup turned to Bleak. They lowered their voices and whispered to each other for a few seconds. Then they turned back to Savannah. "Yep," Bleak said, "that's about it."

Savannah turned her back on them and marched inside. Grabbing her phone from the kitchen counter, she dialed Dr. Liu's office number.

The doctor herself picked up. "Jennifer Liu."

"Hi, Jen. It's Savannah."

"Savannah. I'm so glad you called. I've been worried about you. That was a ghastly thing you had to endure, running into his mother. I am so sorry!"

"I'm all right, thanks," she said. "But I have an enormous favor to ask you."

"Of course. What is it?"

"Dirk says you picked up a suicide there in the hills today."

"Yes, we did. I was just about to start on him."

"Is he really as bad as Dirk says? Or should I say, 'as bad as Dirk smells?'"

Dr. Liu laughed. "Oh, Dirk isn't lying and neither is your nose. This guy is foul even by *my* standards. Why do you ask?"

"I have a score that I really need to settle. My sister and her new husband are death junkies, ghoulies from the word *go*. I think I mentioned them to you before? Well, I think it's time they got a dose of cold reality. Can we pay you a visit?"

She chuckled. "Sure. It's a suicide, not a homicide. I can allow civilians in, if they promise not to contaminate the body in any way."

"Oh, don't worry," Savannah said with an ugly smile. "When they hurl, I'll make sure it's into a sink."

Chapter 26

"Oh, shut that thing, Bates," Savannah told Kenny at the front desk, when she walked in with Jesup and Bleak, "or you'll catch flies in it."

He was standing behind the counter, his mouth hanging wide open. Apparently, Officer Kenneth Bates didn't spend a lot of time with people who wore white makeup on their face, painted their lips and nails blood red and drew bats on their cheeks and snakes on their foreheads.

And what bothered Savannah most wasn't that Kenny was shocked by their attire and makeup. It was that she *wasn't* shocked by it anymore. In fact, she hardly even noticed it.

But Bates was more than noticing the dark-red velvet corset that Jesup was wearing, as well as the black, ripped fishnet stockings she had on under her leather miniskirt. He had gone from mouth-wide-open shock to tongue-hanging lust in ten seconds.

Savannah walked over and began to sign the ledger: "Moe, Curly, Larry."

"Who are these people?" he asked when he finally regained use of a few brain cells. "Are you arresting them? Wait, you can't arrest people, so—"

"These are my *family*!" she said. "So watch what you say about 'em."

"Oh, okay. Whatever."

He leaned over to get a better look at Jesup's legs as Savannah led them toward the hall.

"Hey, Savannah," he whispered. "Do *you* ever dress up in stuff like that?"

"Do you ever wear a real tie, Bates, instead of that lame clip-on?" she asked him, her blue eyes boring holes into his. "A real tie—worn really, really tight, that is. Until your tongue sticks out and swells up and turns black, and your eyeballs pop out of their sockets and down onto your cheeks? I'll get you one. I'd be happy to even tie it around your neck for you."

She herded the happy twosome down the hall toward the autopsy suite. Bleak was practically dancing in his black velvet pants and knee-high riding boots. Jesup seemed slightly less eager, but happy to see her man so excited for a change.

"Wait here," Savannah told them outside the stainless steel doors. "Let me find Dr. Liu, and see if she's ready for you."

She peeked inside the doors and sure enough, there was Dr. Jen suited up in surgical greens, a disposable paper cap over her hair and booties over her shoes. She was standing between the autopsy table and a gurney that had a bagged body on it.

Even with the big fans over the table going full force and the bag still sealed, Savannah got a whiff of the corpse and her stomach lurched.

She had always had a high tolerance for anything visual. Sooner or later, she could get over almost everything she saw in her line of work.

Almost.

But she never got over the smell.

"Did you bring your little gore junkies along?" Dr. Liu said as she snapped on a pair of surgical gloves.

"Oh, they're waiting right outside, as chipper as a couple of kids on Christmas morning."

"So, they're virgins?"

"White as the driven snow. Slice-'em and dice-'em movies—that's it."

Jennifer rubbed her gloved hands together with Vincent Price glee. "Hee-hee, my favorites. Lambs to the slaughter. Bring them in."

Savannah walked back to the door and waved Jesup and Bleak over to her. "It's showtime," she said.

"All right!" Bleak practically ran her down getting into the room. Jesup followed a few halting steps behind.

"Dr. Liu," Savannah said, "I'd like to introduce you to my sister, Jesup, and her new husband of only a few glorious days, Bleak Manifest. Jes, Bleak, this is Dr. Jennifer Liu, the first female coroner ever in this county and the absolute best, too, I might add."

The doctor registered no surprise whatsoever at their appearance. Savannah knew that Dr. Jen traveled in some rather "alternative" groups herself when not on company time, and it appeared to take a lot to shock her.

"It's so nice to meet you," the ME said. "Savannah says that you're particularly interested in the forensic sciences."

"Mostly just the dead bodies," Bleak said. "I'm going to start my own body farm just outside of Vegas."

"When you grow up someday?" Dr. Liu asked with a deadpan smile that didn't betray whether she was serious or insulting him.

"Uh . . . yeah, I guess. I have to get people to donate the bodies and all."

The doctor gave him a too-sweet smile. "Well, there are always some obstacles on the ladder to success."

She walked over to a cabinet, opened a drawer and pulled out three surgical masks and a jar of vapor rub. Handing one to Bleak and another to Jesup, she said, "Here, you'll want to put these on, but smear a big glob of the vapor rub inside the mask first. It helps cut the smell. A little."

Jesup took the mask and rub, and began to do as she was told.

But Bleak shook his head. "Naw, I don't need anything like that," he said. "I can handle stuff like that. I'm . . . like . . . *into* stuff like that."

Dr. Liu gave him a big smile. In fact, she nearly laughed in his face. "O-o-okay," she said. "Whatever you like. But I have a rule in here. If you get sick, you do it in one of these plastic bags." She pulled a couple of large bags from her pocket and held one out to each of them.

Again, Bleak refused.

"Okay," she fixed him with a stern eye. "Then if you throw up, you'd better do it in that sink over there, because anything that misses the sink, *you* clean up. And I'm talking *major* disinfecting, not just a swipe with a paper towel. Got that?"

"Yeah, yeah, whatever."

She offered a mask to Savannah. But Savannah refused as well. "Actually," she said. "I think I'll just wait this one out in the hallway. I've seen my quota of DBs this week." She turned to Jesup. "But I'll be right outside the door if you need me."

Jesup's eyes were big and filled with apprehension. And under other circumstances, Savannah would have warned her or at least felt a bit of compassion for her.

But she needed to know right now what life with Ghoul Boy was going to be like.

Body farm, indeed.

"See y'all later," she said brightly as she walked though the swinging doors and into the hallway.

She glanced at her watch.

She'd give them two minutes. Three tops.

But it was only ninety seconds later when Jesup came crashing through the doorway, her plastic bag over her face. And she was gagging, coughing and hacking like she had eaten five pounds of week-old hamburger.

Savannah suppressed a giggle as she walked over and put her arms around her sister. "Are you all right, sweet pea?" she asked.

"No! Oh, my god! You should have seen—" More gagging, more choking, more retching. "You should have smelled . . . oh . . . that was the worst . . . ah . . ."

Savannah glanced toward the door that was still swinging from the impact. "I guess Bleak's doing okay, though, huh?" she asked, just a little disappointed.

"Oh, no! I think Bleak's dead!"

"Dead! No way! He can't be dead! You can't die just from—"

"I'm telling you," Jesup said, trying to catch her breath. "The doctor unzipped that bag, and we saw, oh, mercy . . . and we smelled, oh, and . . . and Bleak just keeled over right there on the floor, deader than a roadkill skunk."

Again Savannah fought down a fit of giggles. "Well, maybe you should go back in there and try to give him CPR or something. Maybe you can give him the breath of life. Just think how romantic that would be!"

Jesup shook her head. "No way! I'm not going back into that stinkin' room for love nor money. He can just stay dead for all I care. Hell, he sucks anyway. Where's the bathroom?"

Savannah pointed to a door further down the hallway. As she watched her sister's retreating figure, she said, "Oh well, so much for the love of a soul mate."

She knew she should go in there and help Dr. Liu with the recently departed Bleak Manifest. But she knew that Dr. Jen was a whiz when it came to bringing the dead back to life. A simple swipe under the nose with an ammonia inhalant—plain old-fashioned smelling salts—and those in a dead faint usually came right around.

And sure enough, less than a minute later, an even paler than usual Bleak stumbled out with Dr. Liu right behind him.

Savannah had once seen a hound that had tangled with a bear and lost who had more dignity than her brother-in-law displayed at that moment.

"You okay, bro?" she said, trying to interject an adequate amount of pseudo-sympathy into her tone.

He simply moaned, walked over to the wall, put his back against it and slid down to the floor. Dr. Liu shoved a plastic bag into his hand and said, "Just in case."

Then she turned to Savannah. "I'll return to my autopsy in a moment. May I see you in my office? Before you take these two home and put them to bed, I have something I think you'd like to see."

"Sure." Savannah looked down at Bleak. "You just sit there and hold that wall up there, son. It was looking a mite shaky a minute ago. I'll be back directly."

She followed Dr. Liu down the hall and into her office.

As the ME peeled off her gloves and tossed them into a trash can, she snickered and said, "I never even got to lay a hand on the body in there. I barely had him unzipped before they got a good look, a good snootful and bang. Your sister was outta there, and that brother-in-law of yours was on the floor. Pansies."

"I wouldn't ordinarily do that to anybody, but those two have been asking for it right and left. Dirk showed up at my place, stinking to high heaven, and I just couldn't resist."

"I can understand that. Believe me, in my line of work, I run into groupies all the time. They make me sick. It's kind of fun to return the favor."

She reached into her smock pocket and pulled out two pairs of gloves. Handing one pair to Savannah, she said, "Here, put these on." Then she donned a fresh pair herself.

She walked over to a cabinet, unlocked it, and took out a

manila evidence envelope. "I found this on Cameron Field," she said. "It was in the pants pocket of his sweats. I was saving it to show to Dirk, but since you're here, I thought I'd let you have a look at it."

Savannah took the envelope from her and opened it.

Inside the larger envelope was a smaller, beige one, the size that might normally contain a thank-you note or casual party invitation. It appeared to be high-quality linen paper.

"Look inside," Dr. Liu said. "And tell me what you think."

Savannah opened it and found several items. Two were snapshots. The third was a note card that matched the envelope.

When she turned over the first photo and looked at it, her stomach tightened. It was a picture of Dona's gardener, James Morgan, a candid shot of him working in the yard. He didn't appear to know that his picture was being taken.

Flipping the second picture over, Savannah wasn't sure if she recognized the pretty blond woman who was getting out of a car in front of the Papalardo house. But she was about the size and general description of Dona, and didn't appear to be posing or aware she was being photographed either.

"Is this Kim Dylan?" she asked.

"Yes." Dr. Liu's eyes were dark, her face grim.

Savannah's hand began to shake as she opened the note card and looked inside. On it was scrawled some lines, some circles and squares and an *X* on one side.

"It's a map," she said.

"That's what I thought, too."

"It's a map of the Papalardo property and the trails around it. The *X* marks the spot where we're pretty sure Field was standing when he took his shots. You have a clear view of both the front- and backyards from there."

"I figured."

Savannah looked each item over again thoroughly, then carefully slipped them back into the small envelope. She took a deep breath. "This is major," she said.

"Yes, it is. We'll get all of that over to the lab and see if they can pick up any prints on it, other than his, that is."

"DNA off the seal, too."

It was when Savannah was putting the smaller envelope back into the larger one that she smelled something. And the odor sent a series of rapid-fire memory synapses through her brain cells.

"Holy shit," she whispered. "No, it can't be." Her legs turned to jelly beneath her, and she felt like she couldn't breathe. Then a hot surge of anger went through her and the weak feeling disappeared, replaced by pure rage.

"What? Savannah, what is it? What's wrong?" Dr. Liu asked.

But Savannah didn't hear her.

She threw the envelope onto the doctor's desk, turned and headed for the emergency entrance at the far end of the hall.

It wasn't until she was several miles away that she remembered her sister and Bleak back at the morgue.

She took her phone out of her purse and dialed Tammy.

"Moonlight Magnolia Detective Agency," was Tammy's standard salutation.

"I need you to do something," she said.

"Sure, what?"

"Go to the morgue and pick up Jessie and what's-his-name. Give them a ride back to the house. Okay?"

"Yeah, sure. Savannah, you sound funny. Are you all right?"

"No. I'm not. I'm not all right at all. I've never been so mad in all my livin' life!"

"At Jessie and Bleak?"

Savannah shook her head. "No. Sugar, just do me that favor, okay? I'll call you later."

Without waiting for an answer, she hung up and tossed the phone onto the passenger seat.

She knew that in a minute, two at the most, it would ring again. That's how long it would take Tammy to call Dirk and tattle on her, tell him that something was up with Savannah again.

But this time she wasn't going to answer it.

This time . . . she was going to take care of business herself, her own way.

This was one pound of flesh that she wasn't going to share with anybody. Not even Dirk.

Chapter 27

Savannah was sitting at Dona Papalardo's desk in the movie star's library when Dona got home from yet another interview. Juanita had happily allowed her in, though she had given Savannah several wary looks as she ushered her into the library and presented her with a glass of iced tea.

Frequently, Savannah found it difficult to hide her feelings. And today it was impossible.

"Oh, Savannah," Dona said when she walked from the foyer into the library, slipping off her gloves and removing her hat. "I didn't know you were going to be here. What an unexpected, but lovely, surprise!"

Savannah looked into those famous green eyes and didn't see any sort of real pleasure or happiness at seeing her. In fact, Dona looked quite the opposite. She looked suspicious and worried.

And Savannah could easily guess why.

"What are you doing there?" Dona asked, pointing to the two telephones and the piece of paper on the desk in front of Savannah. "I thought you'd have been happy to get out of here and never come back . . . your job here being finished and all."

"Oh, I was. I was delighted to never come back here again."

Savannah's eyes narrowed and turned very cold. "But then . . . I got to thinking."

"Oh, what about?" Dona dropped her gloves, hat, and purse onto an accent table and walked over to the desk.

"Phone calls."

"Phone calls?"

"Yeah."

"Whose phone calls?"

"Oh, mine, Dirk's, yours . . . Cameron Field's."

Yes, Dona Papalardo was feeling very tense, quite worried. And even her abilities as an award-winning actress couldn't hide that. "Why would you do that? And why are you sitting at my desk? Considering that your work is finished here, that's taking liberties, don't you think?"

"I think," Savannah said, her voice as cold as her eyes, "that me sitting behind your desk, taking liberties, is the least of your concerns right now."

"What are you talking about? Phone calls, my . . . concerns?"

Savannah held up an older model, cordless phone. "Recognize this?" she said.

Dona looked at it, thought for a minute. Then shook her head. "No, not really. Why? Am I supposed to?"

"You own it," she said. "It's your phone. But I doubt you use it very often. In fact, I suspect that you didn't even know it existed."

Dona crossed her arms over her chest and lifted her chin a notch. "What are you talking about?"

But the level of fear in those green eyes told Savannah that Dona knew very well the point that Savannah was making.

"It was in your utility room," Savannah said. "You don't spend a lot of time in there, washing, drying, and ironing clothes, do you? I'll bet you didn't even know there was a phone in there."

The color left Dona's face, and she sank onto a chair next to the desk.

"That's right," Savannah said. "You missed one. When you went around the house, room by room, clearing all the numbers off the caller-ID histories from the phones, you forgot this one."

"I don't know what you're talking about!"

"Sure you do. Although, you weren't as smart as you thought you were—besides missing this phone, I mean. The phone companies have records now of every call that's coming and going, and the police can get them like that." She snapped her fingers. "So, you went to a lot of trouble for nothing."

"I told you, I don't know what you're talking about! Are you accusing me of something?"

"Oh, Dona, I haven't even begun to accuse you." She picked up the other phone and showed it to the frightened woman. "This is my cell phone," she told her. Then she tapped the pen she had been using on the paper in front of her. "I've made a little list here of some calls I received. And I've compared them against some calls that you received. And guess what I found?"

Dona said nothing, just stared at her with haunted eyes.

"Uh . . . like this one here." Savannah pointed to one of the entries she'd written. "This is a call that I received from Dirk the day your gardener was shot. Only a couple of minutes after. In fact, I was holding him and he was dying right there in your flower bed when Dirk called me."

Savannah pointed to a number and time directly across the page from that entry. "And here . . . why . . . lookie here. You received a call four minutes before that. And guess what? The caller ID on this utility-room phone says that it was from a 'Field, C.'"

"He was threatening me. It was one of those threatening, obscene calls that he'd been making regularly to me."

"And you didn't bother to mention this to me or the police?"

She shrugged. "I guess it slipped my mind."

"Yeah, right." Savannah pointed to her list again. "And what else do we have here? Oh, yes, Tammy called me to tell me that there was an intruder here in your house. And on this phone . . ." She held up the old telephone. ". . . it shows that you got a call two minutes before that, again from your old buddy, 'Field, C.'"

"Another threatening call, saying that he was going to hurt me." Tears sprang to her eyes. "Savannah, I don't understand why you're doing this, what you're accusing me of. You saw him there in my bedroom; he was going to kill me. But you saved my life and now you're . . . I don't know what this is all about."

"You know damned well what you did, Dona. You hired that son of a bitch to murder Kim and Jack. I've seen the pictures you gave him to identify the targets, and the map you drew for him, showing him the lay of your land here and the best place for him to stand when he killed them. The pictures, the map, they were found on his body at the morgue."

Savannah reached into the top desk drawer and pulled out a box of beige, linen note cards. "And you were stupid enough to use cards from a box right here in your own desk."

"But how . . . how did you know . . . why would you think it was me who . . . ?"

"The envelope reeks of your perfume, Dona. You know, your special blend of perfume that you get whenever you're in Paris. Your own personal, distinctive fragrance that anybody can smell a mile off."

Savannah tossed the pen and phone onto the desk, stood and walked around to stand beside the woman. Her fists were clenched at her sides, her body shaking with fury.

"You set them up to be murdered—Kim and Jack. And now you're going to tell me why."

"No, I mean, I didn't. I didn't do anything wrong, and you're way out of line to be coming here and—"

Dona started to get up from the chair, but Savannah shoved her back down. She leaned over her and placed both hands on the back of her chair, effectively pinning her.

"Why, Dona?" she demanded. "Why have them killed? What did they do to you that was so bad that you'd have them shot down, executed right here on your own land like that?"

Dona lost all composure and dropped all pretenses as she covered her face with her hands and began to sob. "You don't know! You don't know what kind of people they were. What they did to me!"

Savannah stood up, releasing her. She lowered her voice and assumed her pseudo–best-buddy tone that she used to convince a suspect they were among friends. "So tell me, Dona. Make me understand. I want to understand."

Dona seemed to take heart. Hesitantly, she stood and walked behind the desk. She opened a drawer and pulled out the stack of tabloid cutouts that Tammy had discovered earlier. She threw them onto the top of the desk. "Those!" she said. "They are responsible for those!"

"How?"

"She spied on me. And so did he. They came here and asked me for jobs, and I hired them. I had no idea that the only reason why they were here was to snoop around and find out anything they could about my private life and report it to those lowlife scums who print that garbage. They knew each other and pretended not to. They were lovers; they lived together! But here, no-o-o, just faithful servants who were going about their jobs, doing good work for me."

Savannah nodded and smiled sympathetically. "They betrayed you. You gave them a job, paid them money every week, and in return, they deceived you."

"They didn't just take my money." Dona began to cry even harder. "Kim made me believe that she was my friend. She helped me through the hardest time of my life, right after the surgery—stood by me like a sister. And all the time, she was feeding these vultures the most intimate details of my life."

She collapsed onto the chair behind the desk and grabbed handfuls of the articles, crumpling them in her fists. She held them out for Savannah to see. "Do you know what some of these say?" she shouted. "Do you know what she told them about me?"

"I can imagine."

"*No*! No, you *can't*. She . . . she—" The actress choked on the words several times before she could get them out. "She told them about how, after the surgery, I . . . I . . . soiled myself, and my sheets, and my bedcovers. I was sick! I nearly died! I couldn't help myself. But she told them that, and they printed it! The whole world read about how Dona Papalardo, the once beautiful, glamorous movie star, couldn't even control her bowels! How do you think that made me feel? How would that make anybody feel?"

She threw the papers as hard as she could, but they only fluttered like a dirty snowstorm around her. Covering her face with her hands, she sobbed hysterically. "I'm only human. And when people publicly humiliate you, say terrible things about you behind your back like that, print things like that, it hurts."

"I'm sure it does," Savannah said, looking at the pile of papers with their sensational and cruel headlines. "I'm sure it was excruciating. And if I'd been you, I'm sure I would have wanted to kill them, too. But you don't do it, Dona. You scream at them, you fire them, maybe even sue their asses off, but you don't hire an assassin to kill them! How can you do something like that, watch them die a horrible, bloody death like that, and still live with yourself?"

Dona dropped her hands from her face and stopped crying. Her face went hard, cold, expressionless. "I wasn't intending to live with myself," she said. "I was going to die, too."

"What? What do you mean?"

"I hired Field to do three murders: Kim's, Jack's, and mine."

It was Savannah's turn to be shocked. "Yours? You wanted him to kill you, too?"

"Yes, that was the plan all along. For him to kill them, then me."

"But why?"

She shrugged and suddenly looked very tired, much older than her years. "I didn't want to go on living like this. In constant pain, unable to do something as simple as eat the food my body needs to survive without being miserable. Ever since the surgery I've been miserable, depressed, alienating everyone I love. I thought I had nothing to live for."

"So why not just take some sleeping pills? Why hire a hit man to take three lives?"

Dona gave a sad, dry chuckle. She picked up a handful of the papers and shook them in Savannah's face. "Because I wanted these bastards to have something worth printing. They want sensational? I'll give them sensational. How's this for an article? *The Grim Reaper Strikes Three Times,* and this time it's the famous actress herself who is dead. Just as she is poised on the brink of a great comeback, Dona Papalardo is murdered in her posh California coast mansion. Police suspect that her killer is the same murderer who shot and killed two of her staff, in botched attempts to get to her before."

Savannah nodded. "Pretty sensational. It would have been the lead story on the evening news."

Dona smiled. "Ah, yes, a tragic murder mystery that would go unsolved, year after year. Reality-crime shows about it, lots of speculation, conspiracy theories. *That* would have been my legacy. Not *this* crap."

"So, what happened? Why did you hire me if you wanted to get killed anyway?"

"I needed a witness to everything, an outsider, someone to tell the world what had happened. Someone besides a member of my staff."

Savannah thought of the horrible things she had "witnessed" on Dona's behalf. "Gee, thanks for the memories," she said. "But once Field was in the house, why did you call Tammy for help? Why did you have her call me? You had to know I might 'save' you from him. And if you wanted to die . . . ?"

"By then I'd changed my mind. I wanted to live. Mark and I had made up, and I felt so much better after Kim and Jack were dead, like a huge burden had been lifted from me. I didn't even feel so bad physically. I didn't want to die, after all."

"So, you make a quick call to Field, tell him the hit on you is a no-go. I'm sure he'd been content to take the night off and watch TV sports or whatever."

Dona glanced away, avoiding Savannah's eyes. "Well, it was too late to call it off by then, you know . . ."

"No, I don't know. He phoned you minutes before you called Tammy, probably to see if you were ready for him and had left the sliding door open for him to enter, like you'd planned, right?"

Dona didn't reply.

"And you could have told him right then that you'd changed your mind, but you didn't. Why not?"

Again, she didn't reply.

But Savannah knew. She looked down at the crumpled articles. In her mind's eye she saw Dona sitting there at that desk, night after night, reading those words and feeling the pain of betrayal.

"You couldn't risk it, could you?" Savannah said. "You knew what it was like to have people know your deepest, darkest secrets. And you wouldn't have had a moment's peace, knowing that Field was out there, walking around with your secret. Even if it was his secret, too, you couldn't take the chance."

Dona looked a little relieved. "You understand then? You know I did what I had to do, right?"

Savannah reached across the desk and picked up her cell phone. "Oh, I understand, all right. You set me up. With deliberation and premeditation, you put me in a position where I would have to kill somebody, take another human being's life, just so that you wouldn't have to worry. Just so that you'd be sure to get away with the other two murders you engineered. And I have to tell you, lady, that just doesn't sit well with me at all! If you and I were men, we'd probably be dukin' it out right here, right now. In fact, if you weren't a sickly, scrawny-assed chick who doesn't weigh as much as my right thigh, we'd be having a free-for-all. That's how strongly I feel about having you use me as your killing machine."

"But . . . but you said you understood what Kim and Jack did to me, how they deserved what they got. And you said yourself, Cameron Field was a hit man. Who knows how many other people he killed, how many he would have gone on to kill if you hadn't shot him?"

"Well, you're not a judge, and I'm not a jury, so we don't get to decide things like that, now do we?" Savannah dialed Dirk's number on her cell phone. "But we'll find us a judge and jury who can."

Dirk answered with, "Where the hell are you? I've been trying to call you, and you had your phone off. Tammy says that you sounded—"

"Shush," she said. "I'm at Dona Papalardo's place. Get over here as quick as you can. And bring a unit with a cage." She looked at the movie star and gave her a wry smile. "You're going to have yourself a prisoner to transport."

Chapter 28

Savannah stood over the barbecue grill and looked down at the steaks and burgers that Ryan was tending. "I'm telling you," she said, leaning on his shoulder, "if that smells any better, I'm not going to be able to stand it."

He reached down, cut a tiny piece off one steak and slipped it to her, casting a furtive look at Dirk, who was sprawled in a hammock nearby.

"I saw that," Dirk said, peeking out from under the Dodgers baseball cap he had pulled far down over his face. "And I want a bite, too."

Savannah looked at Ryan. "Are you in the mood to walk over there and bite him?"

"Not really."

"Me, either." To Dirk she said, "Sorry, buddy. You'll have to do without."

With some under-his-breath grumbling, Dirk climbed out of the hammock and walked over to the ice chest. As he fumbled inside for his trusty Budweiser, he asked John, who was sitting nearby, if he wanted one.

"No, thank you." John lifted his glass of Merlot. "I'm fine here."

Tammy was sitting beside John, smearing sunscreen on her long legs. "I'll take a Corona," she said, "if you put a lime in it."

Dirk scowled at her, but he pulled out a Corona, walked over to the picnic table, took the top off, and shoved a lime wedge into the bottle.

When she took it from him, she said, "You handled that lime with your bare hands. Are they clean?"

He snatched the bottle away from her. She laughed and grabbed it back. "Just kidding," she said.

John lifted his glass of wine in Savannah's direction. "To our gracious hostess, who knows how to feed us in the style to which we have gratefully become accustomed."

"Here, here," Ryan replied. "And to the Moonlight Magnolia Detective Agency who, once again, brought their man—or in this case—their man and their lady, to justice."

Everyone toasted all the way around, and Tammy said, "Did you see that big special they did on Court TV about Dona Papalardo last night? It was an hour long, all about her life, her hiatus from acting, and then the murders."

"I saw it," Savannah said. "She would have loved it, if she weren't in jail and could have actually seen it, that is. They hardly mentioned the weight issue at all. And they glossed over the surgery problems. She came off as this troubled, complex person who acted out of deep, psychological problems."

"Well," John said, "obviously she *was* troubled on some level."

"Eh, bull pucky." Savannah walked over to the picnic table and began to uncover the salads. "She knew dad-gummed well what she was doing every step of the way. And I have to tell you, I'm still plenty pissed at her. She played me for a jackass, and I just let her do it."

"She had me fooled, too, Van," Dirk said. "She is an actress, you know. And apparently a good one."

"Oh, I forgot to tell you," Ryan said. "We found out a little something about her agent, Miles Thurgood, that you might like to know."

"What's that?" Savannah asked.

"We checked his tax returns and—"

"You can check people's tax returns?" Tammy asked.

"You can if you're a fed," Dirk said, "or even used to be, for that matter."

Ryan nodded. "Let's just say we know some people, who know some people, and anyway . . . That money that Thurgood gave to Kim Dylan? It was actually legitimate. He was acting as her agent, negotiating with the tabloids. The money he paid her was from them, minus his fee."

"No wonder he got nervous when Kim turned up dead," Savannah said. "And then Jack. He may have figured out that Dona had something to do with it, and that's why he got so spooked that day when I was talking to him. He was probably hiding out from her there at the hotel."

"I wonder if he knew that Kim-Penny had a record?" Dirk said. "I doubt it."

"What sort of record did she have?" John asked. "We never heard the particulars."

"She and her boyfriend, James, were wanted in Missouri for blackmail. Seems they worked a similar scam there, hiring on as some big-time country singer's maid and gardener there in Branson. They found out some unsavory things about this so-called wholesome, family entertainer's sex life, and they were blackmailing her with it. But she turned them in to the cops. That's when they split from there and headed out to sunny California."

"Yeah, lucky us," Savannah said, as she walked around the group, handing out plates, knives, and forks.

Dirk came to the table and began to dig into the baked beans, potato salad, and macaroni salad. He glanced toward the house.

"Your sister and brother-in-law haven't even shown their faces the whole time we've been here. What's up?"

"They're breaking up, even as we speak. He's going back to Vegas to divorce her, or get it annulled if it's not too late."

"Don't you just hate it," Dirk said with a smirk, "when these longtime marriages just don't last, even when the people have spent so much time and trouble trying to make it work?"

Savannah reached over and slapped him on the back of the hand with the salad tongs. "That's my family you're insulting there, buddy. Watch it."

She looked at the back door, sighed, and said, "I'll go tell them that the food's on, although I doubt they'll be in the mood to eat. They haven't eaten a single bite of meat since I took them to Dr. Liu's."

Waving an arm to indicate the table and all of its tasty burden, she said, "I'm going inside to check on my kinfolk. Y'all be sure and wait for me . . . like one pig waits for another one."

Inside the house, she noticed a marked quiet, not at all the way her house had been for the past few days. With no insults flying around, no inane cursing bouncing off the wall, she hardly felt at home

The only thing she heard when she entered the living room was someone softly crying.

Jesup was sitting on the sofa, her legs pulled under her, Cleo in her lap. She was slowly stroking the cat's silky coat.

Savannah walked over and sat beside her. "What's the matter, puddin'?" she asked. "Where's Bleak?"

"He's gone." Jesup blew her nose, then leaned her head on Savannah's shoulder. "He left to go back to Vegas. He's going to get the annulment or divorce, or whatever."

"And how do you feel about that?"

"Oh, I want him to. We never should have done anything so stupid as get married. That was a big mistake. I know it now."

"So, why did you?"

"Because he wanted to. He said it would be fun, so I did. Just like he said the Blood Fest would be fun."

"I thought you said you met there?"

"No, I ran into him outside the place. He was going in, and I walked by, and he said I was cute, so I stopped to talk to him. The next thing I knew, I was married."

Savannah put her arms around her and rocked her as she had when she was a young child and had skinned her knees. "That's what happens, honey," she said, "when you let somebody else tell you who you are and what you want to do with you life."

"But I loved him. I really did."

Savannah kissed the top of her head. "I know, darlin', but even the people you love most can't define who you are for you. That's a gift that only you can give to yourself. You can't go through life, being a chameleon, changing constantly to be like the man in your life. You have to find out who you are, and *then* go looking for a man who loves and respects you. Not the other way around."

"Half the time I don't even know what I like."

"Well, it's time to find out, now isn't it?"

Savannah pulled back and looked down at her younger sister's tearstained face. "Just because Bleak is gone, that doesn't mean that you and I can't have a good time on what's left of your vacation."

Jesup brightened slightly. "Yeah?"

"Yeah. You're in southern California. We're the tourist experts around here. I'm all yours now that my job is over. What do you want to do?"

Smiling shyly, Jesup said, "Bleak says it's lame, and he didn't want to go, but . . ."

"Where?"

"Disneyland. I always wanted to go there."

"Well, I think that Bleak is as lame as lame gets, and I'm crazy about Disneyland. So, let's go tomorrow."

"No way."

"Absolutely. There's something I need to do tonight after dinner. But tomorrow you and I will get up at dawn-thirty and stay all weekend."

Her face split in a wide grin. "Oh, wow! Thank you!" She gave Savannah a tight hug and several kisses on her cheeks. "You're awesome."

"Well, hey, how often do you get to celebrate getting rid of a guy like Bleak?"

"Yeah! Really!"

"Are you hungry? Barbecue's ready out there."

"You got your famous potato salad with kosher dill pickles in it?"

"And lemonade and baked beans."

"Yum. Apple pie?"

"And blackberry cobbler. We don't want anybody around here to faint from hunger."

"This is nice," Tammy said, "deciding on the spur of the moment to go on a drive like this. Are you sure that Jesup didn't mind us leaving her behind like that?"

"Naw, Dirk will hang out and watch his boxing match till we get back. She'll have company."

Tammy sat in the passenger's seat of Savannah's Mustang, and Savannah behind the wheel, windows down, drinking in the cool breeze and the magic of twilight. They wound their way through the middle of town, where Savannah lived and headed west, toward the beach.

"I like this time of day," Savannah said. "Always have. The sun setting, the city lights coming on, smells of people's dinners in the air, kitty cats coming out to snoop around and play in the yards. It's the best. And I decided you and I deserve to take a little drive, relax a bit."

"That was some dinner you made."

"Oh, please. I still can hardly breathe. Ryan is amazing with those steaks."

Tammy sighed. "Ryan is amazing, period."

Savannah turned onto Vista del Mar, a palm-lined boulevard that paralleled the beach for more than a mile. Tiny streets crossed it, heading down to the water. And on those two-blocks-long, narrow roads were small, quaint beach cottages of every style imaginable. Some were Cape Cod style, others tiny Spanish adobes, and a few distinctly contemporary.

Savannah turned down one of the streets called Pelican Lane. She and Tammy frequently came down this road for two reasons. One, unlike most of the other streets, it had a wide turnaround at the end, where people could park and take a stroll on the beach. But the second reason why it was a favorite was a cottage, two houses from the beach, on the right.

The "Three Bears Cottage," Tammy liked to call it.

Whoever had built this quaint little house had obviously been a Disneyphile. With its high-pitched roof with its rounded edges, the horseshoe-shaped door, the leaded glass windows and rustic stonework, it looked like something straight out of a fairy-tale forest.

"There's your house," Savannah said as she slowed the car and came to a stop in front of it."

"Oh, look! It's for sale!" Tammy said, jumping up and down in her seat, pointing to the Realtor's sign stuck in the front yard. "I've been watching that house for years and this is the first time it's come on the market. I guess the family who owns it finally decided to sell."

Then her smile fell. "Oh, it's got a 'sold' sticker across it. Wow, that was fast. I was just by here last week and there wasn't even a sign up yet."

"It's really cute, and quite unique. You can't expect that it would stay on the market for very long."

"True." Tammy sighed. "Oh, well, I hope some really nice people bought it. Somebody who'll take care of it and really enjoy it."

Savannah sat, watching her friend's pretty face, as the various emotions played across it. What a truly good person she was. One of the best people Savannah had ever had the privilege to know. She was so grateful to have such a person for a friend.

"I don't think they actually bought it," Savannah said. "More like, just put some serious earnest money down on it, you know . . . to hold it."

Tammy turned to her, confused. "What?"

"You know, earnest money. You give it to the Realtor, and then they promise not to sell it to anybody else while you—"

"I know what earnest money is, but how do you know about . . . ?"

Savannah reached into her purse and pulled out a piece of paper. She unfolded it and handed it to Tammy.

Tammy began to read it aloud, "Earnest money to be applied to down payment on said property at Fifteen Pelican Lane . . . to be held for . . . Tammy Hart. . . . signed E.F. Realty and Savannah Reid and—what? Savannah! What is this?"

Savanna reached over and brushed Tammy's hair back out of her eyes. "It's your new house, sweetie. There's enough money there in the down payment to pay half of their asking price. Your mortgage will be less than you're paying for that studio apartment of yours, so I'm sure you can handle it."

"Oh! Oh! Oh, my god! Are you serious?"

"Serious as can be."

"But how? You don't have that kind of money. I know; I keep your books. I pay your bills!"

"Dona Papalardo paid me a great big bonus . . . before I got her arrested, of course. And once I figured out why—to ease her conscience—I was going to give it back to her. But then I thought about you. I thought about how long you've worked for me and how hard, and how little I've paid you, and how you never, ever complained. Where Dona's going, money's not going to do her a bit of good."

Tears streamed down Tammy's cheeks. She gave Savannah a long, hard hug and got the front of her shirt all wet. "But you should use the money yourself," she said. "I know how bad you need it."

Savannah shook her head. "I don't want it. Really. I don't. This way, something good will come from it. It's what I want, and I don't wanna hear another word of argument about it. Okay?"

Tammy laughed, cried, and kept bouncing up and down on her seat until Savannah was sure she was going to break the springs.

"So, do you want to sit here or go check out the inside of your new house?"

"What? Really? They let you have a key already?"

"Sure." Savannah gave her a big grin, reached into her purse, and pulled out a lock pick. "Right here. Let's go."

Chapter 29

Back at home, Savannah found only Dirk sitting on her sofa, drinking a Bud and eating another piece of apple pie with ice cream melting on top. On the television, his favorite heavyweight had just won back the championship belt for the third time. So, he was in a better than average mood.

"I'm surprised Jessie went to bed so early," she said as she sat down beside him, reached over, and nabbed a bite of his pie.

"She said you're going to take her to see the Mouse tomorrow morning bright and early. She's as excited as a kid on Christmas eve. Said if she can get to sleep earlier, it'll come faster."

"She's a funny kid. Always has been."

They sat, quietly sharing the apple pie, staring at the post-match chatting on TV.

When the pie was gone, Dirk turned sideways on the sofa, facing her. "You and me haven't had a chance to talk since the shooting," he said. "Not really talk. I want to know if you're okay."

She swallowed and looked away. "Yeah, sure."

He reached out, cupped her chin in his hand, and turned her head, forcing her to look at him. "I mean it, Van. Don't bs me. I want to know. How are you doing?"

She shrugged. "I've had some nightmares. But I guess I'm all right."

"You know that was a good shoot, right down the line. Everybody says so. You're in the clear. In fact, if you'd saved anybody other than a gal who's being charged with three first-degree murders, they'd probably be giving you some sort of medal."

She laughed. "Well, that's the breaks. Next time I'll try to save an upstanding citizen."

Then she got very quiet and stared down at her hands that were folded in her lap. "It's not that easy, you know, dealing with it. Even when it's justified, it's hard knowing that you killed somebody."

He reached down and covered her hands with his. She took comfort from the touch, his big, warm hands squeezing her fingers, imparting his concern and affection.

"I'm glad you killed him, Van. I really am," he said with a choke in his voice. "And I'll tell you why."

She looked up and was surprised to see the depth of emotion in his eyes. "Okay," she whispered, not sure of what he would say.

"You know how you make me come over here on Christmas Eve?"

"What?"

"You know . . . every Christmas eve, you have these little parties and you invite Tammy and Ryan and John and me over. And you set out all that fruit and you make us dip it in that chocolate goop you make."

"Fondue."

"What?"

"It's called chocolate fondue."

"Whatever. And you force us to sing Christmas carols and dorky stuff like that?"

"Yeah. So?"

"And you make us sit around the table and decorate those stupid cookies and you get mad if I put boobs on the girl elves or a dick on Santa?"

She stared at him, getting more irritated by the moment. "If you have a point here, boy, you should probably make it before you get slapped upside the head."

He grinned. "My point is . . . as much as I gripe about coming over here and doing those things . . . if I wasn't here with you on Christmas eve, I'd be sitting all by myself in my trailer getting drunk . . . and wishing I was here with you, doing all those things."

She gulped and gave him a sweet smile. "Okay."

He reached up and laced his fingers through her dark curls. "And if, god forbid," he said, letting the curls slip through his fingers over and over again, "if that bastard had shot you, instead of the other way around, and next Christmas . . . you weren't here . . . Van, I couldn't have stood it. I'm telling you, I couldn't have stood it. So I'm glad you killed him. And I'm always going to be glad you killed him. And I'm not going to spend one single minute feeling guilty about it." He paused and took a breath. "And I really, really hope that the day will come when you don't feel guilty about it either."

"Oh, Dirk." She leaned over and kissed his cheek. "That is so, so sweet. I love you, buddy."

"I love you, too, Van."

She smiled and kissed his other cheek. "Good," she said, "because next Christmas we're going to go caroling around the neighborhood here. And Tammy and I have already decided—you get to be a maid a-milkin'. We've got this mop for a wig, and a milk pail, and an old lady's dress and two balloons for your chest, and . . ."